continued . . .

THE GENIUS

POTBOILER

JESSE KELLERMAN

J

JOVE BOOKS, NEW YORK

THE BERKLEY PUBLISHING GROUP
Published by the Penguin Group
Penguin Group (USA) Inc.
375 Hudson Street, New York, New York 10014, USA
Penguin Group (Canada), 90 Eglinton Avenue East, Suite 700, Toronto, Ontario M4P 2Y3, Canada
(a division of Pearson Penguin Canada Inc.) • Penguin Books Ltd., 80 Strand, London WC2R 0RL,
England • Penguin Ireland, 25 St. Stephen's Green, Dublin 2, Ireland (a division of Penguin
Books Ltd.) • Penguin Group (Australia), 707 Collins St., Melbourne, Victoria 3008, Australia
(a division of Pearson Australia Group Pty. Ltd.) • Penguin Books India Pvt. Ltd., 11 Community
Centre, Panchsheel Park, New Delhi–110 017, India • Penguin Group (NZ), 67 Apollo Drive,
Rosedale, Auckland 0632, New Zealand (a division of Pearson New Zealand Ltd.) • Penguin Books
(South Africa), Rosebank Office Park, 181 Jan Smuts Avenue, Parktown North 2193, South Africa •
Penguin China, B7 Jiaming Center, 27 East Third Ring Road North,
Chaoyang District, Beijing 100020, China

Penguin Books Ltd., Registered Offices: 80 Strand, London WC2R 0RL, England

This is a work of fiction. Names, characters, places, and incidents either are the product of the author's
imagination or are used fictitiously, and any resemblance to actual persons, living or dead, business
establishments, events, or locales is entirely coincidental. The publisher does not have control over
and does not have any responsibility for author or third-party websites or their content.

POTBOILER

A Jove Book / published by arrangement with the author

PUBLISHING HISTORY
G. P. Putnam's Sons hardcover edition / July 2012
Jove premium edition / March 2013

Copyright © 2012 by Jesse Kellerman.
Cover images: Arched corridor © Camellia / Shutterstock; Man © Yuri Arcurs / Shutterstock;
Torn paper © R-Studio / Shutterstock.
Cover design by Diana Kolsky.

ISBN: 978-0-515-15302-6

JOVE®
Jove Books are published by The Berkley Publishing Group,
a division of Penguin Group (USA) Inc.,
375 Hudson Street, New York, New York 10014.
JOVE® is a registered trademark of Penguin Group (USA) Inc.
The "J" design is a trademark of Penguin Group (USA) Inc.

PRINTED IN THE UNITED STATES OF AMERICA

10 9 8 7 6 5 4 3 2 1

ALWAYS LEARNING   **PEARSON**

To Gavri

Praise for William de Vallée and the DICK STAPP novels

"There's no one like William de Vallée. Every time I finish one of his books, I feel like washing the blood off my hands. And after *Fatal Deadliness*, I had to take a twenty-minute shower. Dick Stapp sends Mike Hammer to the slammer, and Jack Reacher looking for a preacher. No mystery here; this is a thriller reader's thriller by a thrilling thriller writer."

—Stephen King

"Of all the books I have read this year, this is one of them."

—Lee Child (on *Mortal Grave*)

"If noir is your thing, you won't find a blacker black than the blackness in William de Vallée's postmodern darkness. Every word sent me reeling! Dick Stapp is harder than a body left in the sun, and twice as much fun."

—Robert Crais (on *Risk of Peril*)

"No one does stomach-turning violence better."

—*Milwaukee Journal Sentinel*

"Writing that grabs you by the throat and wrings you like a chicken on the eve of Yom Kippur."   —*Woonsocket Potato Pancake*

"Stand back, Maxwell Smart, there's a new agent in town . . . [Stapp] is a tough guy's tough guy's tough guy, the kind of hero who makes women swoon and men wish they had another testicle."   —*New Haven Calumniator*

"Mr. de Vallée's stock-in-trade are plots twistier than those little wire twisty ties that come with bakery bread but that always go missing, forcing you to spin the plastic bag and tuck its neck underneath in order to maintain freshness."

—*The New York Times Book Review*

ONE **ART**

1.

After one hundred twenty-one days, the search was called off. The Coast Guard had stopped looking after three weeks, but the presumptive widow had paid for a private company to drag the entire Pacific Ocean, or as much of it as they could. With all hope lost, funeral arrangements were now under way. It was front-page news.

There was no obituary as such. A related article outlined the missing man's life and described his many accomplishments, professional and personal. A third surveyed various people connected to him through the business of writing: his agent, editor, critics, and peers. All agreed that William de Vallée had been a master of his craft, a titan whose loss was the world's. One interviewee submitted that the full extent of the tragedy would be felt only in due time, once the initial shock had worn off.

Disgusted, Pfefferkorn tossed the paper aside and resumed eating his breakfast cereal. Nobody had called to ask for his opinion, and it was this that upset him so dreadfully. He had known Bill longer than anyone, including Bill's own wife. She was not quoted in any of the articles, either, having declined to comment. Poor Carlotta, he thought. He considered calling her. But it was impossible. He had failed to call even once since news of the disappearance had broken. Though the odds of finding Bill alive had never been good, Pfefferkorn had been reluctant to offer comfort preemptively, as though by doing so he would be confirming the worst. Now that the worst had come to pass, his silence, however well intentioned, seemed horribly callous. He had made a mistake and he felt embarrassed. It wasn't the first time. Nor would it be the last.

2.

By the next morning, other stories claimed the front page. Pfefferkorn bypassed news of a celebrity divorce, an arrested athlete, and the discovery of a major gas field off the West Zlabian coast, finding what he wanted on page four. The memorial service for William de Vallée, noted author of more than thirty internationally bestselling thrillers, would be held in Los Angeles, at a cemetery catering primarily to celebrities. It was to be a closed ceremony, by invitation only. Pfefferkorn once again felt disgusted. It was typical of the press to feign respect for a person's privacy while simultaneously destroying it. He left the kitchen and went to dress for work.

Pfefferkorn taught creative writing at a small college on the Eastern Seaboard. Years ago he had published a single novel. Called *Shade of the Colossus*, it concerned a young man's bitter struggle to liberate himself from a domineering father who belittles his son's attempts to find meaning in art. Pfefferkorn had modeled the father after his own father, an uneducated vacuum salesman now deceased. The book received mild acclaim but sold poorly, and Pfefferkorn had published nothing since.

Every so often he would call up his agent to describe something new he had written. The agent would always say the same thing: "It sounds simply *fascinating*. Get it on over to me, would you?" Dutifully Pfefferkorn would mail in the material and wait for a response. Eventually he would tire of waiting and pick up the phone.

"Well," the agent would say, "it *is* fascinating. I'll give you that. But to be perfectly honest, I don't think I can sell it. I'm willing to try, of course."

"You know what," Pfefferkorn would say. "Never mind."

"It's not a good time for short stories."

"I know."

"How's that novel coming?"

"Not bad."

"Let me know when you've got something to show me, will you?"

"I will."

What Pfefferkorn did not tell his agent was that the very pages the agent deemed unsellable were not in fact short stories but abortive attempts at a second novel. By his count, Pfefferkorn had started seventy-seven different novels, abandoning each after hearing his first five pages dismissed. Recently, on a lark, he had placed all seventy-seven five-page segments in a single stack and attempted to stitch them together into a coherent whole, an effort that cost him an entire summer but that ultimately yielded nothing. Upon realizing his failure, he kicked out a window in his bedroom. The police were summoned and Pfefferkorn let off with a warning.

3.

The invitation to the funeral arrived later that week. Pfefferkorn set down the rest of his mail to hold the heavy black envelope in both hands. It was made of beautiful paper, expensive paper, and he hesitated to break it open. He turned it over. The back flap was engraved in silver ink with the de Vallée family crest. Pfefferkorn snorted. Where had Bill dug up such nonsense? Pfefferkorn decided it must have been Carlotta's idea. She did have a flair for the dramatic.

He opened the invitation and out leapt a six-inch pop-up cutout of Bill, showing him at his happiest: in his sailing getup, wearing a captain's hat, about to take to the water, a broad smile splitting his broad, grizzled face.

He resembled the older Hemingway. Pfefferkorn had not been to visit the de Vallées in a long time—it pained him to think just how long—but he remembered their yacht, of the kind most often found on the cover of a big, soft, glossy magazine. He assumed it had since been replaced by a more luxe model, one he lacked the wherewithal to envision.

The memorial was to take place in three weeks' time. No guests would be permitted. The invitee was requested to reply at his earliest convenience.

Three weeks seemed a long time to wait for a funeral. Then Pfefferkorn remembered that there was no body and therefore no urgency of decay. He wondered if Carlotta planned to bury an empty casket. It was a morbid thought, and he shook it off.

Though there was never any question as to whether he would attend, he nevertheless made a brief accounting. Between transportation, accommodations, and a new suit (nothing he owned would do), this trip could end up costing him well over a thousand dollars—no trouble for most of Bill's friends, Hollywood types who anyway had to travel no farther than down the freeway. But Pfefferkorn earned a meager salary, and he resented the expectation that he should sink his entire paycheck into paying his respects. He knew he was being selfish but he could not help himself. Just as he was incapable of picturing the de Vallées' latest boat, a rich woman like Carlotta could never grasp how severely a quick nip across the country could damage a person's savings. He filled out his response card and licked the back flap of the tiny return envelope, thinking of Orwell's remark that, as a writer, he could not hope to understand what it was like to be illiterate. He wondered if this might make an interesting premise for a novel.

4.

That evening Pfefferkorn received a phone call from his daughter. She had seen the news on television and wanted to offer her condolences.

"Are you going out there? It looks like it's going to be a big deal."

Pfefferkorn replied that he had no idea how big a deal it would be.

"Oh, Daddy. You know what I mean."

In the background Pfefferkorn heard a man's voice.

"Is someone there?"

"That's just Paul."

"Who's Paul?"

"Daddy. Please. You've met him at least a hundred times."

"Have I?"

"*Yes.*"

"Well, I must be getting old."

"Stop it."

"I can never seem to learn any of your boyfriends' names before there's a new one."

"Daddy. Stop."

"What? What am I doing?"

"Is it really so hard to remember his name?"

"When something's important, I remember it."

"It is important. We're getting married."

Pfefferkorn swayed, gripped a chair, made noises.

"The nice thing to say would be 'congratulations.' "

"Sweetheart," Pfefferkorn said.

"Or you could try 'I love you.' "

"It's just that I'm a little taken aback to learn that my only child is marrying someone I've never met—"

"You've met him *many* times."

"—and whose name I can hardly remember."

"Daddy, *please*. I hate it when you do this."

"Do what."

"Play at being doddering. It's not funny and this is important."

Pfefferkorn cleared his throat. "All right, sweetheart, I'm sorry."

"Now can you please be happy for me?"

"Of course I am, sweetheart. Mazel tov."

"That's better." She sniffed. "I'd like us to all have dinner together. I want you to get to know Paul better."

"All right. Tomorrow night?"

"That's no good, Paul's working late."

"What . . ." Pfefferkorn hesitated. "What does Paul do, again?"

"He's an accountant. Does Friday work?"

Pfefferkorn never did anything in the evenings except read. "It works fine."

"I'll make us a reservation. I'll call you."

"All right. Eh—sweetheart? Congratulations."

"Thank you. I'll see you on Friday."

Pfefferkorn hung up the phone and looked at the picture of his daughter he kept on his desk. The physical resemblance between her and his ex-wife was striking. People had often pointed it out to him, much to his irritation. That his daughter could be anything but entirely his seemed to him a vile affront. He had been the one to raise her after his ex-wife had deserted them and then died. Now he admitted to himself that he had been overly jealous, and foolish to boot. His daughter was neither his nor his ex-wife's but her own, and she had chosen to give herself to an accountant.

5.

Paul cut short his speech on the value of annuities to excuse himself to the restroom.

"I'm so glad we're doing this," Pfefferkorn's daughter said.

"Me, too," Pfefferkorn said.

The restaurant was no place Pfefferkorn had eaten, nor would he ever again. To begin with, the prices were obscene, more so considering the size of the portions. In vain he had searched the menu for something that didn't contain one or more obscure ingredients. Then he had embarrassed his daughter by questioning the waiter as to the identity of a certain fish. Paul had leapt in to explain that it had become fashionable recently due to its sustainability. Pfefferkorn had ordered the hanger steak. It came in the shape of a Möbius strip.

"The wonderful thing about the desserts here," Pfefferkorn's daughter said, "is that they're not sweet."

"Isn't dessert supposed to be sweet?"

"Uch. Daddy. You know what I mean."

"I really don't."

"I mean not *too* sweet."

"Oh."

Pfefferkorn's daughter put down the dessert menu. "Are you all right?"

"I'm fine."

"You're not upset?"

"About Bill, you mean? No, I'm all right."

She took his hand. "I'm so sorry."

Pfefferkorn shrugged. "It's different when you're my age."

"You're not that old."

"All I'm saying is, at a certain point you realize that most of your life is behind you."

"Do we have to talk about this?"

"Not if you don't want to."

"It's depressing," she said. "We're supposed to be celebrating my engagement."

Why had she chosen to bring up the subject of death, then? "You're right. I'm sorry."

Pfefferkorn's daughter sat back and crossed her arms.

"Sweetheart. Don't cry, please."

"I'm not," she said, wiping her eyes.

"I didn't mean to."

"I know," she said. She took his hand again. "So, you like Paul."

"I love him," Pfefferkorn lied.

She smiled.

"I don't know what you've discussed between the two of you," he said, "but I'd like to contribute in some way to the wedding."

"Oh, Daddy. That's very nice of you, but it's not necessary. We're all taken care of."

"Please. You're my daughter. I can't pitch in?"

"Paul's family has already offered to help out."

"Well, I'm offering to help out, too."

Pfefferkorn's daughter looked pained. "But—it's all taken care of, really."

Pfefferkorn understood that he was being turned down out of pity. They both knew he had no money to spend on a wedding. He had no notion of what he'd meant by "pitch in." What could he do? Park cars? He felt humiliated, both by her rejection and by his own impotence. He stared at his knotted fingers as silence settled across the table.

His daughter was correct: the desserts were not

remotely sweet. The donuts Pfefferkorn ordered had the taste and texture of compressed sand. At the conclusion of the meal, he tried to pay, but Paul had already given the waiter a credit card on his way back from the men's room.

6.

The airport newsstands and bookstores all featured prominent displays of William de Vallée novels. Every ten yards or so Pfefferkorn passed another towering cardboard bin, its top crowned by an enlargement of Bill's jacket photo, which had the famous author posing in a trench coat against a background of dark, bare trees. Pfefferkorn, an hour early for his flight, stopped to stare. William de Vallée indeed, he thought.

"Excuse me," a man said.

Pfefferkorn stepped aside to allow him to take a book.

For thirty years, Bill had, unprompted and without fail, sent Pfefferkorn inscribed copies of his novels. Back in the early days, Pfefferkorn had been happy for his friend, gratified that Bill should single him out to celebrate his good fortune. Over time, however, as that fortune continued to grow, and Pfefferkorn's stagnancy became more and more apparent, the gift began to feel like a cruel joke. Pfefferkorn had stopped reading the books long ago—thrillers were not his cup of tea—but in recent years he'd begun throwing the packages straight into the trash. By and by he had gotten rid of the old books as well. Today, first editions of the earliest novels, printed in small batches before William de Vallée became a household name, fetched substantial sums. Pfefferkorn refused to profiteer, donating the books to his local library or slipping them into strangers' bags on the bus.

Standing before the gaudy display, Pfefferkorn decided he owed it to Bill to catch up a bit. He bought the hardcover, walked to his departure gate, and sat down to read.

7.

The thirty-third installment in a series, the novel featured special agent Richard "Dick" Stapp, a brilliant, physically invincible figure formerly in the employ of a shadowy but never-named government arm whose apparent sole purpose was to furnish story lines for thrillers. Pfefferkorn recognized the formula easily enough. Stapp, supposedly in retirement, finds himself drawn into an elaborate conspiracy involving one or more of the following: an assassination, a terrorist strike, a missing child, or the theft of highly sensitive documents that, if made public, could lead to full-blown nuclear engagement. His involvement in the case often begins against his will. *I've had it with this rotten business* he is fond of avowing. Who in real life, Pfefferkorn wondered, avowed anything? For that matter, who *declared, exclaimed, interjected, chirped, chimed in, put in, cut in, piped up,* or *squawked*? People said things, and that was all. Who *sighed heavily*? Or *groaned lustily*? Who *fought to hold back the tears, which came without fail*? Several times Pfefferkorn had to close the book, he was getting so exasperated. Once sucked (or dragged, or pulled, or thrust) back into the maelstrom (net, vortex, spiderweb) of deception (treachery, lies, intrigue), Stapp learns that the mystery he was initially trying to solve is in fact just the tip of the iceberg. A far greater conspiracy simmers beneath, one that raises the specter of ugly events from Stapp's past and that has implications for his personal life. With dismaying frequency he is accused of a crime he did not commit. Stapp's son, a drug addict with whom he has no contact due to Stapp's having been a crummy father, too busy saving the free world to play ball or attend school plays and so forth, tends to fall into jeopardy. Long conversations consisting mainly of leading questions supply a complicated backstory. Trains and flights run on schedule, to exactly the right destinations, allowing Stapp to cover enormous distances in improbably short amounts of time. Despite the fact that his ordeal affords him little food and no sleep, he remains unimpaired when called upon to make passionate love to a beautiful woman.

Captured, he must rely on his ingenuity to escape. A friend is revealed to be an enemy and vice versa. An event or detail that earlier appeared irrelevant comes to play a critical role. Finally, the hero is forced to make a seemingly impossible choice, often having to do with the beautiful woman. Make it he does, though at great cost. For although Stapp is physically invincible, he bears deep emotional scars. Either the woman betrays him or he leaves her, afraid to endanger her. *You're like a moth* he might murmur. *Drawn to what will destroy you.* Then swiftly follow the delivery of vigilante justice and the tying of loose ends in complete defiance of logic or normal rules of criminal procedure. By story's end Stapp is on the run again, his name blackened, his heroism never to be acknowledged, his demons in hot pursuit.

It was a terrible book, even by its own standards: crass and inelegant and sodden with cliché. The plot was overwrought and reliant on coincidence. The characters were flimsy. The language was enough to make Pfefferkorn's throat pucker in distaste. Yet millions of people had rushed to buy it, and millions more would follow suit, especially now that Bill's death was the latest scoop. Were they truly blind to the book's faults, or did they willingly ignore those faults in exchange for a few hours of mindless diversion? Pfefferkorn tried to decide which was worse: having no taste or having taste and setting it aside. Either way, this was not the purpose of literature. He finished reading during his second leg, from Minneapolis to Los Angeles. Rather than leave the book on the airplane for someone else to find, he discarded it while walking to the rental car shuttle bus.

8.

Pfefferkorn checked into his motel with several hours to spare. He decided to take a walk. He put on his tennis shoes and a pair of shorts and ventured out into the glare.

The motel was located along a seedy stretch of Hollywood Boulevard. Pfefferkorn passed cut-rate electronics dealers, sex shops, emporia of movie-related trinkets. A young man handed him a flyer redeemable for two tickets to the taping of a game show Pfefferkorn had never heard of. An unshaven transvestite with foul body odor brushed against him. A woman in hot pants smiled toothlessly as she hawked aromatherapy kits. The streets swarmed with tourists under the impression that movies still got made here. Pfefferkorn knew better. None of the four movies made from Bill's books had been shot in California. Canada, North Carolina, and New Mexico all provided filmmakers with tax breaks that made Los Angeles, however storied its streets, financially unworkable. That didn't stop people from coming to have their picture taken in front of the Chinese Theatre.

A few blocks on, he ran a gauntlet of people brandishing clipboards in support of various causes. Pfefferkorn was asked to lend his voice to the fight against fur, the death penalty, and atrocities allegedly committed by the West Zlabian government. He dodged them all, pausing as he came to a woman kneeling on the sidewalk to light a candle inside a hurricane glass. Bunches of flowers were strewn all around the concrete square wherein William de Vallée's Hollywood Walk of Fame star was set. The woman noticed him staring and offered a smile of shared misery.

"Care to sign?" she asked. She pointed to a card table, atop which sat a red leather–bound book and several pens.

Pfefferkorn bent to the book and leafed through it. There were dozens of inscriptions, many of them quite heartfelt, all made out to Bill or William or Mr. de Vallée.

"I don't think I'll ever get over it," the kneeling woman said.

She began to cry.

Pfefferkorn said nothing. He flipped to the back of the book and found a blank page. He thought for a moment. *Dear Bill,* he wrote. *You were a lousy hack.*

9.

Pfefferkorn pulled the pins from his shirt. It had been years since he had purchased new clothes, and he had been shocked by how expensive everything was. Once dressed, however, he decided the money had been well spent. The suit was dark gray rather than black, a more practical choice if he wanted to get further use out of it. He wore a silver tie. He grimaced to see that he had forgotten to shine his shoes. But it was too late for that. He had less than an hour and he didn't know his way around town.

The desk clerk gave him directions. They were wrong, and Pfefferkorn got stuck in traffic. He arrived at the cemetery chapel as the ceremony was ending, slipping in to stand at the back. The room was packed, the air close with flowers and perfume. He picked Carlotta out with ease. She sat in the front row, her gigantic black hat bobbing and wagging as she wept. No clergy were present. On the dais was a lustrous black casket with brilliant silver fixtures. A life-size version of the pop-up of Bill in his captain's hat stood off to the left. Rock and roll played over the stereo, a song that Pfefferkorn recognized as an old favorite of Bill's. In college, Bill would play the same record over and over until Pfefferkorn couldn't stand it any longer and threatened to break the hi-fi. Bill had always been a creature of habit. He'd kept an immaculate desk, bare save a typewriter, a jar of pens, and a neatly stacked manuscript. By contrast, Pfefferkorn's desks tended to look like a child had been opening presents nearby. A similar distinction held in other parts of their lives. Pfefferkorn wrote irregularly, when the mood took him. Bill wrote the same number of words every day, rain or shine, in sickness and in health. Pfefferkorn had careered through a series of messy love affairs before ending up alone. Bill had been married to the same woman for three decades. Pfefferkorn had no nest egg, no vision for his retirement, no idea of what he ought to do except continue to live. Bill always had a plan.

But what, Pfefferkorn wondered, did those plans amount to in the end? Here, in lustrous black, lay the refutation.

The song concluded. The mourners rose. People were referring to an ivory-colored piece of paper. Picking up a spare, Pfefferkorn saw a map of the cemetery, with arrows indicating walking directions from the chapel to the grave site. On the back was the program for the just-concluded ceremony. Pfefferkorn read that he had been scheduled to speak third.

10.

Last in, first out, he stood at the base of the chapel steps, waiting for Carlotta so he could apologize for his tardiness. Two by two, the mourners poured out. Sunglasses were unfolded or brought down from foreheads. Handkerchiefs were returned to pockets. Frighteningly thin women clung to much older men. Pfefferkorn, who did not own a television and who rarely went to the movies, knew he ought to recognize some of these people. As a group they were exceedingly well dressed, and he felt his new suit put to shame. A woman encrusted in jewels approached him to ask where the bathroom was, reacting with perplexity when he said he did not know. As she tottered away, Pfefferkorn realized she had taken him for a cemetery employee.

"Thank God you've come."

Carlotta de Vallée broke free of the man escorting her and gripped Pfefferkorn fiercely, her woolen jacket bunching itchily against his sweaty neck.

"Arthur," she said. She held him back for inspection. "Dear Arthur."

She was just as he remembered, exceptionally striking,

if not quite conventionally beautiful, with a high, unlined forehead and a Roman nose. The latter had limited her acting career to a few pilots and the odd commercial. She hadn't worked since her thirties. Then again, she hadn't needed to. She was married to one of the world's most popular novelists. Four-inch heels and the hat added to her already imposing stature: she stood five foot ten in bare feet, taller than Pfefferkorn but in proportion to her late husband. Pfefferkorn tried not to ogle the hat. It was an impressive thing, adorned with buttons, bows, and lace, its shape that of an inverted frustum, narrow around the head and widening as it went up, like Nefertiti's headdress.

She frowned. "I'd hoped you would say a few words."

"I had no idea," Pfefferkorn said.

"You didn't get my message? I left it this morning."

"I was on the plane."

"Yes, but I thought you'd get it when you got off the plane."

"That's my answering machine you spoke to."

"Arthur, my God. You mean to say you don't have a cell phone?"

"No."

Carlotta appeared genuinely awed. "Well. It's all for the best. The ceremony went on much too long as it was."

Her escort shifted noisily to signal that he was waiting to be introduced, a gesture Pfefferkorn found imperious given the context.

"Arthur, this is Lucian Savory, Bill's agent. Arthur Pfefferkorn, our oldest and dearest friend."

"Obliged," Savory said. He was extremely old, with an extremely large head. It looked freakish atop his withered body. Thinning black hair was plastered back across his scalp.

"Arthur is a writer as well."

"That so."

Pfefferkorn waved noncommittally.

"Mrs. de Vallée," a young man with a walkie-talkie said. "We'll be ready shortly."

"Yes, of course." Carlotta offered Pfefferkorn her arm and they walked to the grave.

11.

Pfefferkorn stood at Carlotta's side throughout the interment. He was aware of people staring at him, wondering who he was. To block them out, he cast his mind into the past. He and Bill had been in the same class from the seventh grade on, but it was while working on the high school newspaper that they had become friends, each discovering in the other a counterweight. Soon enough they were inseparable, the big, easygoing Polack and the lean, volatile Jew. Pfefferkorn nicknamed Bill "the Cossack." Bill called Pfefferkorn by his Hebrew name, Yankel.

Pfefferkorn recommended books for Bill to read. Bill endorsed Pfefferkorn's grandiose dreams. Pfefferkorn edited Bill's essays. Bill gave Pfefferkorn a lift home whenever they stayed late to finish the layout. Senior year, Pfefferkorn was appointed editor-in-chief. Bill became business manager.

Bill's parents could have afforded to send him to a private college, but he and Pfefferkorn made a pact to go to the state university together. They ran in the same circles, the artistic ones that Pfefferkorn gravitated toward. Those were tumultuous times, and the campus literary magazine was an epicenter of the counterculture. Pfefferkorn rose to become editor-in-chief. Bill served as his ad manager.

At a be-in Pfefferkorn met a tall girl with a Roman nose. She was majoring in dance. She had read some of his stories and was impressed with his vocabulary. He lied and said that he was interested in dance. He fell in love with her instantly but had the good sense to keep his feelings to himself, a choice that revealed itself as far-sighted when he introduced her to Bill and she proceeded to fall in love with him instead.

After graduation, the three of them got a basement apartment together. To make ends meet, Pfefferkorn worked at the post office. At night he and Bill played gin rummy or Scrabble while Carlotta cooked up crêpes or a stir-fry. They would listen to records and perhaps smoke a little dope. Then Pfefferkorn would sit at his desk, typing as loudly as he could to drown out the noise of Bill and Carlotta's lovemaking.

He remembered the first time Bill revealed any literary

aspirations of his own. Prior to then, Pfefferkorn had thought he understood the roles each of them played in their friendship, and it was with some unease that he sat down to read the story Bill had written "for the heck of it." Pfefferkorn was worried it would be either superb and cause for envy or rubbish and cause for an argument. In fact, it fell somewhere in between, and Pfefferkorn felt relief at being able to express honest enthusiasm for the story's strengths while yet retaining his position of dominance. He even offered to mark up the text, a suggestion Bill pounced on. Pfefferkorn interpreted his enthusiasm as an admission that Bill still held Pfefferkorn to be the superior writer and would gladly accept any pearls of wisdom Pfefferkorn cared to drop.

How naïve they had been. Pfefferkorn nearly laughed out loud. The sound of dirt being shoveled atop the grave helped him maintain his composure.

It took Carlotta more than an hour to shake the hands and kiss the cheeks of everyone who had come to pay respects. At her request, Pfefferkorn lingered nearby.

"Hell of a guy," Lucian Savory said.

Pfefferkorn agreed.

"Hell of a writer. I knew from the first line of that first book that this fellow was something special. 'Savory,' said I, 'Savory, behold something rare here. Behold *talent*.'" Savory nodded in confirmation of his own judgment. Then he glanced sidelong at Pfefferkorn. "You probably can't guess how old I am."

"Well—"

"Ninety-eight," Savory said.

"Wow," Pfefferkorn said.

"Ninety-nine in November."

"You don't look it."

"Of course I fucking don't. That's not the point. The point, dingleballs, is I've been around the block. Updike, Mailer, Fitzgerald, Eliot, Pound, Joyce, Twain, Joseph Smith, Zola, Fenimore Cooper. I knew 'em all. I fucked all three of them Brontës. And let me tell you, I never met a writer like Bill. And I never will again, even if I live to be a hundred."

"I think that's likely," Pfefferkorn said.

"What is."

"That you'll live to be a hundred."

Savory stared at him. "You're a smart-ass."

"I just meant—"

"I know what you meant," Savory said. "Fucking smart-ass."

"I'm sorry," Pfefferkorn said.

"Pfft. Any rate, I'm telling you: Bill's name belongs up there with the greats. We could chisel it into Mount Rushmore. Maybe I'll do just that."

"Mark Twain?" Pfefferkorn asked.

"Nicest guy you'll ever meet," Savory said. "Not like that Nathaniel Hawthorne, he was a cunt. You're a writer?"

"Of sorts," Pfefferkorn said.

"Publish anything?"

"A little."

"How little."

"One novel," Pfefferkorn said. "In the eighties."

"Name?"

"*Shade of the Colossus,*" Pfefferkorn said.

"Shitty title," Savory said.

Pfefferkorn bowed his head.

"Not a selling title," Savory said.

"Well, it didn't sell."

"There you go." Savory rolled his tongue around in his mouth. "You should have called it *Blood Night*."

"What?"

"Or *Blood Eyes*. Now those are selling titles. See? I haven't even read it and I came up with two better titles in thirty seconds."

"They don't really relate to the book."

Savory looked at him. "You don't understand this business, do you."

12.

"Never mind him," Carlotta said. "Lucian likes to make himself feel more important than he is. Bill keeps him on out of habit, or maybe compassion. God knows he doesn't need an agent anymore." She paused. "Listen to me. That's what people do, isn't it, use the present tense."

Pfefferkorn squeezed her hand.

"Thank you for coming, Arthur."

"Of course."

"You've no idea how meaningful it is. These people . . ." She gestured to the vanished crowd. "They're nice in a way but they're not our friends. Or, they are in one sense, but you have to understand: this is Los Angeles."

Pfefferkorn nodded.

"I know what they're saying about me," she said. "They think I'm not sad enough."

"Oh, please."

"What they don't understand is that I've been mourning him for months. You can't sustain a fever pitch that long. It's unnatural. I've known more than a few widows like that, going around all day beating their breasts. There's something terribly stagy about it. And wouldn't you know, they always seem to recover as soon as the inheritance check clears."

Pfefferkorn smiled.

"Let them think what they want," she said. "This, here—it's just a formality. It's for everyone else. The real horror is all mine, and it only starts when I'm alone."

Arm in arm, they crossed the burial grounds, parting eddying clouds of midges. The abundant lawns gave off a humidity that drove Pfefferkorn to loosen his tie.

"I expected them to hassle me about burying an empty casket," she said. "But they were darling. They're exceptionally good at dealing with people in a time of grief."

"I bet."

"It's not out of charity," Carlotta said. "It's shameful what they charge. The flowers alone, you can't imagine. And don't get me started on the search company. But I didn't bat an eye. I said find him, whatever it costs.

Although in hindsight I have to wonder if they dragged things out on purpose, to soak me."

"I hope they'd have more scruples than that."

"You never know," Carlotta said. "Money is money."

They stood under the umbrella while the valets ran to fetch their cars.

"That's yours," Carlotta said.

Pfefferkorn looked at his tiny, bright blue rental car. "Point A to point B," he said.

Carlotta's car arrived, an oyster-colored Bentley with the gleam of the showroom floor. The perspiring valet got out to hold the door for her.

"It was good to see you," Pfefferkorn said. "Circumstances notwithstanding."

"Yes," she said. She leaned in to kiss him goodbye but pulled back. "Arthur. Do you really have to go so soon? You can't stay a little? I hate to see you off this way. Come by the house and have a drink first." She clasped her hands to her face. "My God. You've never been."

"Sure I have. I came for his fiftieth, remember?"

"Yes, but that was forever ago. We've moved since then."

Behind the invitation he sensed an accusation. He knew very well how long it had been. But whose fault was that? Then he remembered where he was and why he was there and he felt ashamed for clinging to grudges. Still, he hesitated, afraid to stir up more of his own ill will. He consulted his watch—unnecessarily, as he had already checked out of his motel, his flight didn't leave for seven hours, and he had no pressing obligations other than to return the rental car. He told Carlotta he'd follow her, adding that she'd better not drive too fast.

13.

The de Vallées' new home forced Pfefferkorn to revise his
template for what a Beverly Hills mansion ought to be—
a template established by their previous home. Set north
of the boulevard, behind impenetrable hedges, through
two sets of forbidding iron gates, at the end of a tortuous
driveway snaking through jungly grounds, the house
appeared as if from nowhere, following a final, sharp
turn. Pfefferkorn marveled at the forethought and skill
required to conceal a structure of such immensity until
the very last moment. The house was in the Spanish
Colonial style, a style whose humble materials and lack
of pretense had, until that moment, led Pfefferkorn to
think of it as intrinsically more *heimish* than, say, a super-
modern cage of steel and glass, or the looming, pillared
façades of neoclassicism. Now he reconsidered. The de
Vallée house was born of earth and clay, but it soared,
swelled, and bulged. Turrets and balconies abounded. It
looked like the place to make a valiant last stand against
an invading army. Reinforcing the feeling of besiegement
were a host of security cameras, their lenses winking
through the foliage. Pfefferkorn wondered if Bill had had

a run-in with an obsessed fan. Or perhaps this was simply an example of thickening wealth demanding correspondingly thicker insulation.

Carlotta put the Bentley in the care of the butler and told Pfefferkorn to leave his keys.

"Jameson will handle it for you. Won't you, Jameson?"

"Madame."

"Careful you don't scratch it," she said. "It's a rental."

Pfefferkorn followed her through a mammoth carved wooden door, crossing the foyer and coming to an interior courtyard fragrant with citrus. A mosaicked fountain burbled. Cut flowers stood erect in vases. A chess set awaited players. Chairs awaited buttocks. Portraits smiled, landscapes sprawled, statuary thrust. Every object, living or inanimate, functional or decorative, appeared to Pfefferkorn peerless, including the compact white dog that sprung from its languor to greet them.

"Say hello, Botkin," Carlotta said.

Pfefferkorn stooped to scratch the dog's head. Its velvety coat and pleasant scent spoke of frequent grooming. Around its neck it wore a first-place ribbon. It rolled onto its back and Pfefferkorn rubbed its belly. It yipped happily.

Sensing that this was expected of him, Pfefferkorn asked for a tour. Room by room they went, the dog trotting along at Carlotta's heels. In the basement they visited the indoor swimming pool where Bill did his daily hundred laps. In the theater Carlotta handed Pfefferkorn a remote control as heavy as a dictionary and showed him how to raise and lower the curtain. There was a ballroom where Carlotta danced four nights a week with a professional partner and a music room filled with all manner of instruments, though Pfefferkorn knew for a fact that neither de Vallée could carry a tune. Atop the harpsichord sat a photograph of Botkin, perched on a rostrum, accepting his ribbon.

The tour concluded on the third floor, in what Carlotta called the conservatory. A silver tea service had been laid out and crustless sandwiches prepared.

"You must be starving," Carlotta said.

"I could eat," Pfefferkorn said.

They sat.

"What is this?" he said. "Is this chicken salad?"

"Foie."

"Well," Pfefferkorn said, swallowing, "whatever it is, it's delicious." He picked up a second sandwich. "I couldn't eat like this every day. I'd weigh four hundred pounds."

"You learn moderation," Carlotta said.

Pfefferkorn smiled. So far he had seen very little of Bill's home life that could be described as moderate. "How the hell do you keep it clean? You must have a cast of thousands."

"Honestly, it's not that bad. Aside from Esperanza, there's just the butler, and I'm thinking of letting him go, now that Bill's gone."

"Come on. One person for this whole place?"

"She's very efficient. Bear in mind that I rarely step foot into most of the rooms. You haven't even seen the guest wing."

"Forget it. My knees hurt." He reached for a third sandwich. "I feel like a swine."

"Please."

"They're small," he said. "And I haven't eaten since breakfast."

"You don't have to make excuses," she said, nibbling the corner of a scone. "These *are* good, aren't they." She fed the rest to the dog. "Don't let me take any more."

She stood, stretched, and walked to the window. Her backlit form was lithe, and with sudden, agonizing clarity, Pfefferkorn remembered how much he had loved her. The seams of youth, those lines where disparate traits meet and fuse, had been gently effaced by time, and now he looked at her and saw womanhood in its most complete form. He saw what he had sought in his early lovers, in his ex-wife. All had come up short. How could they not? He was comparing them to her. He watched her for a moment, then set down his food and went to join her.

The window overlooked a stone terrace, which in turn overlooked the grounds, which were in keeping with the rest of the house: at once intricate and overwhelming. Other wings jutted obliquely, massive clay walls and burnt-orange roofs.

"All this," she said.

"It's a beautiful home," he said.

"It's grotesque."

"Maybe a tad."

She smiled.

"I'm sorry I wasn't able to speak," he said.

"It's all right."

"I feel bad."

"Don't. I'm just glad you're here. It's been so long, Arthur. I feel as though I have to get to know you all over again. Tell me about your life."

"It's the same. I'm the same."

"How's your daughter?"

"Engaged."

"Arthur. That's wonderful. Who's the lucky fellow?"

"His name is Paul," Pfefferkorn said. "He's an accountant."

"And? What's he like?"

"What do you think he's like? He's like an accountant."

"Well, I think it's wonderful."

"It will be come April fifteenth."

"You are happy for her, aren't you?"

"Sure I am," he said. "I hope it works out."

Carlotta looked alarmed. "Do you have reason to suspect it won't?"

"Not really."

"Then what's the problem?"

"There isn't any." He paused. "I think I always pictured her with—I know how it'll sound, but—someone more like me."

"And he's the opposite of you."

"More or less." He tapped his lips. "It feels like a rejection of everything I stand for."

"And what do you stand for."

"Poverty, I suppose. Failure."

"Tch."

"I'm jealous," he said.

"Think of it this way. She thinks you're so fantastic a man that she could never hope to find someone *as* fantastic unless she chose someone utterly unlike you."

"That's an interesting interpretation."

"I try," Carlotta said. "When's the wedding?"

"They don't know."

"That's the way it's done these days, isn't it. Get engaged and wait until having children becomes medically impossible. It was different in our day. People couldn't wait to get married."

"They couldn't wait to screw."

"Please. You make it sound like we grew up in the fifteenth century."

"Didn't we?"

"Oh, Arthur, you really are such a *grump*." She pointed below to a narrow path, barely visible, that led into an area of unchecked greenery. "That's the way to Bill's office."

He nodded.

"Would you like to see it?" she asked.

"If you'd like to show it to me."

"I would," she said. "And I think he would have wanted you to see it, too."

14.

They moved through the underbrush, ducking ferns and low-hanging vines, the dog bounding ahead in pursuit of a dragonfly. The light turned murky. Pfefferkorn felt as though he was heading into the heart of darkness. Rounding a mossy outcropping, they came to a glade flecked with dandelions and Queen Anne's lace. Botkin sat by the door to a boxy wooden building, his tail swishing.

"Voilà," Carlotta said.

Pfefferkorn regarded the building. "Looks like a barn," he said.

"It was."

"There you go."

"The previous owner was something of a gentleman farmer. He bred champion goats."

Pfefferkorn snorted.

"Don't laugh," she said. "The good ones go for upwards of fifty thousand dollars."

"For a *goat*?"

"You don't live around here if you're poor. You know the part on a ballpoint pen cap that sticks out? So you can clip it onto something? He invented that."

"My future son-in-law will be impressed."

"Bill loved it out here," Carlotta said. "He called it his refuge. From what, I wanted to know. He never did say."

"I'm sure he didn't mean it literally," Pfefferkorn said. "You know how he could be."

"Oh I know. Believe me." She smiled mischievously. "Sometimes when I'm out here I swear I can smell them. The goats."

Pfefferkorn tried and failed to smell the goats.

"All right," she said. "Let's see where the magic happens."

What struck Pfefferkorn most of all about Bill's office was its modesty. Only a tenth of the barn had been sectioned off and finished, and that was left comparatively spare. Indeed, it was strange to think that such phenomenal wealth as Pfefferkorn had just seen could be produced in a room so plain. Atop a rickety desk were an electric typewriter, a jar of pens, and a neatly stacked manuscript. The familiarity of the arrangement caused Pfefferkorn to shiver.

There had been few embellishments in thirty-some-odd years. There was an easy chair that looked as if it had been slept in a lot. There was a low bookcase filled with Bill's own prodigious oeuvre. On the wall above the desk hung a framed photo of Carlotta, a formal portrait made perhaps fifteen years prior. Below it was a photo Pfefferkorn identified as the source for both the pop-up invitation and the enlargement displayed at the funeral. The uncropped original had been taken at the marina. Bill stood on a dock piled with rope, smiling jauntily from beneath his captain's hat as sunset inflamed a sliver of ocean.

The dog, seeking his missing master's feet, settled morosely beneath the desk.

"I almost went out with him," Carlotta said.

Pfefferkorn looked at her.

"That day, I mean. I changed my mind at the last minute."

"Thank God."

"You think? Don't get me wrong. It's not like I have any notion of us waltzing off together into some spongy afterlife . . . Still. There's guilt." She indicated the manuscript. "That's the new one."

It was hefty, five hundred pages or more. Pfefferkorn wiped the title page free of dust.

SHADOWGAME
a novel of suspense
William de Vallée

Whatever Pfefferkorn's opinion of Bill as a writer, the idea of the novel going unfinished gave him a pang.

"What's going to happen to it?" he asked.

"Honestly, I haven't given it much thought. It hasn't seemed important, given everything else." She rubbed her cheek. "Sooner or later I suppose I'll have to burn it."

He looked at her with surprise.

"I know," she said. "*Très* eighteen seventies. It sounds pointless in the computer age. Believe it or not, he still did all his first drafts on the Olivetti. That's the only copy."

He continued to stare at her.

"What," she said.

"You're going to destroy it?"

"Did you have a better idea?"

"I'm sure his publisher would love to have it."

"Oh, I'm sure they would, too, but Bill never would have approved. He hated anyone reading his unfinished material. That includes me, by the way. Way back in the beginning I used to give him feedback, but it wasn't good for our marriage."

There was a silence.

"You're wondering if I'm tempted to read it now," Carlotta said.

"Are you?"

"Not in the slightest. It would be like listening to him. I don't think I could take it."

He nodded.

"I wish we'd been able to convince you to visit sooner," she said. "Your approval meant the world to him."

Pfefferkorn stared guiltily at the floor.

"It's true." She walked to the bookcase. "Look."

Among everything Bill had ever published there was but a single book by another author. It was Pfefferkorn's novel.

Pfefferkorn was moved.

"In many ways," she said, "you made him a writer."

"Let's not get carried away."

"It's true. You brought him out of the closet, so to speak."

"I'm sure he would have found his way out sooner or later."

"Don't underestimate yourself. He worshipped you."

"Carlotta, please. This is unnecessary."

"You really have no idea, do you?"

Pfefferkorn said nothing.

"I have a very distinct memory," she said. "This was about five or six years ago, I think. A book of his had recently come out and was sitting atop the bestseller list. Bill was out on tour. You know he still liked to tour, after all this time. He didn't have to, but he liked to greet his public. . . . Anyway, one night, he called me from his hotel in New York. It must have been around midnight, three in the morning over there. I could tell right away he was drunk as a skunk. 'Carlotta,' he said, 'do you love me?' 'Of course I do, Bill. I've always loved you.' 'That's good to hear. I love you, too.' 'Thank you, dear. Why don't you go to bed?' 'I can't sleep.' 'Why not?' 'I'm thinking about Arthur.' 'What about him.' 'I have a copy of his book with me.' 'His book? Does he have a new book out?' 'Not a new book, his first book. I have it with me. I was rereading it. It's a marvelous book.' 'I know, it's very good.' 'Not very good. *Marvelous.*' 'All right, marvelous.' 'Do you want to know something, Carlotta?' 'Yes, dear, tell me.' 'I'm going to tell you something I've never told anyone.' 'Tell me, dear.' 'It's very hard for me to tell you this.' 'It's all right, Bill. I love you no matter what.' 'Okay, then, here goes. Are you ready?' 'I'm ready.' 'Here goes. Here it is. Do you know how much money I have?' 'I have a fair idea.' 'More money than God. That's how much money I have. And I swear to you, I swear on my life: I'd give it all, I'd give every single cent, to be able to write like him for one day.' "

There was a silence.

"I wish you hadn't told me that," he said.

"Please don't be angry. I only want you to know how important you were to him."

"I'm not angry."

Light moved across the wall. It was later than he'd realized.

"I should be going," he said.

They walked back to the house. Carlotta ordered the rental car brought around. Pfefferkorn thanked her, kissed her on the cheek, and bent to get behind the wheel.

"Arthur."

Pfefferkorn paused, folded in half. The dog was watching them from the threshold.

"You can't, I don't know, extend your ticket?" She smiled. "The red-eye is always so beastly. You'll be much more productive if you stay the night and work on the plane tomorrow. And how often are you in California? We've barely gotten to talking."

"I have to teach," he said.

"Call in sick."

"Carlotta—"

"What'll they do, put you in detention?"

"It's not that," he said. "I have my students to consider."

She looked at him.

"Let me make a couple of calls," he said.

15.

That evening they dined at an Italian restaurant whose waitstaff knew Carlotta by name. The food was excellent, and Pfefferkorn, normally not a heavy drinker, consumed the other half of a bottle of Chianti.

"Tell me something," he said. "Why did you change your name?"

"You mean when I got married?"

"I mean when Bill changed it."

"I wasn't about to have him be one thing and me another. And which would you rather be: de Vallée or Kowalczyk?"

"Fair enough."

"Bill agonized over that, you know. It was his agent who made him do it."

"Savory."

"He said Kowalczyk was too hard to pronounce."

"Too ethnic."

"Mm. I don't think Bill fully grasped the implications of consenting to be called something else. Remember, he never expected that book to become a series, and he certainly never expected that series to become a hit. When he agreed, I think he had the idea he could still go back to being Bill Kowalczyk afterward, but of course it was too late."

"What I remember about the stories he used to show me," Pfefferkorn said, "is that they weren't any of this cat-and-mouse stuff. They were almost avant-garde."

She nodded.

"I was surprised when the first book came out," he said.

"As was I. Frankly, I didn't care for it. Don't look at me like that. I like them fine now. But at the time I'd never read a thriller in my life. I still don't, except for Bill's."

"What do you read, then?"

"Oh, you know. Those paperbacks with the beefcake in the kilt, and the women are pale and faint three times an hour, and loins drip and members throb and all that."

Pfefferkorn laughed.

"Anything that ends with them galloping across the misty moors is fine by me."

"Now I know what to get you for your birthday."

"A beefcake or a paperback?"

"I can't afford a beefcake."

"I hear they're quite reasonable by the hour, actually."

"I'll look into it," he said.

"Please do." She took a sip of wine, ran her tongue over her teeth. "Bill was always very adamant that what he did shouldn't be considered art."

"I don't believe that."

"It's true. He used to tell people he made chairs. He'd say, 'Every day I get up, I go out to my shop, I sit at my workbench, and I glue and carve and sand. And when I'm done, I'll give you a nice, solid, dependable chair, just right for sitting on. You'll feel very comfortable, sitting on my chair. And by the time you're through sitting on it, I'll be ready with another one, just like the first, and that'll be just right, too.' I think it was important for him to differentiate."

"Between."

"Art and craft. What you did and what he did."

"I don't want to talk about that anymore."

"I'm not saying he wasn't capable of producing art. Just that he was conscious of his choices. He needed there to be a difference." She took another sip of wine. "I don't know if I should tell you this. I suppose it's all past now, but . . ." She shrugged. "He was dabbling in a side project. A literary novel."

"No kidding," he said. "What about?"

"I don't know. I'm not sure he ever got anything on paper. He only mentioned it once or twice. I think he was afraid of how people would react."

He understood she meant him. "Really, Carlotta. Enough."

"Why do you think he still sent you first editions?" she said. "Your opinion meant the world to him."

He said nothing.

"I'm sorry. I'm not trying to make you feel bad. And I don't want to give you the impression that Bill was unhappy. At least I don't think so. He loved building chairs. He might not have set out to become this . . . *god-head*, but it was a role he came to enjoy. His fans are positively rabid. Conspiracy theorists, paranoiacs who read the novels and get wrapped up in this silly world of double-crossing and dirty secrets. Bill played into it, of course, taking those jacket photos with the coat. I used to tell him it was a bad idea, encouraging these people, but he said it was part of the image."

"Did you ever have folks bother you?"

"We've had occasion to hire a private investigator."

"Sounds like a nightmare."

She shrugged. "It's all relative. Remember where we live. Around here nobody gives a damn about a writer. I'll tell you another story. Don't worry, this one's not going to embarrass you. One time we went into a bookstore. I think I wanted a cookbook and we happened to be passing one of the chains, so we went in and got the book and stood in line for the register. Now, behind the counter is this big"—she spread her hands—"I mean absolutely huge display of his new book. There's a photo of him on top, and it's got his name on it. You'd think the clerk would put two and two together. Smile, at least. But—no reaction. We step up to pay for the book and she doesn't bat an eye. Bill hands her a credit card with his name on it, and again—nothing. She swipes the card and puts the book in a bag and tells us to have a nice day." Carlotta sat back. "It was five feet away."

"I wish I could say I was surprised," Pfefferkorn said.

"Well, look, better that than being mobbed every time you go outside. I don't know how these movie stars deal with it."

"They like it."

"Yes, they must, mustn't they? They're exhibitionists."

The waiter approached. *"I dolci, signora."*

"Cappuccino, please."

"And for the *signore*?"

"Regular coffee, thanks."

"Arthur. Aren't we working class."

In the car, Carlotta loaned Pfefferkorn her cell phone.

"Daddy? What time is it?"

Pfefferkorn had forgotten about the time difference. "Sorry, sweetheart."

"You sound funny. Is everything okay?"

"It's just fine."

"Are you drunk?"

"I wanted to let you know that I moved my flight. I'll be home tomorrow afternoon."

"Daddy? What's going on?"

"Everything's fine. I'm catching up with Carlotta."

"All right. Have a good time."

He closed the phone.

"She must be beautiful," Carlotta said.

He nodded.

"The last time I saw her was—God, it must have been her bat mitzvah." Carlotta looked over her shoulder to change lanes. "Every so often I wish we'd had children. Not that often. It was my decision. Bill wanted them. But I was afraid they would turn me into my mother. Which is funny because"—she changed lanes again—"I turned into her anyway."

Back at the house, they made love twice. Then Carlotta showed Pfefferkorn to his own room, where he could rise for his morning flight without disturbing her.

16.

Pfefferkorn couldn't sleep. He switched on the bedside light and reached for the remote control on the nightstand, turning to the news channel. A coiffed woman told him that the prime minister of West Zlabia had released a statement condemning capitalist exploitation and announcing the sale of exclusive rights to the gas field to the Chinese. The East Zlabians were up in arms. He watched for a few more minutes, then turned the television off and leaned back against the headboard, feeling completely awake. His insomnia had nothing to do with guilt, of which he felt none, or none that he was consciously aware of. He supposed he might have suppressed his guilt and that insomnia was the form it took in escaping. To his mind, however, a better explanation was that he was in the grip of newfound possibility. It was irrational, he knew. Nothing had changed. He was still Pfefferkorn, adjunct professor of creative writing. At the same time, making love to Carlotta—something he had fantasized about his entire adult life—had brought him into a state of mind dormant since his early twenties. It takes a woman to make a man feel this way, he thought.

Then he corrected himself. It didn't take just any woman. It took Carlotta.

Seized by a romantic impulse, he pulled back the comforter, put on his dressing gown, and padded downstairs to the terrace, along the way swiping a handful of pebbles from a potted bamboo. His plan was to throw them, one by one, at Carlotta's window, waking her and perhaps arousing a third bout of lovemaking. Once outside in the cold, he felt ridiculous. Even if he successfully determined which of the many darkened windows was hers, he would probably end up breaking the glass.

He scattered the pebbles and sat down on the flagstone, gazing out at the silvery lawns. The night was splendid, the air sweet as nectar. The soothing gurgle of fountains came from points distant. Even a stray chew toy seemed artfully placed, a charming visual blip there to remind the viewer that this was a home, not a museum. Carlotta had called the house grotesque, and while that was partially true, there was also a kind of seemliness to it, a sense that if mansions had to exist, they ought to be just like this. It was probably for the best that Bill had been the one to get rich, as Pfefferkorn's own relationship with money was characterized by that mixture of desire and contempt that comes from never having enough.

Growing up, he hadn't felt jealous of Bill. For one thing, the gap between them hadn't been so glaring. Bill's parents never faced ruin, as Pfefferkorn's often did, but neither were they the Rockefellers. Moreover, having Bill for a best friend enabled Pfefferkorn to thumb his nose at middle-class morality while still getting to ride around in a Camaro. He didn't need money to feel on an equal footing with Bill, because he had his own form of power. Of the two of them, he was the intellectual. He was the Writer.

This paradigm held for so long that he continued to hide behind it long after it had proven false. It didn't matter how many rejection notices he got or how many bestseller lists Bill made. There was one Writer, and it was him. It had to be thus, because otherwise he had no way to exist in their friendship. He quarantined those parts of his brain that whispered, *No, he's the writer, you're a failure,* and as a result he had no concept of how much resentment he had stored up until one night, six years back, when Bill called to say he was coming into town and wanted to get dinner. Pfefferkorn hemmed and hawed. He claimed to have a mountain of papers to grade.

"You have to eat," Bill said. "Come on, Yankel. We'll get steaks. On me."

Looking back, Pfefferkorn was hard-pressed to explain his reaction. Had he been struggling to figure out how he would pay his credit card bill? Had he just gotten off the phone with his agent? Whatever the reason, all the venom came spilling forth.

"I don't want dinner," he said.

"What?" Bill said. "Why not?"

"I don't want dinner," he said again. In a way, it was worse that he wasn't yelling. "I don't want anything, I don't need anything, just enough already."

"Yankel—"

"No," Pfefferkorn said. "No. No. *Enough.*" He was up

and moving now, pacing around his kitchen, squeezing the phone so tightly that he could feel the plastic housing starting to come apart. "Christ, you're arrogant. You know that? Did you ever bother to ask yourself if I liked that name? No, you just assumed. Well, here's news: I *don't* like it. I can't stand it. It drives me up the goddamned wall. *You* drive me up the goddamned wall. Just—leave it alone. Leave *me* alone."

There was a silence. Hurt seeped over the line.

"All right," Bill said. "If that's what you want."

"It is."

There was another silence, longer and more ominous.

"Fine," Bill said. "But listen, Art. Ask yourself this: you're sure you can't think of anything I have that you want? Anything at all?"

"Go straight to hell," Pfefferkorn said and hung up.

Nine months passed before Bill called to apologize. Pfefferkorn made his own grudging apology as well. But the repercussions had been serious and long-lasting. Pfefferkorn had not been to California since. For his part, Bill still sent first editions, and he still inscribed them touchingly, but otherwise communication between them had all but atrophied. Pfefferkorn had concluded that it was sad but better this way. Few friendships were meant to last a lifetime. People changed. Bonds disintegrated. Part of life. So he had told himself.

Now, however, he saw the entire mess as a nauseating victory of pride over love. He began to shiver. He pulled the dressing gown around himself. It was Bill's, far too big for him. Carlotta had loaned it to him. He wrapped himself tighter still and rocked in the moonlight, weeping without sound.

Some time later he stood up, intending to go back to bed. But again he changed his mind. He headed for the office path.

17.

Pfefferkorn stood in darkness, listening to the wind gust through the unused portion of the barn and stubbing his feet against the cold tile. He flicked on the light and sat at the desk, opening drawers. The first was empty. The second contained a box of pens of the same brand as those in the jar. The final drawer contained three reams of paper still in their wrappers.

The wind gusted again.

Pfefferkorn reached for the neatly piled manuscript. He leaned back in the chair. It let out a loud, rusty bark. He read.

If he had expected anything different from Bill's previous work, he was to be disappointed: in both substance and style, the manuscript differed so little from what he'd read on the plane that Pfefferkorn entertained himself with the idea that Carlotta had been mistaken, and that the pages in his hand were not a book-in-progress but the same one on display in airport terminals throughout the world. Three chapters in, he glanced over at the bookcase containing both his and Bill's life's work. The disparity amazed him. Even more amazing was that Bill still thought so highly of him. Surely one would expect that decades of uninterrupted commercial success would go to a person's head. Surely Bill had the right to believe that he, not Pfefferkorn, was the superior writer. And who was to say he wasn't? Pfefferkorn decided that he had been too harsh. Consistency, productivity, broad appeal—these, too, were writerly virtues, as was the ability to repeatedly vary a theme. By the end of its opening sentence, a William de Vallée novel made its reader feel at home. As a student, Pfefferkorn had railed against mass-market entertainment, decrying it as a weapon of the ruling powers aimed at maintenance of the status quo. He gravitated toward writers who employed alienating styles or unconventional themes, believing that these possessed the power to awaken the reading public to fundamental problems concerning the modern condition. He had striven to write in that mode as well. But these were a young man's concerns. Pfefferkorn had long ago stopped believing that his stories (or any story, for that matter) would have a measurable effect on the world. Literature did not decrease injustice or increase fairness or cure any of the ills that had plagued mankind from time immemorial. It was sufficient, rather, to make one person, however bourgeois, feel slightly less unhappy for a short period of time. In Bill's case, the cumulative effect of millions of people made slightly less unhappy for a short period of time had to be reckoned a significant accomplishment. There, at a bare desk in a frigid office in the middle of the night, Pfefferkorn softened his heart toward his dead friend, and to bad but successful writers everywhere.

18.

Dawn broke and he still had seventy pages left. He had to hand it to Bill: the man could spin a yarn. The latest installment of Dick Stapp's adventures began with the murder of a politician's wife but eventually led to far-off regions, as Stapp pursued a suitcase containing nuclear launch codes. Did they really call it a football? Pfefferkorn did not know. He put down the manuscript and stood, twisting to loosen his back. He knelt by the bookcase and took out his own novel, studying the cover, its blue darker than that of the faded spine. There was his name in yellow letters. There, in white, was a pencil drawing of a tree. The tree had been his idea. At the time it made sense to him, but now he saw that it was boring and pretentious. Live and learn, he thought. He opened to the back flap. There was his author photo, taken by his wife on her old camera. In it he was young and thin, staring intensely, chin clutched between thumb and side of forefinger, a pose intended to give him gravitas. Now he

decided that he looked like his head had become detached
and he was trying to keep it in place.

He turned to the title page and the inscription.

> *Bill*
>> *I'll catch you one day*
>>> *love*
>>>> *Art*

Had he really written that? Bill must have been embarrassed by the pettiness of it, although Pfefferkorn could
not remember him saying anything other than thank
you. And such folly. He would never catch Bill, at least
not in terms of numbers. That much should have been
apparent, even back then.

Shaking his head, Pfefferkorn opened the book to a
random page. What he saw astonished him. The text had
been heavily annotated, every sentence asterisked, under-
lined, boxed, or bracketed, some all four. A dense, Talmu-
dic commentary filled the margins. Diction was analyzed,
allusions explicated, scenes dissected for structure. Pfefferkorn riffled the rest of the book and was aghast to discover that it had all been given an identical treatment.
The novel's final paragraph ended in the middle of a page,
and below the closing words Bill had written:

> *YES*

Pfefferkorn turned to the table of contents—it was
clean, which brought him immeasurable relief—then to
the acknowledgments. He read that he had thanked his

agent, his editor, his wife, and various friends who had provided technical advice. He had not thanked Bill.

Stricken, he went back to the title page, intending to rip out the inscription in penance. But he could not bring himself to do it. He replaced the book on the shelf.

He sat for some time in a meditative silence. He thought of his failed novels. He thought of his failed marriage. He thought of Bill, good Bill, kind Bill, bashful Bill, Bill who had ever shown him only generosity, who had admired and studied him, who had loved him and whom he had loved in return. He thought of Bill leaving his mansion to sit in a tiny, ugly room. Bill, typing his two thousand five hundred words, day in and day out. Bill, wishing he had one great book in him. Bill, with his own jealousies, his own regrets. Outside, the birds began to sing. Pfefferkorn looked at the manuscript, seventy pages unread, the rest piled messily and dangling at the edge of the desk, and he thought that Bill never would have been so careless. He thought of Carlotta, the way she had opened herself to him, in punishment and in reward. He thought of his daughter, whose wedding he could not pay for. He thought of his students at the college, none of whom would ever succeed. They had no talent, and talent could not be learned. He thought of life and he thought of death. He thought: I deserve more.

19.

Pfefferkorn waited for the rental car shuttle bus to take him to the departure terminal. In order to fit the manuscript into his carry-on he had had to discard several items of clothing, two pairs of socks and two pairs of underwear and one shirt hastily stuffed into the waste bin of a hallway bathroom that, to his eye, had not been recently used, the bar of soap in the sinkside soap dish still wrapped in ribbon and wax paper.

He stood at the kiosk, waiting for his boarding pass to print.

He stood at the security checkpoint, waiting to be waved through the metal detector.

He sat at the gate in a hard plastic chair, waiting for his group to be called.

Once the plane was in the air and his seatmate asleep, he unzipped his bag, took out the manuscript, and thumbed off the unread portion.

The novel's final scenes were full of action. Pfefferkorn read quickly, his tension growing in inverse proportion to the number of pages left. By the time he reached the second-to-last page, he was on the verge of panic. While the nuclear launch codes had been recovered, the villain responsible for their theft was still at large and in possession of a vial containing a virulent strain of influenza in sufficient quantity to wipe out Washington, D.C., and its environs. With a terrible foreboding, Pfefferkorn turned to the last page.

> coming at them like a bullet.
>
> "Dick!" Gisele screamed. "Dick! I can't—"
>
> A deafening roar cut her off as the bomb detonated. Rocks rained down from the roof of the cave. Dust filled Stapp's lungs.
>
> "Dick . . . I can't breathe . . ."
>
> The weakness of her voice chilled Stapp to the marrow.
>
> "Hang on!" he yelled hoarsely. "I'm almost there."
>
> Like a bat out of hell, Stapp plunged into the icy water

That was all.

Pfefferkorn looked inside his carry-on. Had he missed a page? An entire chapter? But no. Of course the book would end that way. Bill hadn't finished it yet. Disheartened, he put the incomplete completion away and zipped up his bag. He put his head back, closed his eyes, and slept.

20.

Pfefferkorn left his still-packed carry-on beneath the kitchen table and made himself busy. He sorted the mail, he checked the refrigerator, he called his daughter.

"Did you have fun?" she asked.

"For a funeral, it wasn't bad."

"How's Carlotta?"

"Good. She says hello."

"I hope you'll keep in touch with her." Then: "Maybe you could visit her again."

"That, I don't know about."

"Why not? I think it would be healthy for you."

"That's how people get sick, on airplanes."

"That's not what I mean, Daddy."

"Then what do you mean."

"You know," she said.

"I really don't."

"Call her."

"And say what."

"Tell her you had a good time. Tell her you want to see her again."

He sighed. "Sweetheart—"

"Please, Daddy. I'm not stupid."

"I don't have the faintest idea what you're talking about."

"It's good for you."

"What is."

"Having someone."

He had heard this before, notably when she was in her teens and reading a lot of Victorian novels. "I have to go," he said.

"Why do you have to be so stubborn?"

"I have to get to the market before it closes."

"Daddy—"

"I'll call you soon."

Walking down the drizzly avenue, he had to admire how quickly she had deduced the truth. How did they do it, women? It was nothing short of prophecy. He wondered if that might make an interesting premise for a novel.

He slung a plastic basket in the crook of his elbow and wandered through the aisles, distractedly gathering the bachelor's staples: milk, cereal, instant noodles. On his way to the register he passed the floral department and was inspired. A token—a warm hand extended—that was all that was necessary, wasn't it? If Carlotta wanted to speak to him, she could pick up the phone just as easily as he could. He hoped she wouldn't. He wasn't sure he could keep calm. After all, it was only a matter of time before she discovered he had taken the manuscript, and when she did, he would have no ready explanation. Indeed, he couldn't understand it himself. Why would he, of all people, steal an unfinished novel? He had more than enough of those. But of course he had not known it was unfinished. He had taken it thinking it would wrap up nicely. He told himself that he'd merely wanted to finish reading it. But if so, why take the entire thing? Why not just the last seventy pages? What had he been thinking? He blamed fatigue, stress, grief, postcoital delirium. He argued to himself that he had not stolen but borrowed, and he decided that he would return the manuscript as soon as he had the chance. But if that had been his intention all along, why not leave a note? Why cover up his deed, as he had done, placing the old title page atop a pile of blank paper, so that anyone walking into the room would see nothing amiss? These were not the deeds of an innocent man.

He walked home. He put away the groceries. He avoided looking at the carry-on, which seemed to radiate with the aura of the stolen manuscript. Hoping to ease his nerves, he moved the bag to the back of the coat closet.

The website provided the option of including a card with his bouquet, but none of the choices seemed suitable. Neat descriptors—bereavement, thanks, love, apology—did not capture the complexity of the circumstances. In the end, he settled for "Just Because."

21.

"They're lovely, Arthur. Thank you. I've put them on my nightstand."

"My pleasure," he said.

"I'm so glad you stayed."

"Me, too."

"But—you don't have any regrets, do you? You shouldn't," she said, as if he had answered in the affirmative. "If there's any lesson to be learned from all this, it's that life is precious. We could both walk out of our houses tomorrow morning and get hit by a bus."

"That would be some rotten luck."

"Wouldn't it, though. My point is we're too old to get hung up. Be happy now, that's what Bill always said. Well, that's what I want."

"By all means."

"That applies to you, too, Arthur."

"I am happy," he said.

"Happier, then."

"Everything in moderation," he said.

"Funny man. When can I see you again?"

"Come anytime," he said, instantly regretting the

invitation. His apartment was unfit for a woman of any class, let alone Carlotta. "There's a nice hotel a few blocks away," he said.

"Really, Arthur. A hotel? Anyway, I hate planes, they're so dehydrating. No, I insist: you must come here as soon as you possibly can, and I won't let you argue with me."

"Well—"

"I know it's a long trip."

"I have a job," he said.

"Oh, who cares."

It frustrated him, her refusal to acknowledge that forgoing work was not an option for most people. "It's not that simple," he said.

"And why not."

"Do you know what a round-trip ticket costs?"

She whooped with laughter. "*That's* your excuse? You silly man, *I'll* pay for your ticket."

The echo of his argument with Bill was unmistakable, and Pfefferkorn fought to suppress his anger and shame. "Absolutely not," he said.

"Arthur," she said, "please. There's no need to be prideful."

There was a long silence.

"I've said the wrong thing, haven't I?"

"No."

"I've insulted you."

"It's all right."

"I'm sorry."

"It's all right, Carlotta."

"You understand what I meant to say."

"I understand."

"Only for us to be happy. Both of us. That's all I want."

There was a silence.

"Call when you can," she said.

"I will."

"And, please—try not to be angry."

"I'm not."

"All right," she said. "Good night, Arthur."

"Good night."

"Thanks again for the flowers."

"You're welcome."

"They really are lovely."

"I'm glad," he said. But he was thinking that he should have chosen a more expensive bouquet.

22.

Pfefferkorn had a system, refined by many years of experience, for classifying his creative writing students. Type one was a nervous, fragile girl whose fiction was in essence a public diary. Commonly explored themes included sexual awakening, eating disorders, emotionally abusive relationships, and suicide. Next there was the ideologue, for whom a story functioned as a soapbox. This student had recently returned from a semester abroad in the Third World, digging wells or monitoring fraudulent elections, and was now determined to give voice to the voiceless. A third type was the genre devotee, comprising several subtypes: the science-fiction hobbit, the noirist, and so forth. Last, there was the literary aspirant, dry, sarcastic, and well-read, prone to quote, with a veneer of calm condescension occasionally (and then spectacularly) shattered by an explosion of nastiness. Pfefferkorn himself had once been of this type.

Although the last three types were predominantly male, a high absolute number of type-ones led to a preponderance of women in Pfefferkorn's classes.

There was a fifth type, naturally, so rarely seen as to not merit its own category, and whose nature moreover rendered the act of categorization irrelevant: the true writer. In all his years Pfefferkorn had encountered three of them. One had gone on to publish two novels before becoming a lawyer. The second had grown rich writing for television. The third taught creative writing at a small college in the Middle West. She and Pfefferkorn corresponded once or twice a year. The first two he had lost touch with.

It was common for professional educators to say that they lived for the rare birds, a sentiment Pfefferkorn found unforgivably self-important. It was only to the vast, mediocre herd that the actual work of teaching applied, and then only to dubious effect. Talented students had no need of the classroom. Teachers liked talented students because talented students made teachers look good while requiring no effort on the part of the teacher.

One week after his return from California, Pfefferkorn sat in a room with ten untalented students, conducting a workshop. He did not participate in the conversation other than to nod and to offer smiles of encouragement to the fragile young woman whose story was up for dissection. She wore an oversized sweater with a button that said FREE WEST ZLABIA, and as the criticism grew progressively more rancorous, she retreated into her clothes like a turtle protecting itself, first retracting her arms into her sleeves, then pulling the hem of the sweater down over her hugged knees. Another day, Pfefferkorn might have come to her defense, but presently he was absorbed in worry. He had put his conversation with Carlotta on a permanent loop in his brain and was analyzing it for some hint that she knew what he had done. He couldn't find any, but that didn't mean she hadn't gone into the office in the last week. She hadn't called. Was her silence furious? Ambivalent? Embarrassed? He didn't know, and he worried. He worried further that he had been too quick to take offense at her offer of a plane ticket. He did miss her. On the other hand, if he was too old to get hung up, he was also too old to become a kept man. That he should have to negotiate with himself for these tattered scraps of dignity was itself humiliating.

He let a week pass. The phone didn't ring. He went to class. He came home. He listened to his daughter talk about her ongoing quest for a wedding venue. Another week went by. He avoided looking at the coat closet. He read the paper. William de Vallée had ceased to be newsworthy. The economy was down. Fuel prices were up. Tempers in the Zlabian valley continued to flare, with shots being fired across the border. Pfefferkorn didn't pay attention to any of it. He had more important things on his mind than the squabbles of people in faraway places. He reread the file where he kept his ideas for future novels. Every single one stank. It had been a full month and Carlotta still had not called. Maybe she had burned the pile of paper on the desk without looking at it. Maybe she'd forgotten about it. Maybe she had left it out for him on purpose. Maybe it had been a test and he had failed. Or maybe she meant it as a gift and his fear was baseless. He took the carry-on out of the coat closet and piled the manuscript neatly on his desk. He stared at the thick block of paper for hours on end. He had known what he intended to do all along, hadn't he? He still felt conflicted, of course. He had to work on himself, argue with himself, convince himself. He sat on the edge of his bed, unfolding and examining Carlotta's words—*be happy now*—taking them first as a pardon, then as permission, and finally as a command. The time for excuses had ended. The time had come to act.

23.

One of Pfefferkorn's more shameful secrets was that he had once tried to write a popular novel of his own. Fed up with being perpetually broke, he took a few days to sketch the plot—it was a murder mystery set at a small college on the Eastern Seaboard—before sitting down to bang out a quick and dirty ten chapters. His daughter, then thirteen, noticed the pile growing on his desk and beamed with pride. Indeed, it was the only time since publishing his novel that he had gotten any further than the first five pages, and while he detested every word he'd written, he had to admit feeling some satisfaction in seeing any book of his achieve a third dimension.

The problem was the ending. In his zeal to entertain he had constructed six distinct, wildly complicated plotlines, giving but the slightest consideration to how they might ultimately intertwine. He soon found himself stymied, spinning in place like a man whose six dogs have all run off in different directions. Frustrated, he reversed tack, stripping away all but one of the plotlines, leaving him with a mere forty pages. Attempts to expand these pages proved ham-fisted and futile. He tried introducing a romantic interest, only to discover, to his dismay, and over his loud mental protests, that his protagonist was a latent homosexual. To increase the suspense he murdered another administrator. He murdered a student. He murdered a hapless janitor. Bodies kept piling up and still he had fewer than twenty-five thousand words. It didn't take much, he discovered, to kill someone in print, and there was only so much page space one could reasonably fill with gory descriptions.

In a fit of pique he caused the campus quadrangle to be detonated.

After much floundering he threw the manuscript in the trash. His daughter came home from school and, seeing the empty spot on the desk, the dustless rectangle where once their hopes for a better future had lain, ran to her room and locked the door, deaf to his entreaties.

As he sat at his computer, plagiarizing Bill's manuscript, Pfefferkorn thought often of those days. He regretted having given up so easily. He might have done his daughter proud after all. But there was no sense fretting. She was getting married and he had work to do.

The theft of *Shadowgame* had begun with Pfefferkorn placing the manuscript in his carry-on, but it was not complete until eleven weeks later, when he finished retyping the text. He would have finished far sooner had he not chosen to fix some of the more infelicitous phrasing. For instance, it was characteristic of special agent Richard "Dick" Stapp to perform difficult physical feats *in one fluid motion*. Pfefferkorn didn't care for the expression one bit. It was better to say *fluidly*, or *smoothly*—or, better yet, to apply no modifier but rather to plainly state the action in question and allow the reader to envision it. In redacting the manuscript, Pfefferkorn tallied twenty-four instances of movements taking place *in one fluid motion*, striking all but three from the final text. Two he left in because he felt he owed it to Bill to not eliminate whole-sale what was obviously a pet phrase. The third *in one fluid motion* came when Stapp simultaneously answered his cell phone and floored an attacker, a spectacular move that began with Stapp's hand darting to his belt clip and removing the phone before proceeding in a sharp, shal-low arc up toward his face to answer the call, the resultant jutting elbow striking his assailant in the solar plexus, leaving him—the assailant—"sinking to his knees, gasp-ing for breath" (a phrase that itself cropped up again and again, along with "snapped his neck," "dove for cover," and "chambered a round") while he—Stapp—calmly said *I'm gonna have to call you back*. In this case, Pfefferkorn decided the phrase meant something: it conveyed that two fundamentally disjointed movements were being car-ried out with such precision and ease that they appeared harmonious. He doubted that any but the most careful reader would intuit the thought behind the words, but games like this kept him entertained throughout the revision process. They also helped him convince himself that his efforts were not wholly without artistic merit.

He scrubbed out all the shouts, exclamations, declara-tions, and avowals, leaving in their stead a simple "said." He mopped up inappropriate tears and scraped down the ugliest dialogue. Names, dates, and locations had to be changed. Last, there was the matter of the non-ending. It was to this, the most daunting task, that Pfefferkorn turned his attention for a full month.

An unstated rule of William de Vallée novels held that justice must be done—to a point. The sadistic minions, the brainless goons, always met an untimely end, but the mastermind often escaped to plot another day. This lack of resolution was important for two reasons. First, it implied that there were more adventures to be had. There was, too, a certain pleasurable chill in the suggestion that evil still lurked. In this day and age it was implausible to suggest that good would ever fully prevail. The contemporary reader required a touch of moral and narrative ambiguity. But only a touch. In constructing his new ending, then, Pfefferkorn strove mightily to achieve this delicate balance.

He killed off Dick Stapp.

Or at least he appeared to. It was unclear: a cliff-hanger. And Stapp was not Stapp, for Pfefferkorn had rechristened him Harry Shagreen.

What remained after Pfefferkorn had finished his tinkering was an extraordinarily odd hybrid of his and Bill's writing styles. Some might quibble with the ending, but Pfefferkorn thought there was more than enough justification for buying the manuscript in its present form. He printed it out. He printed out the new cover page. The new title was *Blood Eyes*. He put the book in the mail to his agent and waited for a response.

TWO **COMMERCE**

24.

Pfefferkorn was rich. His novel *Blood Eyes* had been on the bestseller list for one hundred twenty-one days. His publisher had chosen the book as the lead title for the fall list and had consequently poured ample funds into promoting it, taking out ads in newspapers and magazines of national repute as well as on the Internet. Now Pfefferkorn's embossed foil name was visible at airports, supermarkets, and discount warehouse stores, on library shelves and in the hands of reading groups. Boarding a busy bus or a subway car in a major American city without seeing at least one person engrossed in a copy would present a challenge. The novel had been reconstituted as an audiobook, an abridged audiobook, an electronic book, an "enhanced" electronic book, an "amplified" electronic book, a "3-D" electronic book, a graphic novel, a pop-up book, a "3-D" pop-up graphic novel, as manga, in Braille, and in a large-print edition. It had been translated into thirty-three foreign languages, including Slovakian, Zlabian, and Thai.

The success of the book was not strictly commercial. Critical acclaim had been lavish. Among the phrases oft repeated were "far better written than your average thriller" and "turns the genre on its ear." Several reviewers had singled out the ending for its deft touch.

Pfefferkorn had granted scores of interviews and had been the subject of countless blogs. He had attended a convention of thriller aficionados who anointed him "Rookie of the Year." He had shaken so many hands and inscribed so many copies that his wrist had begun to ache. His publisher had established for him a website and encouraged him to engage in the new social media. He responded personally to every letter and e-mail. The volume of correspondence was smaller than he would have expected, given his sales figures. Most people didn't have the time to write, it seemed. Those who did tended to fall at the far ends of the bell curve, either blindly adoring or else filled with rabid, foam-flecked hatred. The former greatly outnumbered the latter. For this, Pfefferkorn was glad.

He was given to understand by his agent that there was no longer any money for book tours. Amortizing the cost of a flight, a hotel, a media escort, and meals against the number of books the average author could expect to sell at any given event invariably resulted in a net loss— making it all the more remarkable that the publisher had decided to send him to eleven cities. He was met everywhere by large, enthusiastic crowds. It took him a while to get the hang of public speaking. At first he stammered. Then he spoke too fast. He told himself that an audience was basically a roomful of students. With this in mind he was able to relax, and by the end of the tour, he felt slightly disappointed that it was over.

Despite the speed and force of the changes being wrought in his life, he tried to keep a level head. His luxuries were few. He found a new apartment, bigger than his old one but far less than what he could have afforded. At his daughter's behest he acquired a cell phone, and he would occasionally take a taxi rather than the bus— although never to work. That he did not quit his job was a fact he made a point of mentioning in interviews. Teaching, he said, had always been his first love. He said this not out of guile. It was a lie he had come to embrace, as it helped him convince himself that his values remained unchanged. He was still Pfefferkorn, adjunct professor of creative writing. Waiting on the corner for the number forty-four, he would note his position on the bestseller list, then deliberately deflate his sense of satisfaction by turning to the front page. One glance at the headlines was all it took. Everything was right with the world, which was to say: everything was appalling. A babysitter had murdered her charges by supergluing them to the blades of a ceiling fan and running it on high. A senator had been indicted for hiring a prostitute, then refusing to pay with anything other than bulk-sized bags of nougats. The president of East Zlabia had survived an assassination attempt for which the West Zlabians were denying responsibility. Members of the international community were calling on both sides to exercise restraint. It was business as usual. Violence, poverty, and corruption still reigned. So he had made a little money. So what?

Pfefferkorn met the parents of his future son-in-law. They all gathered for dinner at a restaurant Pfefferkorn's daughter had picked out. This time his steak came in the shape of an Escher fork, which made it difficult to eat, as it kept disappearing each time he tried to cut into it.

An agreement was reached: Pfefferkorn was to assume half the cost of the wedding. As father of the bride, he was bound by tradition to pay more, but Paul's parents refused to budge. Pfefferkorn, understanding that they did not want to look cheap or mercenary, did not press. Any arrangement was fine with him so long as he was not excluded. Throughout dinner he watched the clock, and at a predetermined moment he excused himself to the restroom. On the way back he gave the waiter his credit card, paying for the entire meal and leaving a generous tip.

25.

One worry remained, of course: Carlotta, with whom he had not spoken in close to a year. Pfefferkorn assumed that she had read his novel. For him to have suddenly produced a blockbuster thriller was an awfully convenient coincidence, and if he were her, he would be unable to resist a quick peek. When she did, the similarities to *Shadowgame* would be unmissable. True, she had claimed never to read Bill's books before completion. But what husband didn't talk about his work with his wife, if only casually? At minimum Bill must have described the basic premise to her. Pfefferkorn therefore had to conclude that she did know, and that her lack of response was deliberate. Every day that her call did not come reconfirmed that she was waiting for the right time to turn the tables on him—waiting until his fame reached its apex, so that his downfall would be all the more painful. He had never taken her for a cruel woman, and to imagine her scheming against him like this distressed him in the extreme.

He had but one way to protect himself. Bill's original typewritten manuscript, wrapped in a plastic bag and stashed under Pfefferkorn's new kitchen sink, was the only extant copy. Without it, there could be no proof of his misdeed, so he fed it, five pages at a time, into his new fireplace.

Seeing the paper blacken and shrink made him feel a trifle safer. Even so, he did not relish the idea of Carlotta knowing his secret. He feared her scorn far more than any public exposure. He wondered if he had blown his last shot at happiness. Several times he picked up the phone to call her, only to lose his nerve and hang up. Be a man, he told himself. Then he wondered what that meant.

26.

Soon after *Blood Eyes* began to make waves, calls started to come from Hollywood. Acting on the advice of his film agent, Pfefferkorn held out for more money, although he twice allowed himself to be flown to California to take meetings with loud men in turtlenecks. He enjoyed expensive lunches at no cost. He thought it comical and sad that the richer one was, the less often one had to pay for things.

"They want to meet you," his film agent said. "This one looks like it might be legit."

She had said as much the first two times, but Pfefferkorn packed his carry-on and flew to Los Angeles.

"A. S. Peppers," the producer said, using the nom de plume Pfefferkorn had chosen after his surname was deemed too difficult to pronounce, "you're a *star*."

The assistant producers sitting along the wall nodded obsequiously.

"Thanks," Pfefferkorn said.

The producer's secretary poked her head in to announce that the head of the studio urgently needed to speak to the producer.

"Dang it all," the producer said, standing up. "Well, you're in good hands."

Pfefferkorn sat while the assistant producers ignored him and gossiped for forty minutes.

"Sorry 'bout that," the producer said, returning. "We'll be in touch."

Pfefferkorn's cell phone rang as he was walking across the studio lot.

"How'd it go?" his film agent asked.

"Great."

His hotel was located on a posh stretch of Wilshire Boulevard. He took a walk, passing a small group of people picketing a department store. Crossing the street to avoid them, he was then confronted by a woman who bade him to stop the atrocities in West Zlabia. He moved on.

Alone in his suite, he did the same thing he had done on his previous two trips to Los Angeles: he dialed Carlotta's number on his cell phone, stopping short of pressing CALL. Be a man, he thought. He picked up his room phone and instructed the hotel valet to bring around his rental car.

27.

Pfefferkorn announced himself to the intercom. A moment later the gates parted. He inadvertently stomped the gas, spinning out on the gravel. He palmed his chest and told himself to keep it together. He checked himself in the rearview mirror, wiped the sweat from his brow, and drove slowly up the driveway.

Carlotta stood by the front door, the dog peering out from between her ankles. She wore black leggings and a man's shirt and was without makeup or jewelry. Like him, she appeared to be perspiring. Like him, she seemed skittish and circumspect.

The butler held the car door for him.

"Jameson," Carlotta said, "you'll park Mr. Pfefferkorn's car, please."

"Madame."

The rental car dipped down the path and out of sight.

They stood, looking at each other. Pfefferkorn came forward, holding out his gifts: a bouquet of flowers and a romance novel. Carlotta put up a hand.

"Don't touch me," she said.

Pfefferkorn stiffened. His stomach dropped. He

wished he hadn't given the butler his keys, so that he could leap back in the car and speed back to his hotel.

"I'll be going, then," he said.

"Oh, I don't mean *that*," Carlotta said. "I'm filthy right now."

The dog yipped happily, rushed forward, and began humping Pfefferkorn's leg.

"Botkin," Carlotta said. "Botkin. Just give him a good kick, he'll get the message."

Pfefferkorn knelt and gently pried the dog away. It rolled over, and he rubbed its stomach. "I should have called." He gave the dog a pat and stood up. "I'm sorry."

They smiled at each other.

"Arthur," Carlotta said. "Dear Arthur. Welcome back."

28.

"Jesús, I'd like you to meet my dear friend, Arthur Pfefferkorn. Arthur, this is my tango partner, Jesús María de Lunchbox."

The man's silk shirt was unbuttoned to the navel, flashing open as he bowed to Pfefferkorn and revealing a tan, muscular torso.

"Nice to meet you," Pfefferkorn said.

The man bowed again.

"Let's call it a day," Carlotta said. "Monday, then? The usual time?"

"*Señora,*" Jesús María said. He moved gracefully across the ballroom to collect his bag before bowing a third time and slipping away. Carlotta stood toweling off her neck and chugging from a bottle of vitamin-fortified water. She noticed Pfefferkorn frowning at the empty doorway. "What."

"Are you," Pfefferkorn said. "Eh."

She giggled. "Oh, Arthur."

"It's not my business," he said.

"Arthur, please. You really are too silly. He's queer as a three-dollar bill."

Pfefferkorn was relieved.

"Anyway," she said, "I'm not sure what right you have to complain. It's not like you've been around."

"I'm sorry."

"It's as much my fault as yours." She sighed. "We're like a couple of children, aren't we."

He smiled.

"Let me get cleaned up," she said. "Then you can tell me all about it."

29.

They ate at the same Italian restaurant, ordered the same delicious wine, stuffed themselves with pasta. He thought he had never seen her so beautiful, her strong features mellowed by the liquid flicker of candlelight.

"You must be very busy these days," Carlotta said.

"Off and on."

"You were in town," she said. "I saw the poster at the bookstore."

His nerves had been deflating over the course of dinner, but under her unwavering stare, terror ballooned anew, larger than before, and he braced himself for the pinprick that would burst him in an instant.

"You didn't call," she said.

He said nothing.

"Why?"

"I didn't want to upset you."

"Why in the world would that upset me?"

"We didn't exactly leave things on a major chord."

"All the more reason to call," she said.

"I'm sorry."

"Silly man," she said. "I forgive you."

The waiter arrived with dessert menus. When he had gone, Pfefferkorn girded himself to ask the question hanging around his neck like an anvil.

"Did you read it?"

She did not look up from the menu. "Of course."

There was a silence.

"And?" he said.

Now she looked up. She cleared her throat. "Well, like I said, I'm no thriller expert. Bill is my only point of comparison. But I thought it was very good."

He waited. "That's it?"

"Don't be such a writer. I said it was very good."

He wasn't looking for praise, though. He was looking for exoneration. He studied her closely as she debated out loud whether to order dessert. He sought a clue. Some preoccupation around the eyes. Some tightness in the lips. Some backward-canted posture of concealed revulsion. He waited and waited, yet all she seemed to care about was whether the strawberry zabaglione was worth the calories. At first he wouldn't allow himself to accept what was happening. But it kept on happening, and by "it" he meant "nothing." Nothing was happening, because she had no idea what he had done. It was the stuff of bad novels, but it was true. It struck him then that the stuff of bad novels was far more likely to occur in real life than the stuff of good novels, because good novels enlarged on reality while bad novels leaned on it. In a good novel, Carlotta's motivations were far more complicated than they appeared. In a good novel, she was withholding her accusations so she could spring them on him later to achieve an unexpected end. In the bad novel of life, she simply didn't know. His troubles ended here. That she did not seem to care for *Blood Eyes* was beside the point. It mostly wasn't his book. He wanted to jump up and sing. He was safe. He was free.

"*Signora?*"

Carlotta relinquished the menu and ordered a cappuccino.

"And the *signore?*"

"Same," Pfefferkorn said.

The waiter departed.

"If you knew I was in town, why didn't you come to the reading?" Pfefferkorn asked.

"I didn't want to upset you."

"That's the same excuse I used," he said.

"Well, I thought you were angry at me."

"I wasn't."

"It was a reasonable assumption based on our last conversation."

"Why is it," he said, "that when I misjudge you I'm wrong, but when you make the same misjudgment of me it's reasonable?"

"Because," she said.

"Right," he said.

30.

He extended his ticket and they spent a blissful ten days eating, laughing, and making love. There was a refreshing abruptness to their romance, a welcome dispensing of preliminaries, as they enjoyed each other for their own sakes. Bill's name seldom came up, and when it did it was spoken with a kind of abstract fondness, as though he were a memorable character in a novel they had both enjoyed. The triangle had collapsed into a line, one that ran directly from Pfefferkorn's heart to hers.

She drove him to the airport herself.

"Let's not wait another year, please," she said.

"I don't plan on it."

"I can come there."

"That won't be necessary," he said.

It wasn't necessary, because he could now afford to fly across the country every few weeks. He soon became a regular in coach—this a concession to a lifetime of frugality—growing friendly with the stewardesses who worked the route, enough so that they would slip him freebies or sneak him into business class if the flight was empty. Exiting the airport, he would find the Bentley idling curbside, Jameson at the wheel, a cold bottle of seltzer waiting in back.

Los Angeles was growing on him. Like every city, it was a lot more enjoyable when you had money. Carlotta took him to quality restaurants. They browsed boutiques. They lounged at the beach club where the de Vallées were members. These were activities he could not have tolerated before, because he would have been too embarrassed to let Carlotta pay. In most instances, she still did pay —she had a way of effortlessly dispensing with the bill when he wasn't looking—but it bothered him less, for he knew that, were she to forget her credit cards, he had the ability to step in and save the day. Pfefferkorn had heard it said that money was freedom, and this was true in the usual sense: having money enabled him to go places previously closed to him and acquire items previously out of reach. However, there was another, less obvious sense in which money was freedom. Money bred self-acceptance, liberating him from a sense of inadequacy. At times he felt ashamed that he had come to evaluate himself in such crude, stark terms. But the feeling swiftly passed, and he was once again able to enjoy himself.

31.

"You're not offended, are you, Arthur?"

"Not in the slightest."

It was a Saturday morning, three weeks before Pfefferkorn's daughter's wedding, which Carlotta had just said she would not be attending. The remains of breakfast in bed were on the nightstand. The smell of strong coffee lingered. Pfefferkorn shifted, rustling the sheets and slopping the disordered newspaper to the floor. He moved to retrieve it but she tugged him back.

"Leave it," she said.

He relaxed again and she relaxed against him.

"It was thoughtful of you to invite me," Carlotta said.

"Her suggestion."

"Now you really are making me feel guilty."

"I'm sure she won't even notice. She's trapped in a bubble of self-absorption."

"Well, she is the bride."

"I didn't say I blame her," he said, "only that she won't care."

"I can go," she said unconvincingly.

"Not if you don't want to."

There was a silence.

"I do and I don't," she said.

He said nothing.

"It would be hard for me, I think, to see her all grown up."

"I understand."

She shook her head. "It's not that it makes me feel old. I mean, yes, it makes me feel old. But that's not what I'm afraid of."

There was a silence.

"You make choices," she said. "You can't know how you'll feel about them twenty years down the line."

He nodded.

"It was my decision," she said. "It always was. Bill tried to change my mind but I had it made up."

She fell silent. He felt a wet tickle on his bare shoulder.

"Hey, now," he said.

She apologized. He brushed the hair from her forehead and kissed her cheeks.

"You don't suppose it's not too late?" she said.

"Anything's possible."

She laughed and wiped her eyes. "Hooray for modern medical science."

"You'd really want to start with that, now?"

"Probably not," she said.

"It's very tiring," he said.

"So they say."

"Trust me."

"That's another thing Bill always talked about. What a good father you were."

"How would he know?"

"We admired how you managed it on your own."

"I didn't have a choice."

"Take some credit, Arthur."

He said nothing.

"You must wonder, sometimes," she said. "If things had turned out differently."

He did not answer her. He had spent thirty years fleeing that question, and only now, when it no longer mattered, had he come to some kind of peace.

"I'm sorry," she said.

"It's all right."

They lay together without speaking. He had never been anywhere as silent as the de Vallée mansion. There was no settling of wooden joints, no sigh of air-conditioning. According to Carlotta, that had been the goal. Peace and quiet, privacy and solitude. The whole house had been insulated to the utmost degree, and Carlotta and Bill's master suite especially. Pfefferkorn told himself that he had a right to stop thinking of it as "Carlotta and Bill's." He had a right to think of it as Carlotta's alone, or possibly Carlotta's and his. Then he told himself not to be bothered by technicalities.

She sat up. "Let's do something fun today."

"Seconded."

She peeled back the duvet and headed to the bathroom. He heard the hiss of hot water. He bent over the side of the bed and picked up the paper. The headlines were uniformly depressing: terrorism, unemployment, global warming, performance-enhancing drugs, Zlabian unrest. He left the paper on the bed and went to join Carlotta in the shower.

32.

Every cost associated with the wedding ended up being triple what Pfefferkorn had been quoted. He didn't care. He was set on giving his daughter everything she wanted. At her second fitting, she had spied, from across the store, a different gown, a thrilling one, the right one. Pfefferkorn did not blink. He wrote a check. The mother of the groom had insisted the caterer use premium organic ingredients. Pfefferkorn did not protest. He wrote a check. The bandleader had expressed the view that five pieces were insufficiently festive. Nine would be better, he said, and Pfefferkorn, taking out his checkbook, agreed. What began as a simple afternoon affair soon swelled into an entire hosted weekend, with meals and entertainment provided throughout. Pfefferkorn wrote one check after another, and when the appointed day arrived, and he saw his daughter's joy, he knew he had chosen correctly.

The party was over. Pfefferkorn, his tuxedo wrinkled and damp, sat alone in the reception hall, listening to the clatter of chairs being stacked. One by one, the guests had come up to him to pump his hand and offer congratulations before stumbling off toward the complimentary valet. Pfefferkorn's literary agent had been among the last to leave, and it was his parting words that Pfefferkorn was mulling over.

"Great party," the agent had said. "Give me a call when your ears stop ringing."

Pfefferkorn knew what was coming. In the wake of *Blood Eyes*'s success, he had allowed himself to be coaxed into signing a lucrative three-book deal. The deadline for the first draft of the next Harry Shagreen novel was fast approaching and nobody had seen a sample chapter. The publisher was getting nervous. Pfefferkorn sympathized. They were right to be nervous: he had yet to write a word. At the time of the signing, he had turned in a plot summary, but it was sketchy and improvised, and in the ensuing months it had proven worthless. He had not begun to panic, although he could see panic around the corner. He did not have a plan. He never did. Bill would have had a plan. He was not Bill.

"Don't be sad."

His daughter and her new husband were walking toward him, hand in hand. She was barefoot, slender, her radiant face framed by tendrils of hair that had come loose at her temples. The sheer beauty of her caused Pfefferkorn's chest to tighten.

"I know," she said. "Kind of an anticlimax."

"I'm just depressed thinking about the bill," Pfefferkorn said.

She stuck her tongue out at him.

Pfefferkorn addressed his new son-in-law. "I take it your folks are all settled."

Paul's parents were spending the night in the hotel before driving home in the morning. Pfefferkorn had quietly paid for them to be upgraded to a suite.

"They're super," Paul said. His tie was gone and his jacket pockets bulged with the bride's shoes. "You're the man, Dad."

There was a silence.

"Well," Paul said, "the chamber of consummation awaits."

Embarrassed, Pfefferkorn looked away.

"Go on," Pfefferkorn's daughter said. "I'll meet you up there."

"But I want to carry you across the threshold."

"Then wait for me outside."

"A man can only wait so long."

"I'll be there soon."

Paul smiled and strode off.

"Sorry about that," Pfefferkorn's daughter said. "He's hammered."

She pulled out a chair and sat, and together they watched as the hotel workers began to disassemble the dance floor.

"I hope it's okay he called you Dad."

"As long as I can call him Junior."

She smiled and took his hand. "Thank you for everything."

"You're welcome."

"I know it turned out to be more than you expected."

"It was a bargain," he said.

A section of parquet was carted away.

Pfefferkorn felt he should say more—offer a piece of

advice, perhaps. But what could he say that would not ring hollow? She knew better than anyone what a disaster his own marriage had been. For many fathers, it would have been easy, and sufficient, to say *I love you*. To Pfefferkorn this was unthinkably trite. If one could not express something in an original way, one ought not to express it at all, and so he never did. There were other, older reasons for his silence. Forced to be both mother and father, he had done neither job well, and during his daughter's adolescence, when she started throwing his mistakes back at him, he had responded by lacquering his heart, one thin layer at a time, until it was impenetrable. He saw himself without any other option. If she had ever understood how frightened he was of losing her affection, he would have forfeited his already tenuous authority. Even now, he found himself skirting emotion by resorting to practicalities.

"Always come to me if you need help."

"We'll be fine, Daddy."

"I'm not saying you won't. Life costs a lot more than it did when I was your age. You're young, but that doesn't mean you should suffer."

"Daddy—"

"Say you will, please. For me."

"Okay," she said. "I will."

"Thank you."

More parquet was lifted.

"I want you to know how proud I am of you," she said.

Pfefferkorn said nothing.

"I've always believed in you. I knew you had it in you.

I've always known it would happen for you, and now that it has, I'm just . . . so happy."

Pfefferkorn felt mildly sick.

The final piece of the dance floor was removed.

"It comes apart so fast," his daughter said.

There was a silence. Lights began to blink off.

"I think that's a sign," she said.

He let go of her hand.

"Have a good night, Daddy."

"You, too . . . Sweetheart?"

"Yes?"

He paused. He understood that she was leaving him, and that this was his last chance to tell her anything.

"Careful he doesn't drop you," he said.

33.

Pfefferkorn met his agent for lunch.

"Great party."

"Thanks."

"I've been to my fair share of Jewish weddings, but that was one of the best, if not the. *Love* that hora."

"It's a fun time."

The agent's salad arrived, layered in a tall vase. He

worked his fork down inside and stabbed a quantity of lettuce. "So, then," he said. "Back to the grind."

Pfefferkorn nodded, buttering his roll.

"How's that coming, if you don't mind my asking."

"It's coming," Pfefferkorn said.

"I understand completely," the agent said. "I'm not trying to rush you."

Pfefferkorn chewed.

"This is an organic process. You're a writer, not a vending machine. You don't push a button and bang, out it comes. Although you might be interested to know how excited everyone is. I talk to other editors, I go to Frankfurt, all I hear is, what's Harry Shagreen's next move. It's up to me, of course, to shield you from all that, so you can work."

"Thanks."

The agent held up a hand. "You never need to thank me for doing my job." He tilted the vase to get to the bottom of his salad. "So you've been making progress, though."

Pfefferkorn regretted not having ordered an appetizer. He had finished his roll, and now he had nothing to put in his mouth. He took a long sip of water and wiped his lips on his napkin. It was starchy. "I've had a few thoughts," he said.

"That's good enough for me," the agent said. "I'm not going to ask you anything else."

"It's all right," Pfefferkorn said. "We can talk about it."

The agent put down his salad fork. "Only if you want to."

Pfefferkorn had spent the previous few days preparing

for this moment, but now he felt unequal to the task. He took another sip of water. "It seems to me," he said, "that the crux of the issue is the relationship between book one and book two. Last time we had both a nuclear threat and a biological one. So the question is, how do you top that?"

"Exactly. How."

"There's the pat answer, of course. Come up with something even more threatening."

"I like it already."

"But, see, then you run into a new problem."

"Which is."

"You're getting dangerously close to self-parody."

"Right," the agent said. "How so."

"I mean, it's possible to make the situation even more apocalyptic, but if we do that, we run the risk of becoming cartoonish."

"Huh," the agent said. "Okay. So—"

"So I look at this as an opportunity for Harry Shagreen to face down a new kind of enemy. One that nobody has ever faced before."

". . . okay."

"One he's totally unprepared for."

"Okay. Okay. I like it. Keep going."

"One that brings him to the brink of total collapse."

"That's good. That's *very* good."

"Harry Shagreen," Pfefferkorn said, "is going to face down the most terrifying adversary imaginable."

"Yeah?" the agent said. He was bent across the table. "And?"

"And it's going to change him forever."

"Fabulous. Brilliant. I love it."

"I'm so glad," Pfefferkorn said.

"So," the agent said, "who is it."

"Who's what."

"Who's he going to fight."

"It's not a who so much as a what," Pfefferkorn said.

"Okay, what."

"Crushing self-doubt," Pfefferkorn said.

There was a silence.

"The barramundi," the waiter said. "And the filet, medium."

"Thank you," Pfefferkorn said.

"Enjoy."

The silence resumed. Pfefferkorn, aware of having ruined his agent's day or possibly even his year, engaged in cutting up his steak, which was in the shape of a Klein bottle.

"Huh," the agent said.

Pfefferkorn ate without appetite.

"Hnh," the agent said. "Hah."

There was a silence.

"I know it's unorthodox," Pfefferkorn said.

". . . yes."

"But I see it as having breakthrough potential."

". . . could be," the agent said.

"I think so," Pfefferkorn said.

"Yeah, no no no no no, it definitely could be. Eh."

There was a silence.

Pfefferkorn cut meat.

"All right, so," the agent said. "Look. I think it's really

creative, I think it's original. So, you know, that's all, that's fantastic. You know, and I think that's great. Ahhm. At the same time, I think you'll agree that the creative process is, ah, a questioning process, so I think it's worth our while here to ask ourselves a couple of questions."

"All right," Pfefferkorn said.

"All right. So. Uh. So, I'm a reader. I bought your first book, I loved it. I'm in the bookstore, hey, look, he's got a new one. I take out my credit card, I go home, bam, I'm in bed, I'm curled up, I'm turning pages . . . and I'm saying to myself, 'You know . . . *this* . . . is kind of uncharted territory.'" The agent paused. "You understand what I'm saying?"

"Nobody said it was going to be simple," Pfefferkorn said.

"Right, but—"

"I think it's a necessary step for me. Artistically."

"Okay, but, be that as it may, you have to remember, people have certain expectations."

"If I'm not happy with it, it's not going to be a good book."

"One hundred percent. I'm not debating that. I'm just saying, from the perspective of your readership, is this what I think I'm going to get when I pick up an A. S. Peppers? And the answer, okay, the answer, if we're being honest here, is, not so much."

"And that makes it bad."

"Who said bad? Did I use that word? You used that word. Nobody's saying bad. I said *different*."

"That's the point of art," Pfefferkorn said.

The agent pinched the bridge of his nose. "Let's please not get wrapped up in theory."

"There's an audience for this kind of book," Pfefferkorn said.

"I'm not saying there isn't."

"I'd read it."

"Not everyone's as smart as you."

"Why do we insist on underestimating the intelligence of the American public?"

"I'm not saying those people aren't out there, okay? The question is: the audience for that kind of book, is it *your* audience. You're not starting from scratch. People know the name A. S. Peppers, they know what he writes, and they have those things in mind when they plunk down their twenty-four ninety-five. A novel is a contract. It's a promise, *to* the reader, *from* the writer. You're asking people to trust you. And, but—but look. I can see how strongly you feel about this. I'm not saying it can't be done. I'm saying it's all in the execution."

Pfefferkorn said nothing.

"If anyone can make it work," the agent said, "it's you."

"I appreciate the vote of confidence."

"That's my job," the agent said. He still hadn't so much as glanced at his entrée. "So. When can I expect to see some pages."

34.

It could have gone worse. He hadn't been rebuffed out-right. And he agreed with his agent that constructing a thriller around a man battling his own sense of inade-quacy was strictly a question of execution. The more dar-ing the proposition, however, the more finesse required to carry it off, and Pfefferkorn knew his own limitations. Perhaps there existed someone capable of writing such a book. He was not him.

He sat at his desk, answering fan e-mail. A woman asked if he would take a look at her novel. Pfefferkorn thanked her for her interest, explaining that it was his policy never to read unpublished material. An elderly lady chastised him for his use of profanity. For kicks he drafted a long, profanity-laced reply, then scrapped it, responding that he was sorry he had offended her. A community cen-ter in Skokie invited him to deliver the keynote at its annual authors' luncheon. He referred them to his speak-ers bureau. He handled the remainder of the queries in short order, leaving him no choice but to click on a file labeled "novel 2," bringing up the half page of text he had managed to produce in eleven months of work.

For Harry Shagreen, life was never simple.

It wasn't great literature, but it served its purpose. It was what followed that made him cringe.

Shagreen was a marked man.

"For God's sake," Pfefferkorn said.

He deleted the sentence. Then he deleted the sentence that followed, and the next, until he was left with his opening line and the germ of a conversation.

"Make it a double," Shagreen said.
"You've had enough," the bartender said.

Pfefferkorn had had enough as well. He deleted the dialogue. He did a word count. So far, his new blockbuster novel was seven words long.

35.

"I hate to say I told you so," Pfefferkorn's daughter said.

They were at her apartment, sitting on the sofa while Paul finished making dinner. Pfefferkorn had mentioned that he was flying to California in a few days' time. His daughter smirked whenever Carlotta's name was mentioned, as if she'd known all along they'd end up together.

"Then don't say it," Pfefferkorn said.

"I won't."

"Except that by not saying it, you're still saying it."

"Oh, Daddy. Lighten up. I think it's sweet. What's on the agenda?"

"There's a party for the Philharmonic."

"Sounds glamorous."

"Boring," he said.

"So jaded, so fast."

"It doesn't take long," Pfefferkorn said.

From the kitchen Paul yelled that dinner would be ready in five minutes.

"He's such a magician," Pfefferkorn's daughter said.

Pfefferkorn bit his tongue. He had been the victim of his son-in-law's cooking on a few too many occasions. Invariably, something went awry—a pot boiled over, a pudding failed to set—and substandard equipment, rather than the chef's lack of skill, was blamed.

Paul popped his head in. "We can start with the salad, if you're hungry." He was wearing an apron that said **Culinary Ninja**.

"Yum," Pfefferkorn's daughter said.

They filed into the eat-in kitchen. The apartment was the same postage-stamp one-bedroom Paul had lived in as a bachelor, and with the arrival of a second person, it had begun to feel a bit like a refugee camp. Pfefferkorn had made sure to use the restroom before sitting down, knowing that once he got into his chair, he would be unable to leave without Paul sliding the entire table out, which necessitated scooting over the watercooler, which in turn involved removal of the freestanding butcher block.

"We have too much stuff," Pfefferkorn's daughter said as Pfefferkorn sucked in his gut.

The salad was complicated, with exotic seeds and rinds. Pfefferkorn had to be told which bits to swallow, which to chew but spit out, and which were strictly aromatic.

"This is amazing," Pfefferkorn's daughter said. "Where'd you get the recipe?"

"The Internet," Paul said.

Pfefferkorn used his fork to pry a husk from between his front teeth. "Delicious," he said.

"Thanks, Dad."

"It has such a nice smokiness to it," Pfefferkorn's daughter said. "What is that?"

"Something's burning," Pfefferkorn said.

Paul lunged for the oven door. An acrid black cloud billowed out. Pfefferkorn's daughter ran to the sink and began filling a bowl with water. Pfefferkorn, coughing, strove gamely to extricate himself from behind the table.

"Wait," Paul yelled.

Pfefferkorn's daughter doused the interior of the oven. Hissing and sizzling ensued. Grease spattered everywhere. Pfefferkorn's daughter shrieked and dropped the bowl, which shattered. Paul dove headfirst into the steaming oven, hoping to salvage the chicken, but it was soaked and charred beyond repair. He beheld it and moaned.

Pfefferkorn's daughter said consoling things as she bent and gathered shards of the bowl in her bare hands.

"Can somebody please help me here?" Pfefferkorn asked. "I'm stuck."

By consensus, the oven was the culprit. Pfefferkorn and his daughter returned to the sofa to let the kitchen air out.

"We're at the end of our rope with this city," she said. "It's like living in a zoo."

"Where else would you go?"

She named a suburb.

"It's not that far," she said. "You can be at our house in thirty minutes."

"You make it sound as if you've got the place all picked out," he said.

"I do," she said.

She led him to the closet Paul used as a home office and showed Pfefferkorn the listing on the computer. "Isn't it so pretty?"

"The pictures are nice," he said.

"You should see it in real life."

"You've been there?"

"Our broker took me last Sunday."

"You have a broker?"

"She's the number-one person in the area," she said.

"That's nice," Pfefferkorn said.

"I was wondering," she said, "if you wanted to come out and see it yourself."

"Honey? Dad?"

"We're back here. I'm showing him the house."

Paul appeared, plastic bags of takeout hooked on his fingers. "Nifty, right?"

Pfefferkorn looked at the images on the computer screen. "You said it."

36.

Following the party for the Philharmonic, Carlotta retired early, complaining of a headache and a sour stomach. As a precaution, they elected to spend the night apart. By now Pfefferkorn knew his way around well enough to find his own linens, and after tucking her in with tea and aspirin, he headed downstairs.

He paced the library restlessly, prying down volumes and putting them back. He wasn't in the mood to be sedentary. He was in the mood for activity. Specifically, he was in the mood for sex. He had hidden his disappointment from Carlotta, but his body had expectations. He scolded himself, remembering Oscar Wilde's remark about a luxury once sampled becoming a necessity. He wondered if that might make an interesting premise for a novel.

Aiming to burn off some energy, he went down to the pool room. He had gotten in the habit of swimming a few laps every day. He was no Bill, that was for sure, but at his age even moderate exercise accrued enormous benefits. He had trimmed down noticeably and could now swim for thirty minutes without needing to stop and catch his breath. He usually went in the afternoons, during Carlotta's tango session. She had tried to get him to join her, but he didn't like dancing any more than Bill had, and moreover, he didn't care for that Jesús María de Lunchbox character, what with his silk shirts and buttery pectorals.

He swam lazily for a while. He got out, dried himself with a fresh towel from the pyramid the maid kept stocked atop the smoothie bar, and redonned his dressing gown. It was designer, a gift from Carlotta so he wouldn't have to keep borrowing Bill's too-big one.

Upstairs, he examined the paintings, the sculpture, the furniture. He made a sandwich, took two bites, and discarded it. A nameless agitation had taken hold of him. He went outside to the terrace and crossed the lawn to the office path.

37.

He had not been in the barn since the night of his theft. By the look of it, neither had anyone else. The place had become a shrine by default, everything just as he had left it except now wearing a loose gray pelt. He erupted in sneezes and rubbed his watery eyes. There was the easy chair, the desk chair, the desk. The bookcase, the books, his book. The photographs. The jar of pens. What appeared to be a manuscript but was in fact a pile of blank paper with a title page.

A running fantasy had him discovering a cache of Bill's unpublished novels. He would have settled for much less than a full text. An outline would have helped. But of course no such thing existed, and if it did, he doubted his ability to realize anything from it. He had never suffered from a shortage of ideas, only a shortage of follow-through.

He fetched out the copy of his first novel, the one Bill had so lovingly pored over. He reread his snide inscription. Now that he was no longer poor, the idea of reducing a friendship as profound as theirs to a race felt beyond childish.

Someone tapped on the door.

There was nothing inherently wrong with him being here, but the memory of his sin draped over the present, and he felt a spasm of guilty panic. The maid and butler had gone for the day. That left Carlotta. Why wasn't she in bed? He waited for her to leave. There was another tap. He opened the door. The dog trotted past and plopped down beneath the desk.

Still clutching the copy of his novel, Pfefferkorn sat in the office chair, rubbing Botkin's back with his foot. He listened to the wind gusting through the unused portion of the barn. He inhaled deeply in search of goats. He closed his eyes. He opened his eyes and the photos above the desk had changed. No longer was it Bill in his sailor's getup, smiling jauntily. It was Pfefferkorn. He had Bill's beard and moustache. Carlotta's portrait had changed as well. Now the photo showed Pfefferkorn's ex-wife. Pfefferkorn stared in horror. He tried to get up but he was pinned to the chair. He opened his mouth to scream and he woke up. Outside, morning was breaking. The dog was gone. The door to the office was ajar. His novel was on the floor, fallen from his limp hand. Pfefferkorn picked it up, tucked it inside his dressing gown, and hurried back toward the main house before Carlotta awoke and found him missing.

38.

He left four days later, taking with him the annotated copy of *Shade of the Colossus*. He did not mention to Carlotta that he was borrowing it, and had he been pressed for an explanation, he could not have supplied one. Perhaps something about the barn compelled him to steal books.

His flight landed in time for him to catch a late dinner. He directed the taxi to his neighborhood sushi bar. He ordered without consulting the menu, laid the novel flat on the table, and started to read. A twenty-five-year-old work of failure seemed like an odd place to look for inspiration, but who knew? Obviously Bill had seen value in it.

Much of the book was flawed. Pfefferkorn could accept that now. He spared a thought for his first editor, a motherly woman who had since passed away. She had tried to get him to inject more humor. He had resisted, and eventually he had worn her down. He remembered her telling him, in a heated moment, that he was the most stubborn person she'd ever met. The word she used was "mulish." He smiled. I've changed, Madelaine, he thought. I've grown old.

For all its youthful excesses, though, Pfefferkorn thought it a worthy piece of art. There were passages of authentic beauty. He had chosen to mask the story's autobiographical roots by making the protagonist a painter rather than a writer. The final third described the protagonist's return home following his first successful exhibition. His father, the old tyrant, has fallen into a coma, and it is the son who makes the decision to withdraw life support. It remains ambiguous whether this is an act of mercy or one of vengeance. What is evident is that the power to carry it out has been made possible by his art. The closing paragraphs suggest that his next step is to attain the moral strength to focus that power.

Pfefferkorn poked at his red-bean ice cream, wondering if there was some way to convert the book into a blockbuster. He could make the father a gangster, and the son the policeman assigned to take him down. Father versus son, blood ties leading to spilled blood. It sounded promising. Certainly he needed to get something on paper, and fast. His agent had been leaving him voicemails in a tone of barely contained hysteria. Pfefferkorn had not called him back. Nor had he acknowledged the half-dozen e-mails from his editor. His current editor was young, scarcely older than Pfefferkorn's daughter, and while he tended to be deferential, it was clear that his patience was all but gone. He had hitched himself to Pfefferkorn's star and now he stood in danger of being brought crashing to earth. Again, Pfefferkorn sympathized. Lots of people depended on him. His daughter did. Paul did. *He* depended on him, if he hoped to continue flying across the country every few weeks. The future looked bleak. His ice cream had turned to a gloppy mauve puddle. Pfefferkorn asked for the check. The tip he left was smaller than usual.

39.

"Well? What do you think?"

"I think it's very nice."

"Oh, Daddy. That's the best you can do?"

They were standing in the dining room of the gigantic house Pfefferkorn's daughter wanted to buy. The real estate agent had stepped outside to take a call.

"What did she mean by that," Pfefferkorn asked, " 'Great bones'?"

"It means it has a lot of potential," Pfefferkorn's daughter said.

"What's wrong with it the way it is?"

"Nothing's wrong with it, but it's somebody else's taste. That's the way it always is. There's always going to be some work."

Pfefferkorn, a lifelong renter, wondered where his daughter had learned these things. "If you say so."

"I'm thinking we could knock out this wall. You know, like an open kitchen. Don't you think it would be fantastic for parties? Of course, we'll need to change the countertops."

"Of course."

"So you like it."

"I like that it makes you happy," he said.

"It does. It really does. Can't you see us raising a family here?"

It was the first time she had ever spoken of children. He had always made a point of saying nothing. The choice was hers. Hearing her raise the subject on her own filled him with an indescribable mix of emotions.

"I think it's a lovely house," he said.

"Me, too," his daughter said.

"And," he said, his head tingling with the excitement of a man about to push in all his chips, "I want to give it to you."

His daughter's eyes widened. "Daddy. That's not why I—"

"I know," he said.

"But we can't—I mean, Paul won't allow it."

"That's your job," he said. "You work on him."

"Daddy. You really mean it?"

He nodded.

"Oh," she said. "Oh, oh, oh."

"Sweetheart. What's wrong?"

"Nothing," she said. "I'm just so happy." She put her arms around him. "Thank you."

"Of course."

"Thank you so much."

"Of course," he said again, less confidently this time. "Eh. Sweetheart?"

"Yes, Daddy?"

"I forgot to ask about the price."

She named a number.

"Mm," he said.

"Trust me, it's a steal, even at asking."

"Mm-hm."

She released him. "You don't have to do this."

"I want to."

She embraced him again. "I love you so, so much."

Pfefferkorn tried to remember what he was due to be paid for the delivery and acceptance of his next novel. He tried to calculate whether it would be enough to pay for the entire house or whether they would need to take out a mortgage. He didn't know the first thing about real estate finance. Whatever the case was, he couldn't afford anything unless he turned in a book. The present word count stood at ninety-nine, including the title and dedication pages. He wondered if making an outlandish offer was his subconscious's way of motivating him to get to work. Or perhaps he could not bear to see his daughter disappointed. With the wedding, he had set a high standard, one he now felt compelled to meet and exceed. He pulled away so she wouldn't feel his heart starting to pound.

"Daddy? Are you okay?"

"I'm fine."

"You look a little green," she said. "Do you want to sit down?"

He shook his head. He managed to produce a smile. "Question for you," he said.

"Yes, Daddy?"

"When I'm old and pissing my pants, where's my room going to be?"

"Stop."

"Oh, I get it. You're going to put me in a home."

"Daddy. *Stop.*"

"Never mind, then."

40.

Pfefferkorn's success had at once heightened and undercut his stature as a professor. On the one hand, demand for his creative writing classes had grown, with long waiting lists established. With so large a pool available to him, he had the ability to control the composition of the class. However, he tended—stupidly, he thought—to admit a disproportionate number of literary types. These were the very students who tended to be snobbish about his work, comporting themselves with disdain, as though he could not possibly teach them about real literature when he had made a fortune writing trash. Even his good reviews provided grounds for scorn, signaling the death of critical integrity. The fact that his first novel had been literary fiction did not impress anyone. Nobody had heard of it. Pfefferkorn often wondered if he ought to go back to shepherding fragile young women.

The story under discussion that morning centered on an old man nearing the end of his life. He was tending his garden, oblivious to how its flourishing mocked his own senescence. The old man then watched a film in which the growth of flowers was shown, sped up, so that they went from seedling to full bloom to wilting to dead, all in a matter of seconds. This sequence was described in minute detail. The story ended with a cryptic fragment of dialogue.

The author was a twenty-year-old boy named Benjamin who came to class dressed in a homburg. His grasp of the aging process was limited to lurid descriptions of the male body in decay, although Pfefferkorn did acknowledge that the young man wrote with impressive confidence about urogenital problems and arthritis. Still, in Pfefferkorn's opinion, the story lacked emotional insight. Indeed, it made no attempt whatsoever to penetrate the old man's psyche at all. It was as if the author had laid the character on a slab and left him there. When Pfefferkorn attempted to raise this critique he met a blistering counterattack, not only from Benjamin but from a host of like-minded supporters. They argued that Pfefferkorn's understanding of character was antiquated. They abhorred writers who overexplained. Pfefferkorn defended himself by citing avant-garde and postmodern writers whom he enjoyed, stating that even these seemingly stone-faced works had at their center a moist, beating core of humanity. "That is total bullshit," Benjamin said. "We're all robots," a hard young woman named Gretchen said. Pfefferkorn asked her to explain what she meant by that. "I mean we're all robots," she said. Heads nodded. Pfefferkorn was confused. "You can't all be robots," he said, not knowing what argument he was making or why he was making it. These students did not speak the same language as he did. He was tired, too, having slept badly for several months running. His doctor had prescribed him a sedative, but so far it had proved ineffective, lulling him to the cusp of sleep but not beyond, so that he spent his waking hours in a fog. He saw himself through his students' eyes and he saw weakness. "I am not a robot," he repeated firmly. "How do you know?" Gretchen said. "Because I'm not," Pfefferkorn said. "Yes," she said, "but how do you know?" "I'm human," Pfefferkorn said. "If you cut me, I bleed." "If you cut me," she said, "I bleed motor oil." This was agreed upon by several of the students to be very funny. Pfefferkorn, feeling the beginnings of a migraine, was glad when the hour was up.

That evening he sat at his desk with two large piles in front of him. One was a long-neglected stack of mail. The other was made up of hundreds of stories his students had written over the years. He had always kept copies on the off chance that one of them became famous and the story turned out to be valuable. That was not his present purpose in browsing. Rather, he was trying to find something he could use. A recent Herculean effort had pushed the word count to one hundred ninety-eight, but he still hadn't gotten past the second page. Perhaps somewhere in this yellowing tower of mediocrity was the key to kick-starting his creativity. He told himself he wouldn't steal anything word for word. That wasn't his style. All he needed was to get the juices flowing.

Four hours and two hundred pages later, he put his head in his hands. He was headed for the rocks.

He turned his attention to the mail. Most of it was junk. There were bills, many of them overdue. His agent had sent royalty statements, along with a few medium-sized checks—nothing to sneeze at, but nothing that would cover a large suburban house, either. A padded envelope contained paperbacks of the Zlabian edition of *Blood Eyes*, all but one of which he planned to get rid of. Already his new office was overrun with author's copies. He crumpled a circular and spied an envelope addressed to him in a large, shaky hand. It was postmarked several weeks prior. There was a return address but no name. He opened it. Inside were several folded pages and a note written on heavy-stock cardboard.

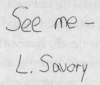

See me —

L. Savory

Pfefferkorn shuddered as he remembered Bill's agent with the huge, veiny head. There was no phone number on the note. Nor had Savory indicated when to come. Was Pfefferkorn supposed to show up at the return address at a time of his choosing? How would Savory know he was coming? It was an altogether bizarre—and officious—way to schedule a meeting. Schmuck, Pfefferkorn thought. He had no intention of honoring the request until he unfolded the enclosed pages. Then he understood immediately.

41.

Lucian Savory's office was downtown, not far from Pfefferkorn's agent's office. The next day Pfefferkorn stepped from the bus and was pummeled by a blast of wind, funneled through a chasm of high-rises. He hurried into the lobby, locating Savory's name on the directory and taking the elevator to the penthouse.

No other tenants shared the floor, leading Pfefferkorn to expect a suite of offices, fronted by a secretary or three. He was surprised to be met at the door by Savory himself.

"About fucking time," Savory said. "Come in."

Pfefferkorn stepped into an enormous room, perfectly beige and almost as bare. Two beige chairs stood on opposite sides of a beige desk. A bank of beige file cabinets ran the length of one beige wall. The color scheme gave him the sensation of being smothered in putty.

"I would've called first," Pfefferkorn said, "but you didn't leave a number."

"I don't have a number," Savory said. He looked exactly as he had at the funeral. Pfefferkorn assumed that someone at such an advanced age would show greater daily wear and tear. But Savory was like a living fossil. He shuffled behind the desk and sat down. "I take it you finally decided to wise up."

"You didn't give me much choice."

Savory smiled.

Pfefferkorn sat down. He took out the pages and flattened them on the desk. The first page read

SHADOWGAME
a novel of suspense
William de Vallée

"Some of your edits were decent," Savory said. "I'll grant you that much."

"Thanks," Pfefferkorn said.

"Nice title."

"It was your idea."

"Still, you had the good sense to use it."

Pfefferkorn said nothing.

"Did you think I wouldn't know?" Savory said.

"I thought I had the only copy."

"What the hell gave you that impression?"

"Carlotta told me he never showed his unfinished work."

"Not to her, maybe. And then you went ahead and

used my title? It's like you were screaming for my attention."

Pfefferkorn shrugged. "Maybe I was."

"Oh," Savory said, "I see. It was a cry for help. You wanted to get caught."

"Sure," Pfefferkorn said.

"Some sort of deep-rooted Freudian thing. 'Spank me.'"

"Could be."

"That's one theory," Savory said. "I have my own, though. Want to hear it? Here goes. You didn't bother to take any of that into account because you're a lazy, greedy son of a bitch with poor executive function."

There was a silence.

"That's possible," Pfefferkorn said.

Savory slapped the desk. "Well, we'll never know."

Pfefferkorn looked at him. "What do you want from me."

Savory cackled. "Perfect."

"What is."

"I was taking bets with myself whether it would be that or 'Why are you doing this to me.'"

"I don't see why we have to drag it out. Just tell me how much you want and I'll tell you if I can afford it. Otherwise we have nothing to talk about."

"*Au contraire,*" Savory said.

42.

"A spy?"

"Not quite," Savory said, "but for simplicity's sake, we can call it that."

"But that's ludicrous," Pfefferkorn said.

"Says you."

"I've known Bill since I was eleven."

"And therefore."

"He wasn't a spy."

"Since you seem intent on picking nits, fine: he wasn't a spy. He was a courier."

"He was a writer," Pfefferkorn said. "He wrote thrillers."

"The man never published a single thing of his own invention," Savory said. "We gave it all to him. William de Vallée was a perfect fraud, and by that I mean in creating his cover, we all did a perfect job, including Bill. He was a major asset, the result of thousands of man-hours and millions of dollars. You can't imagine how disappointed we were to lose him."

"I have no idea what you're talking about," Pfefferkorn said.

"Every Dick Stapp novel has contained encrypted directives for operatives embedded in hostile territories where standard means of transmission have proven too difficult."

"I still have no idea what you're talking about."

"Code," Savory said.

"Code?"

"Code."

"Bill wrote in code."

"I told you, he didn't write anything. The Boys did."

"What boys."

"*The* Boys. Capital B."

"Who're they."

"That's not important."

"They're not important but they get a capital B?"

"All information will be given on a need-to-know basis."

"And I don't need to know."

"Bingo."

There was a silence. Pfefferkorn looked up at the ceiling.

"What," Savory said.

"Where are the cameras."

"There aren't any."

Pfefferkorn stood. "When does the TV crew jump out?"

"Sit down."

Pfefferkorn walked around the room. "Ha ha," he said to the walls. "Very funny."

"We have a lot to discuss, Artie. Sit down. Or don't, I don't care. But time's a-wasting."

"I don't believe you."

Savory shrugged.

"I don't believe any of it," Pfefferkorn said. "How can that make sense? Delivering secret messages out in the open. It's preposterous."

"That makes it all the more difficult to detect. Try sending an e-mail to North Korea and see how far you get. But a top-notch thriller penetrates like nobody's business. He wasn't the only one, mind you. Most blockbuster American novelists are on our payroll. Anything with embossed foil letters, that's us."

"But . . ." Frustrated, Pfefferkorn aimed to score a hit. "Wouldn't it make more sense to use the movies?"

Savory sighed in a way that suggested Pfefferkorn was terribly slow.

"Jesus," Pfefferkorn said. "Them, too?"

"If you think things are bad now, just imagine what might've happened if we'd allowed you to sign a film deal. We've been playing catch-up as it is."

"I'm not following you at all."

"What do you know about Zlabia?" Savory said.

43.

Pfefferkorn told him what he knew.

"That's not much," Savory said.

"Sue me."

"Let me ask you this: when did your first novel come out?"

"Nineteen eighty-three."

"Not that first novel. Your other first novel."

"About a year ago."

"Can you think of anything in recent Zlabian history that happened around then?"

Pfefferkorn thought. "They tried to kill whatsisface."

Savory cackled. "Gold star for you. For the record, whatsisface's name is East Zlabian Lord High President Kliment Thithyich, and he's a very rich, violent, and unstable man, the sort of fellow who doesn't take kindly to being shot in the ass."

"What does my book have to do with any of this?"

"Let's start by reminding ourselves of one key fact. It wasn't *your* book. Was it."

Pfefferkorn said nothing.

"'In one fluid motion,'" Savory said.

"What?"

" 'In one fluid motion.' That was the flag. The manuscript you stole wasn't even finished, and then you had to go ahead and have your way with it."

"It needed trimming," Pfefferkorn said.

"Not the kind you gave it. Do you know how many 'in one fluid motions' you deleted?"

"It's cliché," Pfefferkorn said. "It's meaningless."

"Seriously, take a guess. How many."

Pfefferkorn said nothing.

"Twenty-one," Savory said. "Three of them you left in. That's seven-eighths of the code, destroyed. You turned it into cryptographic Swiss cheese. God knows how the operatives made anything out of it. But obviously they did, because next thing we know, the president of East Zlabia is in intensive care. At first we assumed it was the West Zlabians. Everyone did. They've been at each other's throats for four hundred years. But then we get a coded transmission from one of our Zlabian sleeper cells that the operation had been a failure. Well, that set off a scramble. What operation? We hadn't called any operation. It wasn't long till we figured out what the message referred to. What stumped us was how the order had been set in motion. In the first place, the manuscript you stole had nothing to do with shooting Thithyich, at least not until you mangled it. It was supposed to be a plain old recon directive. In *West* Zlabia, no less. More to the point, it never should have been released, because after Bill died we ordered all his files destroyed." Savory touched his lips philosophically. "Although given what you did to it, one could argue that the book was, in fact,

destroyed. Neither here nor there. Somehow it missed the shredder and got into your hands, leaving us with a pantsload of angry East Zlabians. Thing about Thithyich is, despite being a merciless tyrant, he's quite the populist. Born dirt poor, 'one of us,' all that jazz. To you and me he's a run-of-the-mill post-Soviet autocrat. To your average East Zlabian peasant grinding it out at subsistence level in a thatch-roofed hut filled with six, maybe eight, kwashiorkoric children who have, collectively, no more than ten, maybe twelve, teeth, he's Jack Fucking Kennedy. Try to see it from their side. They're upset."

"I shot the president of East Zlabia," Pfefferkorn said.

"The power of literature," Savory said. "Whatever. The important thing now is to stop the bleeding." He stood up. "That's where you come in."

Pfefferkorn was alarmed. "Where."

Savory shuffled to the file cabinet and began opening drawers. "We need someone to fill the position vacated by Bill. Seeing as how you've already gone ahead and preempted us . . . where the hell did I . . . and over and above that, established superb brand recognit—ah." He found what he was looking for: a thick manuscript bound with rubber bands. He brought it over and dropped it heavily on the desk in front of Pfefferkorn.

"Tag," Savory said. "You're it."

44.

The title page read *Blood Night*.

"I think you'll find that it expands upon the themes begun in *Blood Eyes*," Savory said. "Additionally, there's a lot of good character development, some real poetry to the descriptions of weather. Killer sex scenes. The Boys are proud of it, and rightfully so."

"This is outrageous," Pfefferkorn said.

"Quit being such a prima donna."

"It's blackmail."

"The word is *collaboration*."

"Not if I don't have a choice, it isn't."

"Oh, you always have a choice," Savory said. "But why in the world would you say no? I guess you could, but then you really are done with publishing. Let me let you in on a little secret, Artie: you haven't got any talent. I read your first book. It was a piece of dreck. Here's another secret: I've read your interviews. I've been to your new apartment building. I've seen enough to know that you like being a published author. Of course you do. Your new life is a hell of a lot nicer than your old life. You'd be a fool to give it up. And for what? It's not like

I'm asking you to do anything you haven't done already. I'm giving you the chance to keep your reputation, serve your country, and build up a decent retirement fund in the process. It's the best deal imaginable. You should be spit-shining my asshole."

Pfefferkorn said nothing.

"You can always say no. You can walk out of here right now. I'd hate for you to do that, though. Never mind the headache it makes for me. Never mind that. It's more that I'd hate to see you suffer. You do understand, don't you? I'll expose you. I'd have to. It's the only fair thing to do. What a field day the press would have with that, huh? Just imagine. You'll be trash, and so will your agent, your publisher, and your family. Everyone within fifty miles of you will reek."

"If you expose me," Pfefferkorn said, "I'll expose you."

Savory smiled. "Go for it. I'm sure everyone will believe you."

There was a long silence.

"Does Carlotta know?" Pfefferkorn asked.

"She's clueless."

"I don't want her to find out."

"She won't unless you tell her."

There was a silence.

"What really happened to Bill?" Pfefferkorn asked.

"Hand to God," Savory said, "it was a boating accident."

There was a silence.

"The flag is 'Hurry, we don't have much time.' Got that? So do me a favor. Don't touch that phrase. Come to think of it, don't monkey around with it at all. It's fine the way it is. Resist the urge to mark your territory and everything will be fine." Savory stood up and put out his hand. "Do we have a deal?"

45.

"I love it," Pfefferkorn's agent said.

"Thanks."

"I'm not gonna lie: you had me sweating there, all that stuff about—but, look, the important thing is to realize what we have, and what we have is a gem. A rock-solid grade-A twenty-four-carat gem."

"Thanks."

"The thing that sets you apart," the agent said, "is character development. The daughter—sorry, you know I'm terrible with names."

"Francesca."

"Francesca. She is just a fabulous character. That bit where she steals the ruby from her grandmother's necklace and replaces it with the piece of glass taken from her broken locket that her dead mother got from the man she loved before Shagreen who—it's fantastic, not just the idea itself but the way you handled it, the subtlety—this guy the mother once loved, and then we're given to understand maybe Shagreen might've had something to do with his death . . . I mean, come *on*."

"Thank you."

"Layers upon layers."

"Thank you."

"*Great* title."

"Thanks."

"Good. Well, if you're ready, I'm going to get this over to them today and start pressing for the D-and-A."

"I'm ready."

"Excellent. Cause as they say on the Ferris wheel, here we go again."

46.

Blood Night met with unanimous approval at the publisher, who decided to rush the book to press in time for beach-read season. The accelerated schedule was made possible by the fact that the manuscript required almost no editing. Pfefferkorn's editor wrote to him that, aside from a handful of typos caught by the copy editor, the text was "as close to word-perfect as I've ever seen." Savory had informed Pfefferkorn of these typos in advance. "If there wasn't anything to fix," he told Pfefferkorn, "it would look fishy." Pfefferkorn thought it looked mighty fishy regardless, but the publishing machine had too many parts, moving at too great a speed, for anyone to dare derail its operation by questioning why a book was better than expected.

Watching *Blood Night* barrel along toward publication, he felt a strange sense of gratification. It wasn't the novel he'd always dreamed of writing, but nor was it pure schlock, and he took some small amount of credit for laying the groundwork that had enabled the Boys, as Savory referred to them, to flesh out Harry Shagreen's personal life. They had given him a hobby, playing full-contact Scrabble. They had assigned a sizable role to his daughter, a character mentioned in passing in the first novel. (Pfefferkorn had reconfigured her out of Stapp's son.) A former math whiz turned drug-addled cat burglar with a heart of gold with a gaping hole in the shape of her father's missing love, Francesca Shagreen screamed off the page, and the final scene, with Shagreen dragging her into the emergency room, was a serious tearjerker. Pfefferkorn was perturbed to catch himself choking up as he read it. It wasn't unusual for a writer to get sentimental about his characters. But the operative word was "his." He had no more ownership of these characters than Bill had. Like Dick Stapp or Harry Shagreen, Pfefferkorn was a man who couldn't let emotions cloud his judgment. He had a mission. Duty called.

47.

Except he didn't know what the mission was, and his duty—to send in the novel, sit back, and let events play themselves out—turned out to be far harder than he had anticipated. Against all odds, he was going to accomplish something he had long thought impossible: he was going to publish a book that changed the world. It might be a large change. It might be a small one. It might be a change he approved of, politically and morally. It might not. He had no idea, and he agonized over the thought that he had sold his soul. He was surprised at himself. He had never been much of an activist. Even during his student days, his crusades had been primarily artistic, rather than political, in nature. Moreover, he had assumed—incorrectly, it seemed—that his soul was already gone, sold on the cheap along with the first manuscript. To combat his anxiety, he ran through all the good things that had come about as a result of his deal with Savory. He no longer had his agent, editor, and publisher breathing down his neck. He had been able to put an offer in on the house his daughter wanted. These had to count for something, didn't they? Besides, the mission's aims weren't necessarily objectionable. He just didn't know. But his conscience would not be quieted, and as the publication date loomed, he began to feel suffocated by a sense of powerlessness.

He went downtown to see Savory.

"I need to know what the message is."

"That's not important."

"It is to me."

"You're going to have to learn to live with ambiguity," Savory said.

"It's about the Zlabias, right? Tell me that much."

"Bill never asked," Savory said. "It's better if you don't, either."

"I'm not Bill."

"You're having qualms," Savory said. "That's to be expected. You have to remind yourself that your government has your best interests in mind."

"But I don't believe that."

"You goddamned boomers always have to drag everything before a fucking ethics committee. Do you think we beat the Nazis sitting around worrying about hurting people's feelings? Go home, Artie. Buy yourself a watch."

He didn't buy a watch. Instead, he spent several afternoons at the university library, enlisting the help of a friendly student worker (who became even friendlier after Pfefferkorn handed him a hundred-dollar bill) to make photocopies of the front pages of all major American newspapers for the two weeks following the publication of every Dick Stapp novel. It came to more than a thousand pages in total, and he stayed up all night, jotting down the headlines in a notebook he had divided by subject. The pattern that emerged confirmed his hunch: the novels of William de Vallée anticipated every twist of Zlabian political fate from the late 1970s on. On the half-dozen occasions Pfefferkorn could not find a coup or riot linked in time to the publication of a Dick Stapp novel, he assumed there was cloak-and-dagger going on, the kind of stuff that would never be known outside select circles. He shut the notebook, his heart racing. He was blithely toying with the fate of people whose countries he couldn't find on a map.

He looked at the clock. It was eight thirty a.m. He ran downstairs to find a cab.

As he rode along, he prepared his speech. I want out, he would say. Or: I've had it with this rotten business. Savory would try to dissuade him, of course, and then would come the threats. He would have to stand tall. Do your worst, he would say. I am not your tool. Mentally, he revised: I am not your plaything.

He got in the elevator and pressed the button for the top floor. Listen here, he would begin. I am not your plaything. No: *you* listen here. That was better. It made clear who was in charge. He tried again, once with Savory's name and once without. Using Savory's name pinned Savory to the wall, giving him no way to pass the buck. On the other hand, it gave Savory an identity, and Pfefferkorn was aiming to reduce the man, to make him as small and squashable as possible. You listen here. It had a staccato rhythm, like a handgun. You listen here, Savory, sounded more like a slice from a sword. He still hadn't made up his mind when a chime sounded and the elevator opened. He stepped briskly forth to knock.

There was no answer. He knocked again, assertively. Still there was no answer. He tried the knob. It turned. "You listen here," he said, stepping into the doorway. He went no further. The room had been stripped bare.

48.

Pfefferkorn called his agent.

"We need to hold the book."

His agent laughed.

"I'm serious," Pfefferkorn said. "It can't go out the way it is. There are too many mistakes."

"What are you talking about? It's perfect. Everybody says so."

"I—"

"*You* said so yourself."

"I need to make changes."

"Look," the agent said, "I understand you've got butterflies, but—"

"It's not butterflies," Pfefferkorn shouted.

"Whoa there."

"Listen to me. Listen. Listen: I need you to call them up and tell them we're going to hold it another month so I can make revisions."

"You know I can't do that."

"You can. You have to."

"Are you hearing yourself? You sound nuts."

"Fine," Pfefferkorn said. "I'll call them myself."

"Wait wait wait. Don't do that."

"I will unless you do."

"What is going on here?"

"Call me back after you've spoken to them," Pfefferkorn said and hung up.

Forty-five minutes later the phone rang.

"Did you talk to them?" Pfefferkorn asked.

"I talked to them."

"And?"

"They said no."

Pfefferkorn began to hyperventilate.

"You have a first printing of four hundred thousand," the agent said. "They're already shipped. What do you expect them to do, pull them all? Look, I understand how you feel—"

"No," Pfefferkorn said. "You don't."

"I do. I've seen this before."

"No, you haven't."

"I have. I've seen it dozens of times. This is not unusual. You're having a normal response to a stressful situation. You've got people counting on you, the stakes are high. I get it, okay? I know. It's a lot to shoulder. That doesn't change what you've done. You've written a fantastic book. You've done your job. Let them do theirs."

Pfefferkorn stayed up all that night as well, rereading the book and dog-earing every instance of a character hurrying for lack of time. The pace was supercharged—

he could all but hear a ticking clock—and he counted nineteen flags. He copied out the surrounding paragraphs, studying them for patterns. Who am I kidding, he thought. He needed the decryption key or whatever. He needed training. He went online and read about code breaking. Nothing he tried worked, although he did accidentally discover that the instructions on his washer/dryer formed a substitution code for the opening scene of *Waiting for Godot*.

Pfefferkorn despaired.

49.

"Poor Arthur."

No sooner had he gotten on the phone with Carlotta than he realized he'd made a mistake. He had called seeking solace, but how could she give it to him when he couldn't tell her the truth? Instead, her sympathy came off as grating.

"Bill always got like this right before a book came out. Like something terrible could happen."

Pfefferkorn said nothing.

"You're two of a kind," Carlotta said.

"You think?"

"Sometimes I do, yes."

"Am I a good lover?" Pfefferkorn asked.

"What kind of a question is that?"

"Am I?"

"Of course you are. You're wonderful."

"I've had to shake off a lot of rust."

"If so, I never noticed."

"Am I as good as Bill?"

"Arthur. Please."

"I won't be offended if you say him. It's only natural. He had more time to learn what you like."

"I like *you*."

"Be honest," he said. "I can handle it."

"It's a ridiculous question and I'm not going to answer it."

"I'm afraid you just did."

"I did no such thing. I refused to answer a ridiculous question. That's all."

There was a silence.

"I'm sorry," he said. "I've been under a lot of strain."

"I know," she said. "I'm sure it'll be a smashing success."

That was precisely what he was afraid of. He wondered how Bill coped. Presumably it got easier with each go-around. Also, the chain of events was elaborate enough to make his contribution appear relatively minor and therefore forgivable. He wasn't pushing a button or pulling a trigger. He was publishing a book.

"Are you excited for the tour?" she asked.

"I'm looking forward to seeing you," he said.

"I'm bringing a big crowd to the reading."

He felt a frisson of dread. He preferred to keep her away from anything at all having to do with the book. He didn't want her tainted. "I thought you had a tango session that night."

"I canceled it."

"You shouldn't," he said.

"Arthur, don't be absurd. I can dance whenever I want."

"But it makes you so happy."

"I'd much rather see you."

"Please," he said. "It'll make me nervous if you're there."

"Oh, stop."

"I'm serious," he said. "Don't come."

The words came out harsher than he had intended, and he hastened to clarify. "I'm sorry. But it really will trip me up."

"Well, we don't want that, do we."

"Please don't," he said. "Not tonight."

She sighed. "I know. I'm sorry."

"Never mind that. Let's plan to meet afterward. Pick someplace relaxing. Will you do that for me, please?"

"Of course."

"Thank you."

"Travel safely," she said.

"Thank you."

"Arthur?" She paused. "I love you."

"I love you, too."

He hung up and paced around his apartment. It was eleven p.m. In ten hours the first bookstores would open and *Blood Night* would be unleashed upon the world. He had stock signings all the next day and his first reading at seven thirty. He had a grueling three weeks ahead of him. He needed to rest. But there was no way he was getting any sleep, not tonight. He turned on the television. He watched the first twenty seconds of a special report about the Zlabian crisis before switching the television off and getting up to pace once more.

The aspect of Pfefferkorn's new reality to which he had devoted the least amount of attention was the implications it held for his past. He had been strenuously ignoring that line of thinking, afraid of where it might lead. Whole swaths of his identity had been formed in reaction to Bill. He had defined himself as a writer unwilling to sacrifice art for the sake of material gain: the anti-Bill. But it made no sense trying to be the opposite of something that did not exist, and it devastated him to grasp that he had spent his life wrestling a phantom.

And in the final analysis, how worthwhile had that struggle been? Where had it gotten him? Certainly he hadn't distinguished himself through his writing. What made him so different from Bill, other than his own, mulish insistence that they *were* different? What if he, not Bill, had been the one recruited for clandestine activities? Would he be the one married to Carlotta? Would he have a daughter? Would he even be alive right now? The fabric of the universe had been irreparably shredded, and through the holes he saw new worlds, some tantalizing, some terrifying beyond belief.

High atop a shelf in his closet was a box containing old snapshots he had never found the time to organize. Desperate for evidence of an independent self, he hauled it down and dumped it out on the floor. He knelt and grabbed the topmost photo: a black-and-white image of a much younger him hunched over a desk at the university literary magazine. A plaque read

ARTHUR S. PFEFFERKORN, DICTATOR-IN-CHIEF

—a gag presented to him by Bill in honor of his managerial style. Where, Pfefferkorn wondered, had he gotten the idea that he had an artistic birthright? His mother had never finished high school. His father never read anything more sophisticated than the racing form. He himself had not been a studious child, preferring to listen to baseball games on the radio or to sneak cigarettes from his father's coat pocket. When had the transformation occurred? How had he become who he had become? He used to think he knew, but now everything seemed up for grabs. He picked up another photo and was startled to see himself mouth-kissing his daughter. But it was not his daughter. It was his dead ex-wife. The resemblance that so often annoyed him here verged on pornographic. He hurriedly turned the snapshot over. His ex-wife would be in lots of these photos, if not most. It gave him pause. How much of those years did he want to revisit? He remembered the day she called to tell him she was dying. *I want to see her.* It was an extraordinary demand to make of a seven-year-old girl who hadn't seen her mother in three years. To bring her into that room, with its tubes and its smells . . . But he couldn't rightly say no. A mother was a mother. His daughter had refused to come, though, and Pfefferkorn's ex-wife had called to scream at him. *You're poisoning her against me.* He tried to reason with her but it was no use. A month later, she was gone.

He picked up another photo.

There they were: he and Bill, Piazza Navona, their shadows humpbacked by large canvas rucksacks. The summer after graduation they had wandered across Europe. In those days a rail pass cost eighty-five dollars. Bill paid for those as well as for their airfare, using money he'd gotten from his grandparents as a graduation gift. Pfefferkorn had always intended to reimburse him. He never had. He wondered about the real origins of Bill's "graduation gift." Grandparents? Or the Boys? Was Bill working for them as early as then? Pfefferkorn could never know. He felt doubt beginning to hollow out his memories. He remembered a night in a Berlin hostel (it was West Berlin back then), opening his eyes to catch a glimpse of Bill leaving the room at two in the morning. The next day Bill pled insomnia. *I went for a walk.* Pfefferkorn remembered it and doubted. Berlin, of all places—and like that, his happy memories of the city caved in on themselves. He doubled over as though gutshot. It hurt to breathe. Eventually he rose to his hands and knees and reached for another photo. Their high school prom. He saw the ruffled cuffs and the powder-blue tuxedos and their shining red faces. But he doubted. He doubted all of it. The memory imploded. He reached for another and the same thing happened. And another and again. Piece by piece his history disappeared. The cursing parakeet they kept in the apartment. Bill's green Camaro. The canoe trip with their young wives. The first time Bill held Pfefferkorn's daughter. He knew he should stop. He was destroying himself. He could not stop, not until the sun came up. He had gone through the whole box and his life lay in shambles. He had thought himself done with grief, yet here he was, sobbing again. Not for the death of a friend but for the death of a friendship. He wept for the friend he never had.

50.

The book tour for *Blood Night* was bigger and fancier than that for *Blood Eyes*. He went to more cities. He flew first class. He stayed in swanky hotels, one of which celebrated his arrival with flowers, fruit, and a quarter-scale replica of the novel rendered in chocolate and icing. He used his cell phone to take a picture.

One thing that had not changed from the first tour was the roster of media escorts who met him along the way. These were amiable, attractive women between the ages of thirty-five and sixty who loved to read. At each airport one would be waiting outside the baggage claim, holding a copy of his book. She would smile and say how nice it was to see him again. She would spend the morning shuttling him around to local bookstores to sign stock. Over lunch she would make a fuss over photos of Pfefferkorn's daughter in her wedding gown. More stock signings were followed by a two-hour break at the hotel so Pfefferkorn could shower and shave. In the evening the media escort would pick him up and drive him to his reading. The next morning she would show up before dawn to get him to his next flight. These women made an otherwise dreary routine more humane, and Pfefferkorn was grateful for them all.

It helped matters that they could be genuinely optimistic: every event was packed. Publishers bemoaned the fact that fewer and fewer people read fiction, while those who did got older and older. Within a few years, they predicted, there would be no market left. Seeing his various and sundry fans, Pfefferkorn decided things couldn't possibly be as bad as all that.

He took questions.

"What inspired this book?"

Pfefferkorn said it had just come to him one day.

"Do you do a lot of research?"

As little as he could get away with, he answered.

"What's next for Harry Shagreen?"

Pfefferkorn said he didn't want to spoil the surprise.

Every night he returned to his suite drained. He ordered room service, changed into a bathrobe, and girded himself for the most harrowing part of his day: reading the newspaper.

Boston, Providence, Miami, Washington, D.C., Charlotte, Chicago, Milwaukee, Minneapolis, St. Louis, Kansas City, and Albuquerque passed without incident. He began to wonder if he had made a mistake. Maybe it wasn't Zlabia he was in charge of. He flew to Denver. His daughter called to say they were getting their dining room set delivered. She thanked him and mentioned that the pillows she had custom-ordered for the den ended up costing more than expected. He invited her to put the difference on his credit card. She thanked him again and told him to keep out of trouble. "That's me," he said, running his finger down the column headed *International News in Brief.* "Mr. Trouble." He flew to Phoenix. The owner of the mystery and thriller specialty store was a delightfully wry woman who took him to a Polynesian restaurant. He remained morose throughout the meal, glancing over her shoulder whenever she took a sip of her mai tai. Above the bar was a television tuned to a cable news channel. He was waiting for a graphic that said breaking news. He flew to Houston. The manager of the independent bookstore presented him with a logo mug and what he called "the sickest but best book of the year." It was a how-to called *Kid-A-Gami: 99 Fun Shapes to Fold Your Infant Into.* Pfefferkorn put it in his carry-on for his flight to Seattle but did not take it out. Instead he scoured three different papers. He had stopped looking exclusively for articles about Zlabia. Every piece of bad news made for a potential indictment. A dam burst in India, leaving sixty thousand people homeless. His doing? The Middle East convulsed and sparked. Him? The rebel forces closing in on a South American capital,

the millions of anonymous Africans dying by the hour—
any of it could be him. It then occurred to him that he
was delegating an unjustified degree of authority (and
responsibility) to himself. He wasn't "in charge of"
squat. He was no Dick Stapp. He was no Harry Shagreen.
He was a flunky, a pawn—making his complicity even
more debasing. He flew to Portland. His media escort
took him for the best donuts in town. In nineteen days
of travel he had yet to hear about a catastrophe he did not
feel culpable for. But he would never know. Whatever the
event was, it might have already taken place. It might also
take place in a month, a year, two years, ten. He flew to
San Francisco. The bookstore owner was a kindly older
man with a fondness for opera. It was raining, warm
summer rain, and the inside of the store smelled like shoe
leather. A slovenly fellow with a beard like a mop asked
him to address the presence of Marxist themes in his
writing. He returned to his hotel. He dined alone. He
went upstairs, put on a bathrobe, and stretched out on
the bed. He scanned the laminated channel guide. There
were multiple news stations. He turned on the television
and watched baseball until he fell asleep.

51.

Dragomir Zhulk, the prime minister of West Zlabia, was dead. He had been killed by a sniper's bullet while walking to work. While most security analysts presumed that his death was retaliation for the attempted assassination of Kliment Thithyich, others believed that the killers belonged to a splinter group within Zhulk's own party. The splinter group itself had released a statement blaming the Americans. The secretary of state refused to dignify this accusation with a response, reiterating instead his country's support for East Zlabia ("our long-time and historical ally") and cautioning that the use of force by either side could be considered cause for intervention. The Russians had released a statement denouncing "these acts of terroristic aggression." The Swedes had convened a fact-finding committee. The Chinese had taken advantage of the momentary distraction to execute a jailed dissident. A prominent French intellectual had written that the situation "inarguably supplied a manifest example of the shortcomings of reactionary identity politics as applied to the realpolitik of statecraft during a post-structural epoch." It was front-page news.

Pfefferkorn felt frayed. He was having a hard time keeping track of all the players. Worst of all—or best, he couldn't decide—nobody had discerned the truth, which was that Dragomir Zhulk had been killed by a thriller that had just that morning hit number one on the best-seller list.

"Morning," his media escort said. "Coffee?"

Pfefferkorn gratefully accepted the proffered cup and climbed into the waiting car.

An hour later he was sitting in the first-class lounge with the obituaries spread out before him, staring at the grainy image of the man he had murdered. Dragomir Ilyiukh Zhulk was wiry and bald, with small black eyes set behind efficient-looking steel-rimmed glasses. An engineer by training, he had studied in Moscow, returning to his homeland to help build West Zlabia's nuclear power plant, for many years the world's smallest working reactor, until an accident forced it to close. He had climbed the Party ladder, becoming first minister of atomic research, then minister of science, then deputy prime minister, and finally prime minister, a title he had held for eleven years. He was widely regarded as an unrepentant ideologue, a man for whom the fall of the Berlin Wall had proven only that the Russians were not fit to inherit the Marxist-Leninist mantle, and whose greatest vice, if it could be called that, was a passion for Zlabian poetry. He lived monkishly, shunning the large security force favored by his East Zlabian counterpart, a decision that had proven costly. His first marriage, to a school-teacher, had ended with her death. Five years ago he had remarried, this time to his housekeeper. He left no children.

The flight to Los Angeles was called. Pfefferkorn walked to the jetway, discarding the paper in the trash.

52.

His Los Angeles reading was on the small side—a blessing in disguise, as Pfefferkorn wanted to get it over with as fast as humanly possible. Afterward, his media escort drove him to the restaurant Carlotta had picked out. He went straight to the bar to order a stiff drink. The television was tuned to images from the Zlabian front. Troops marched. Mini-tanks rolled. A commentator in a corner box was explaining that no fence separated East and West Zlabia, only an eight-inch-high concrete median strip running down the middle of Gyeznyuiy Boulevard. "You have to remember," he said eagerly, "this is a conflict that has been raging in one form or another for four-hundred-plus years. Ethnically speaking, they're one people." The byline identified him as G. Stanley Hurwitz, Ph.D., author of *A Brief History of the Zlabian Conflict*. He appeared exhilarated by the carnage, as though he had been waiting all his life for his moment to shine. The anchor kept trying to cut him off but he went right on talking, citing lengthy passages of some little-known Zlabian poem that was apparently the source of all the fighting. Pfefferkorn asked the bartender to change the channel. The bartender found a baseball game. At the end of the inning, Pfefferkorn checked his watch. Even for Carlotta, thirty minutes was unusually late. He draped his jacket over the bar stool and stepped outside. Her home phone rang and rang. Her cell phone went straight to voicemail. He returned to the bar and asked for a third drink. He nursed it as long as he could bear before trying Carlotta again. There was still no answer. By this time he had been waiting for more than an hour. He paid his tab, apologized to the maître d', and asked him to call a cab.

53.

Pfefferkorn stood at the mouth of the driveway to the de Vallée mansion. The gate was open. In all his visits he had never once seen it left that way. He leaned forward, his hands on his hips, and started to hike up. The driveway was steep. He began to pant and sweat. Why had he told the cabbie he would walk the rest of the way? Perhaps it was his mind's way of slowing him down. Perhaps he already knew he did not want to know what awaited him. As he climbed higher, the thrum of the boulevard died away. All those trees and hedges and gates and heavy clay walls were there to maintain privacy and quiet. But they had another consequence. They ensured that nobody on the outside would hear you scream.

The second gate was also open.

He ran the last hundred yards, cresting the hill and sprinting for the open front door. He barged inside, calling Carlotta's name. From a distant room came the dog's crazed howls. Pfefferkorn ran, slipping on the polished floors. He made wrong turns. He backtracked. He stopped calling Carlotta's name and called for the dog instead, hoping it would appear to lead him to the right place. The howling grew more urgent but no closer, and he ran from room to room, at last skidding to a halt in front of the ballroom. Frantic scrabbling, nails on wood. He threw open the double doors. The dog shot past, yelping. Pfefferkorn froze on the threshold, staring at the dance floor, at the glazy lake of blood and the human form heaped at its center.

THREE **A NOVEL OF SUSPENSE**

54.

"How did you know the victim?"

"He was Carlotta's dance partner."

"What kind of dance?"

"It matters?"

"We'll decide what matters, Pfefferkorn."

"Answer the question, Pfefferkorn."

"Tango."

"That's a pretty sexy dance, huh, Pfefferkorn?"

"I suppose."

"How long have you known Mrs. de Vallée?"

"We're old friends."

"'Friends.'"

"Recently it's become more than that."

"Now there's an image I didn't need."

"TMI, Pfefferkorn. TMI."

"You asked."

"What do you think of the victim?"

"What do you mean what do I think?"

"Were you close with him?"

"We didn't fraternize."

"That's a big word, Pfefferkorn."

"Don't play games, Pfefferkorn."

"I'm not playing games."

"So you didn't 'fraternize.' "

"No."

"Did you like him?"

"He was fine, I guess."

"You guess."

"What am I supposed to say? He worked for Carlotta."

"Don't lie to us, Pfefferkorn."

"We'll know if you do."

"I'm not lying."

"Someone's doing sexy dances with my more-than-friend, I have an opinion."

"Well I don't."

"You been drinking, Pfefferkorn?"

"I had a few drinks at the bar."

"What kind of drinks?"

"Bourbon."

"What kind of bourbon?"

"I don't remember."

"You like bourbon but not any specific brand."

"I'm not a drinker, I asked for bourbon."

"If you're not a drinker, how come you asked for bourbon?"

"I was in the mood for a drink."

"Is that right?"

"Yes."

"Something bothering you?"

"Something you're nervous about?"

"Something you feel guilty about?"

"Something you want to tell us?"

"You can tell us, Pfefferkorn. We're on your side."

"We're here to help you. You can trust us."

Silence.

"So that's how it's going to be, huh?"

"I'm doing my best to answer your questions."

"We haven't asked a question."

"Which is why I'm not answering."

"You always this sassy, Pfefferkorn?"

"I'm sorry."

"What for?"

"Being sassy."

"Anything else you're sorry for, Pfefferkorn?"

"Anything else on your mind?"

"On your conscience?"

"Anything else you'd like to share?"

"I'll tell you whatever you'd like to know."

"Let's cut the baloney, Pfefferkorn. Where's Carlotta de Vallée?"

"I told you. I don't know. I came to look for her and I found . . . that."

"You don't want to tell us what you found?"

". . . it was horrible."

"You think so?"

"Of course I do."

"You didn't have anything to do with it?"

"What? *No.*"

"There's no need to get touchy, Pfefferkorn. It's just a question."

"Do I look like the kind of person who could do that?"

"What kind of person do you think does that?"

"Someone obviously very disturbed."

"What makes you say that?"

"You're telling me you don't find it disturbing?"

"Where's Carlotta de Vallée?"

"I don't know."

"Why don't you take a break and think about it."

Alone in the interrogation room, Pfefferkorn shut his eyes tightly against the image of Jesús María de Lunchbox's mutilated corpse. He wasn't sure he'd ever be able to eat rigatoni again. Just as he was starting to feel better, the door swung open and the detectives reentered. Canola was a smiling black man with large, feminine sunglasses. Sockdolager was white and unshaven. His shirt wasn't rumpled, but only because his paunch was straining it so hard.

"Okey-dokey," Canola said. "Let's try this again."

Pfefferkorn surmised that the purpose of asking the same questions over and over was to trip him up. For a fifth time he narrated the events of the evening. He described his concern upon finding the gates open. He described the dog shrieking to be let out.

"You tell a good story," Canola said. "No wonder you're a writer."

"It's not a story," Pfefferkorn said.

"He didn't say it was untrue," Sockdolager said.

"I was just complimenting you on your fine grasp of narrative structure," Canola said.

He allowed himself to be questioned for several more hours before asking for an attorney.

"Why do you need an attorney?"

"Am I under arrest?"

The detectives looked at each other.

"Because if not," Pfefferkorn said, "I'd like to go."

"All right," Canola said agreeably.

He stood up.

Sockdolager stood up.

Pfefferkorn stood up.

"Arthur Pfefferkorn," Sockdolager said, "you're under arrest."

55.

Not wanting to frighten his daughter over what would surely turn out to be a giant misunderstanding, he used his call to phone his agent. Nobody answered, though, and after further processing he was shown to a cell occupied by a young gang member covered in tattoos.

"What about my phone call?" Pfefferkorn said to the guard.

"Ain't my fault," the guard said.

"But—"

The door slammed shut.

Pfefferkorn stood agape.

"Don worry, *ese*," the gang member said. "You get use to it."

Pfefferkorn avoided looking at his cellmate as he climbed up to the empty top bunk. He had a notion that it was unwise to stare at people in jail. They might take it the wrong way. He lay down and tried to think. His arraignment was scheduled for the morning. Where did that leave him for now? Locked up like some common criminal? What about bail? What about parole? What about time off for good behavior? He didn't know how any of this worked. He had never been arrested before. Of course he hadn't. He was a law-abiding citizen. He tossed and turned with indignation. Then he thought about Carlotta and his anger became anguish. Anything might be happening to her. If the police believed they had solved the case by arresting him, they were bringing her that much closer to death—if she wasn't dead already. Time was slipping away. He felt as though he were buried up to his neck in sand. He moaned.

"*Ese*. Chill out."

Pfefferkorn clenched his fists to keep still.

A little later, a buzzer sounded.

"Chow time," the gang member said.

The dining room walls reverberated hellishly with the noise of men eating and talking. Pfefferkorn took his tray and sat alone, slumped, his arms crossed over his chest. He needed to make that call.

"Not hungry?"

Pfefferkorn's heart contracted unpleasantly as his cellmate sat down across from him.

"So, *ese*, what you do?"

Pfefferkorn frowned. "Nothing."

"Nothing?"

"No."

"Then why you here?"

"I'm being accused of a crime I didn't commit," Pfefferkorn said.

The gang member laughed. "Hey, what a coincidence. Me, too."

He flexed one forearm, causing the Virgin Mary to shimmy lewdly. Gothic lettering spanned the hollow of his throat.

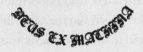

"*Ese,*" the gang member said, "you lookin at something?"

Pfefferkorn averted his eyes again. "No."

The chow room clattered and boomed.

"You know what that means?" the gang member said.

Pfefferkorn nodded.

"Okay, then," the gang member said. He stood. "Eat up."

56.

"Pfefferkorn. Derecho. Let's go."

"Rise and shine, *ese*."

Pfefferkorn stirred. He felt god-awful. He'd spent most of the night awake. Rarely did the other inmates cease hollering and stomping, and anyway, he was too wound up from imagining Carlotta in various states of peril. He had nodded off shortly before daybreak. The color of the light told him it wasn't much later than that now.

"Move it."

Pfefferkorn and his cellmate stood in the corridor, facing the wall. The guards patted them down and escorted them out of the cell block toward the elevator.

"No talking," a guard said, although nobody had said anything.

A van was waiting to transfer them to the central courthouse. They were shackled to their seats. The engine started and the van crept toward the security gate. The driver flashed a badge. The arm went up. They pulled onto the streets of downtown Los Angeles.

Pfefferkorn was immersed in one kind of anxiety, enough so that at first he did not realize the van had pulled onto the freeway. When he did notice, he was not in sufficient possession of his faculties to be surprised. Only after they exited the freeway and started driving uphill did it occur to him that they should have arrived at their destination some time ago, and a second kind of anxiety came to the fore. He couldn't tell where they were, because the van's back windows were blacked out, and the grate protecting the driver made it hard to see through the windshield. He glanced at his cellmate. The man appeared perfectly at ease. Pfefferkorn didn't like it.

"Are we almost there?" he called.

Nobody answered.

The road got bumpy. Pfefferkorn glanced at his cellmate's shackles. He reasoned that whatever was happening had to be happening to his cellmate as well—hence their common state of shackledness. He tried to make this make him feel better. It didn't work.

The van pulled over. The driver got out and came around to open the back door. A blast of unfiltered sunlight caused Pfefferkorn to squint. What he saw did not compute. Instead of a parking lot or an urban street, there was barren hillside and a dirt road.

"Where are we," he said.

The driver did not answer. She—it was a she—unlocked Pfefferkorn's cellmate. Though Pfefferkorn was still half blind, he was able to detect a familiarity in her face.

"What's happening," he said.

"Relax," Pfefferkorn's cellmate said, rubbing his wrists. He no longer had a gangbanger accent. He got out of the van. The door closed. Pfefferkorn heard them talking. The gang member was complaining about being itchy. The driver murmured a reply and the two of them laughed. Pfefferkorn cried for help, his voice bouncing around the inside of the van. He jerked helplessly at his chains.

"You're going to hurt yourself," the driver said, opening the back door. The gang member was behind her, clutching something sharp and glinting.

Pfefferkorn slid away from them in terror.

"Take it easy," the gang member said. His jail uniform was gone and his entire mien had changed. The driver was also out of uniform. With their youthful freshness, they could have been students of his. Then Pfefferkorn saw: they *were* students of his. The young man was Benjamin, author of the pretentious short story about getting old. Pfefferkorn didn't remember him having so many tattoos. Then again, Pfefferkorn didn't remember him being a gang member at all, so perhaps his memory was not to be trusted. The driver was Gretchen, she of the robots. She took the syringe from Benjamin, who cracked his knuckles and got ready to pounce.

Pfefferkorn pressed himself back into the unforgiving wall. "No."

Benjamin tackled him and pinned his arms. Pfefferkorn fought. He had no chance.

"I have a family," Pfefferkorn said.

"Not anymore," Gretchen said.

The needle sank into his thigh.

57.

He was in a motel room. He knew this upon opening his eyes, before he had moved. The moldy air, the cottage-cheese ceiling, the line of gray light crossing it: these were proof enough. He rose up on his elbows. For a motel room, it was below average. The television set was bolted crookedly to the dresser. The carpet was mangy. The bedspread was a rough synthetic fabric printed with pink hibiscus blossoms as big as hubcaps. He was naked. The thought of that fabric against his skin gave him the willies. He leapt to his feet and was hit with a wave of nausea. He staggered to the wall and leaned against it, taking deep breaths until he could stand on his own.

He stepped to the window and drew back the curtain a few inches. His room was on the second floor, overlooking a parking lot. A search turned up neither telephone nor clock. The dresser drawers were empty, the walls bare. The nightstand contained a Gideon Bible. The television's power cord had been snipped, leaving a quarter-inch stub. He checked the closet. It was without so much as a hanger. Another wave of nausea sent him running for the bathroom. He fell to his knees and vomited up a caustic orange stream. He sat back, hugging himself and shuckling, his body damp and quivering.

The toilet rang.

Pfefferkorn opened his eyes.

The ringtone was an irritating and ubiquitous thirteen-note ditty. Coming from within the toilet tank, it assumed an echoey, sinister quality.

I must wake up, he thought. I must stop this nightmare.

Everything continued to exist.

Wake up, he thought.

The toilet rang and rang.

He pinched himself. It hurt.

The ringing stopped.

"There," he said. He felt that he had attained a small victory.

The toilet once again began to ring.

58.

A phone had been duct-taped to the underside of the tank lid. He peeled it free. The caller ID said WOULDN'T YOU LIKE TO KNOW. He was afraid to answer but more afraid not to.

"Hello," he said.

"Sorry it had to be this way," a man's voice said. "I'm sure you can understand."

Understand what? He didn't understand anything.

"Who are you?" he yelled. "What is this?"

"It's not safe to talk over the phone. You need to get moving."

"I'm not going anywhere."

"You will if you want to live."

"Goddammit," Pfefferkorn said, "don't you threaten me."

"It's not a threat. If we wanted to do something to you, we would have done it already."

"That's supposed to make me feel better?"

"It's not about your feelings," the man said. "It's much bigger than that."

"What is?"

"You'll know soon enough. Now get moving."

"I don't have any clothes."

"Look up."

Pfefferkorn looked up. The bathroom ceiling consisted of foam tiles two feet square.

"You'll find what you need in there."

Pfefferkorn climbed onto the toilet and slid aside a ceiling tile. A plastic shopping bag fell out, hitting him in the face. He found brand-new khakis wrapped around a pair of white running shoes. One shoe held balled white gym socks, the other a pair of white briefs. Last, there was a black polo shirt. He held it up. It hung to his knees.

He heard the man talking and picked up the phone.

"—win any best-dressed awards, but it'll do."

"Hello," Pfefferkorn said.

"Ready?"

Pfefferkorn pulled on the underwear. "I'm going as fast as I can."

"Inside your nightstand is a Bible. Taped to page one hundred twenty-eight you'll find three quarters."

Pfefferkorn, one leg in the khakis, hopped to the nightstand. He was angry at himself for having missed the quarters. In unsticking them he took care not to tear the delicate paper. The verse revealed was John 8:32: "And ye will know the truth, and the truth will make you free."

"In a minute you're going to leave your room," the man said. "Don't do it yet. Down the hall to the left you'll find vending machines. I want you to buy a grape soda. Is that clear? Once I hang up, this phone will cease to function. Drop it in the toilet tank before you leave."

"But—" Pfefferkorn said.

He was talking to the air.

59.

The man had instructed him to go left, but Pfefferkorn turned right, toward the stairs, and went down to the first floor in search of a phone. There was movement in the window of the motel's front office. He did not go in, concerned that the clerk might be in league with his abductors. He crossed the parking lot, hoping to get his bearings.

The motel was on the side of a freeway running through the desert. Baked earth kissed bleached sky. He could have been anywhere in the American Southwest. Setting out on foot was out of the question, so he waited, hoping to flag down a passing car. None came. He was left with two choices: solicit help from the clerk or obey the mysterious caller's instructions.

A bell rang as he entered the office. A clock on the wall read six fifty-seven. Behind the desk, a small television set was tuned fuzzily to the morning news. Two well-formed people made light banter about a plane crash.

An obese young man emerged from a back room. "Can I help you."

Pfefferkorn inferred from the clerk's apathy that the fellow knew nothing of Pfefferkorn's captivity. This was both encouraging and discouraging. On one hand, he could speak without fear of alerting the mysterious caller. On the other hand, everything he could think to say sounded insane.

"Would you mind please printing out a statement of charges?"

"Room number."

Pfefferkorn told him. The clerk typed with two fingers. It looked as though the act required intense concentration. A graphic flashed on the television screen.

TOP STORIES

"Good morning," the male anchor said. "I'm Grant Klinefelter."

"And I'm Symphonia Gapp," the female anchor said, "and these are our top stories. A renowned suspense novelist is sought by police."

Pfefferkorn's jacket photo appeared on the screen.

Pfefferkorn felt the blood leave his head. His knees began to jellify and he braced himself against the counter. Meanwhile the clerk was still typing, his tongue poking between his teeth.

"Following a daring jailbreak, bestselling author A. S. Peppers is wanted for questioning in connection with the brutal slaying of his Lambada instructor."

Pfefferkorn listened as the news anchors cheerfully proceeded to implicate him in Jesús María de Lunchbox's murder. The clerk finished typing and pressed a button. A printer whined. Pfefferkorn's jacket photo was shown again, accompanied by the number for a tip hotline. A reward was being offered.

"Sad stuff," Symphonia Gapp said.

"Indeed," Grant Klinefelter said. "When we come back: more trouble on the Zlabian border."

"And later: a local kitten does his part to win the war on terror."

"Anything else?"

The clerk was holding out the statement. Pfefferkorn took it. The motel's address was printed at the top of the statement. It listed a route number Pfefferkorn had never heard of, in a town he had never heard of, in a state adjacent to the one in which he had been abducted. The box marked name of guest brought an unwelcome shock.

The room had been rented to Arthur Kowalczyk.

"Anything else," the clerk said again.

Pfefferkorn shook his head absently.

The clerk lumbered out.

Pfefferkorn remained standing there, leaning against the counter, the jingle of the commercial fading away, the walls fading away, the dusty heat and the desert glare fading, fading away, everything canceling itself out. Only one sensation remained: a strange, nonphysical itch insinuating itself throughout his entire body, starting from his chest and spreading to the tips of his toes, the back of his throat, the hairs on the tops of his thighs. He was paranoid. It had happened that easily. Much like Harry Shagreen, or Dick Stapp, or any man ensnared in a tangled web of deception, treachery, lies, and intrigue, he did not know whom to trust. Unlike Harry Shagreen or Dick Stapp, Pfefferkorn had no experience upon which to draw. He headed back to the second floor.

60.

The vending machines were set in a nook around the bend in the hall. One sold snacks, another sold drinks, and a third dispensed ice. The sight of packaged food behind glass turned Pfefferkorn's stomach. He fed the quarters into the drink machine and pressed the button for a grape soda.

The machine hummed.

A can banged into place.

Pfefferkorn waited. Was that it? He was now out of instructions, and he had spent all his money on a beverage he did not want.

He took the soda. The label read *Mr. Grapey*. The drink contained one hundred sixty calories, no fat, no cholesterol, fifty-three milligrams of sodium, forty-seven grams of sugar, no vitamins, look in your back pocket.

I'm hallucinating, he thought.

He rubbed his eyes.

The words remained.

He reached into his back pocket and removed a slip of paper the size and shape of a fortune-cookie fortune. On it were printed two words.

TURN AROUND

Pfefferkorn turned around.

Not three feet away, where ten seconds prior there had been nobody, a man now stood. Pfefferkorn could not fathom how he had gotten there so quickly and quietly. Yet there he was, a medium-sized man in a shapeless charcoal suit. Pfefferkorn could not tell his age, due to a full eighty percent of his face being hidden behind the largest, bushiest, most aggressively expansionist moustache Pfefferkorn had ever seen. It was a moustache with submoustaches that in turn had sub-submoustaches, each of which might be said to be deserving of its own area code. It was a moustache that vexed profoundly questions of waxing, a moustache the merest glimpse of which might spur female musk oxen to ovulate. It was a moustache that would have driven Nietzsche mad with envy, had he not been mad already. If the three most copiously flowing waterfalls in the world, Niagara, Victoria, and Iguazú Falls, were somehow united, and their combined outputs rendered in facial hair, this man's moustache would not have been an inaccurate model, save that this man's moustache also challenged traditional notions of gravity by growing outward, upward, and laterally. It was an impressive moustache and Pfefferkorn was impressed.

"I'm afraid you've been misinformed," the man said.

61.

Moustaches or no moustaches, Pfefferkorn knew at once who he was talking to.

"Jameson?" Pfefferkorn asked. "Is that you?"

The moustaches moved in a disappointed way. "For the purposes of this operation," Jameson said, "you should refer to me as Blueblood."

Pfefferkorn followed him to a black coupe at the rear of the parking lot.

"Why are you wearing that ridiculous getup?"

"All information will be provided on a need-to-know basis."

They peeled out onto the highway.

"Can I at least see some identification or something?" Pfefferkorn asked.

"Field agents don't carry ID. My official picture wouldn't match my face, anyhow."

"I'm not sure why I'm supposed to trust you."

"Have you seen the news? I cut you loose and you'll either be in jail or dead by sundown. If not both. And sooner. So it's in your interest to listen to me.

But"—Jameson/Blueblood veered onto the shoulder and slammed on the brakes—"it's your call."

Pfefferkorn stared out at the shimmering blacktop. He had no food, no water, and no money. His clothes didn't fit and he had a headache. He could run, but where? He could seek help, but from whom? There was a reward posted for his capture, and he was one of the most famous writers in the world. Not as high-profile as a movie star, perhaps, but still.

"Well?" Blueblood/Jameson said. "Do you accept?"

"Accept what."

"Your mission."

"How am I supposed to answer that? I have no idea what I'm committing to."

Blueblood rooted around under his seat. "This might help."

He tossed a manila envelope in Pfefferkorn's lap. Pfefferkorn opened it and withdrew a photo. It was pixelated and blurry, a still taken from a video. It was what they called a "proof of life" picture. It showed a newspaper with yesterday's date. The newspaper was being held up by Carlotta de Vallée. She was dirty. Her makeup was smeared. Her left temple was matted down with dark crust. She looked petrified. She had a right to be. There was a gun to her head.

62.

The safe house was a four-story log cabin on a private lake. Pfefferkorn clambered out of the seaplane and took in a lungful of piney air.

"Go on ahead," Blueblood said. "I'll be there in a minute."

Pfefferkorn walked up the dock toward the house. The front door opened.

"Howdy doody," Canola said. "Glad you could make it."

He ushered Pfefferkorn to an elegant room appointed with bear-skin rugs and Craftsman furniture. A stag's head hung over a stone fireplace roomy enough to spit-roast a yak. There was a stately grandfather clock and a long conference table polished to a mirror shine. If not for the presence of a bulletin board tacked with a map of the Zlabias and a ceiling-mounted projection screen, it would have made an appropriate setting for a state dinner party, especially one whose menu called for yak.

"Take a load off," Canola said. "Op com will be by soon to brief you. Hungry?"

Pfefferkorn nodded.

"Sit tight."

Pfefferkorn fiddled with the knickknacks on the mantel. Muted voices drifted down the hall. He tried to eavesdrop but got nothing.

Canola returned with sandwiches and ice water. "Lunch is served," he said.

Pfefferkorn bit into an egg salad on seven-grain.

"Sorry about all the rough stuff," Canola said. "You understand."

Pfefferkorn, chewing, nodded. He didn't understand, but he was beginning to sense that it was better for him to pretend he did.

Canola grinned. "I gotta say: you looked real scared when we cuffed you."

A voice in the hallway said, "Did someone say lunch?" Sockdolager entered and spied the food. "Don't mind if I do," he said. He stuffed half a sandwich into his mouth and spun around a chair to sit backward, grinning through crumbs at Pfefferkorn. "What's new, puddytat?"

"Everything," Pfefferkorn said.

The "detectives" chuckled.

Pfefferkorn set down his sandwich and went to study the map. Together, the two Zlabias made a shape akin to a misshapen root vegetable. That both fit onto a single sheet of paper while yet maintaining enough fineness of resolution to label the individual streets spoke to how tiny the countries were—neighborhoods, really. Why was it that violence always burned hottest in cramped, obscure places? The dividing line, Gyeznyuiy Boulevard, cut clean up the middle of the map, ending at the top of the page in a plaza labeled, on one side, *Square of the*

Location of the Conclusion of the Parade of the Commemoration of the Remembrance of the Exalted Memory of the Greatness of the Sacrifices of the Magnificent Martyrs of the Glorious Revolution of the Zlabian People of the Twenty-sixth of May, and on the other side, *Adam Smith Square.* Along the bottom edge of the map bulged a blank space marked *Dzhikhlishkh Nuclear Exclusion Zone.*

"It'll all be on the exam."

Pfefferkorn turned. The speaker was a young man with ash-brown hair neatly parted along the right side. He wore a bland suit and an understated necktie held in place by an American flag pin.

"For the purposes of this operation," he said, "you can call me whatever you'd like, Dad."

63.

"We downloaded this from the de Vallées' home security system," Paul said.

Pfefferkorn watched the computer screen. It showed closed-circuit footage of the ballroom. Carlotta and Jesús María de Lunchbox were dancing the tango. The video had no sound. It made them look like they were having very well-coordinated seizures. A minute or so into the video, they pulled apart with identical expressions of terror. Eight masked men rushed into the frame. Four of them grabbed Carlotta. Pfefferkorn was proud to see her fight like a champion. She could have been an actress in a silent movie, exhibiting "The heroine struggles courageously." The men carried her off screen. Meanwhile the other four men were busy with Jesús María. Three of them restrained him while the fourth took out a boning knife.

Paul pressed pause. "I think you know what happens next," he said.

Pfefferkorn was shaken. "Where is she," he asked.

In answer to this question Paul closed the file and clicked on another. A new window filled the computer screen. The video was the source for the still photograph Blueblood had shown him. Carlotta was sitting in front of the same blank, scarred concrete wall. The same gun was to her head. She was holding the newspaper. She sounded scared but in control of herself. She repeated the date. She said that she was fine and being treated well. She said that she had been taken captive by the Revolutionary Movement of the Twenty-sixth of May. She said that in order to secure her safe return, the U.S. government would need to hand over the workbench. She said a few more things Pfefferkorn couldn't make heads or tails of, either. Then she said something that stood his hair on end.

"The delivery must be made by American novelist Arthur Pfefferkorn. He must come alone. If anyone else comes, or if he fails to deliver the workbench, I will be—"

The image froze. Paul closed the window.

"Let's not worry about that part," he said.

If Pfefferkorn was shaken before, he was really quite badly shaken now. He was like a martini inside a rock tumbler being held by a detoxing epileptic standing on stilts atop a trampoline inside the San Andreas Fault. He stared at the blank blue screen, the afterimage of Carlotta's face dancing before him.

"Tell me everything you know," Paul said.

64.

Pfefferkorn told him everything he knew, starting with the theft of the manuscript. When he came to the part about the note from Lucian Savory, Paul said, "He's a double agent."

"You say that like it's the most obvious thing in the world."

"Don't feel bad," Paul said. "We only just found out about it ourselves."

He clicked another file. Up came a photo of two men greeting each other.

"This was taken three weeks ago at Khlapushniyuiyk Airport, East Zlabia. I'm sure you recognize Savory."

The sight of that bulbous forehead caused Pfefferkorn's blood pressure to rise.

"Three guesses who he's shaking hands with."

The second man was hugely tall and broad as a bear. An entire carton of Marlboros jutted from one pocket of his tentlike sportcoat. In the background was a contingent of expressionless men armed with machine guns as well as a squad of improbably buxom women wearing the uniforms of the Dallas Cowboys cheerleaders.

"I have no idea," Pfefferkorn said.

"East Zlabian Lord High President Kliment Thithyich," Paul said.

"The guy I shot?"

"You didn't shoot him."

"I didn't?"

Paul shook his head.

"Thank God," Pfefferkorn said.

"If I were you, I wouldn't start congratulating myself just yet. You did kill Dragomir Zhulk."

"Oh."

Paul minimized the photo of Savory and Thithyich. "A lot of what Savory told you was true. The books were coded. Bill did work for us. And you were his intended replacement. But the part about *Blood Eyes* causing Kliment Thithyich to get shot was bullshit."

"Then who shot him?"

"He did."

"He shot himself? Why?"

"To create a pretext for invading West Zlabia," Paul said. "He's already filthy rich—casinos, mostly, plus some telecom and media—but control of the West Zlabian gas field would bump him up to the big leagues. He's tried rallying international support for an invasion through more respectable channels. You might've noticed his campaign to promote awareness about West Zlabian human rights violations? It didn't catch on. The opposite, in fact: Thithyich actually lost a few neutral-to-favorable percentage points, probably because, as our own polls indicate, ninety-six percent of people haven't heard of either Zlabia, and eighty-one percent of those that have can't tell them apart. You can imagine how antsy Thithyich must be getting if he's willing to fake an assassination attempt. It hurts, getting shot in the ass."

"Then why didn't he invade?"

"Because he's a chicken. Remember, before the Wall came down, we propped up guys like him as a bulwark against the Soviets. They have the most grotesque sense of entitlement. He was counting on our support as part of any offensive. We've since made it clear that we have no intention of getting involved in another war for the sake of lining his pockets."

"So there was no code in *Blood Eyes*?"

"There was, but it was a dummy—a call-and-response code. We wanted to test whether your name brand would have sufficient penetrance to be useful for future operations. And did it ever. Perfect score."

"But I mangled it," Pfefferkorn said.

"Mangled—"

"The flag. 'In one fluid motion.'"

"That wasn't the flag."

"It wasn't?"

"No."

"Then what was?"

" 'Sank to his knees, gasping for breath.' "

It depressed Pfefferkorn to realize that he had let such a wretched cliché slip through the cracks. "How did you know I would take the manuscript in the first place?" he asked.

"We knew. We have a profile on you running back to the seventies. You were emotionally needy, financially strapped, alternately self-congratulatory and self-loathing, led to believe that your more successful friend held you to be the superior writer. It was the perfect storm of ego and greed. And, like I said, you showed big promise. We were all set to bring you in and give you the hard sell when forty percent of our covert network, including all of Zlabia, was scrapped due to budget cuts. Believe that? Thirty-three years of work—gone, overnight." Paul shook his head forlornly. "Politics."

"How does *Blood Night* fit into all of this?"

"Thithyich got wind of the cuts. From Savory, presumably. So he hurried up before our operatives in the field were recalled and had Savory slip you a doctored code—"

"Blood Night."

"Right. Sayonara, Dragomir Zhulk."

"Let me get this straight," Pfefferkorn said. "Thithyich got Savory to get me to get my publisher to get your men to do his dirty work."

"Give him points for creativity. We don't communicate with the operatives directly. They only scan for the flags. There was no way for them to tell the difference

between a real code and the doctored one. It was a mas-
terstroke. With Zhulk gone, nobody's driving the bus.
There are at least half a dozen factions vying for control:
the Party, sure, but also the anarcho-environmentalists,
the Trotskyites, the Chomskyites, the nihil-pacifists, the
open sourcers. It's a total free-for-all. All the East Zlabians have to do now is pick their moment and they'll waltz
right across the border."

Pfefferkorn massaged his temples. "So who kidnapped
Carlotta?"

"That would be the May Twenty-sixers. West Zlabian
counter-counter-revolutionaries. Third-generation hard-
liners raised during perestroika on a steady diet of disin-
formation, believing themselves the last great hope for
Communism and dissatisfied with what they perceive as
Zhulk's passivity, although ironically, it's his propaganda
machine that created them in the first place. They've seen
Thithyich building up his forces and they're spoiling for
a fight. They're also short on firepower. So that's what
they're asking for."

Pfefferkorn thought. "The workbench."

Paul nodded. "Capital W. Encryption software. You
plug in a source code and out pops a blockbuster thriller,
complete with message. Our working theory is that the
kidnappers came to the mansion looking for it. They
didn't find it, of course, because we erased it, remotely,
after Bill died. So they took Carlotta instead."

It dawned on Pfefferkorn that she had been at the house
at his insistence. If he had allowed her to come to his reading, like she'd wanted to, she would be safe right now.

"We have to get her back," Paul said. "She's too valuable to leave out in the field."

Pfefferkorn found it disturbing that such an accounting could be made at all. "She's an agent, too."

"One of the best. Co-architect of the original ficto-cryption program."

"So you're going to hand over the Workbench."

"No way. Are you kidding? It would give them the capacity to generate an endless supply of encoded blockbuster thrillers. It would give them access to most of our worldwide covert arsenal." Paul paused. "Including several dozen nukes."

"Oh, God."

"We'll use a dummied version. It'll produce authentic-looking novels but the codes will be gobbledygook. Your challenge is to sell the Twenty-sixers on it."

There was a silence.

"Why do they want me?" Pfefferkorn asked.

"I was hoping you might be able to shed some light on that," Paul said.

Pfefferkorn shook his head.

"It's highly irregular," Paul said. "You're not a trained agent."

"No kidding."

"I'd much rather send a strike force."

"I'd much rather you did, too."

Pfefferkorn stared at the map, at its impenetrable combinations of consonants. "And if I say no?"

Paul did not reply. No reply was necessary.

Pfefferkorn looked at him. "Who *are* you."

"I'm family," Paul said.

There was a silence.

"Please tell me she's not in on it, too," Pfefferkorn said.

"Your daughter? No." Paul put a hand on Pfefferkorn's arm. "And let me just say, for the record, because I'm sure you're wondering: I really do love her."

Pfefferkorn said nothing.

"It didn't start out that way, but I do now. And I want you to know that, whatever your decision, whatever the result, you have my word that she'll be taken care of."

Pfefferkorn regarded him skeptically. "You framed me for murder."

"Just showing you what we're capable of. In case you got cold feet."

"You stranded me naked in a motel."

Paul shrugged. "We had reward points that were going to expire."

Pfefferkorn said nothing.

"Carlotta really does love you, too. I know what it must look like, but that's the truth. One of the reasons we picked you as Bill's successor was because you already had an established relationship with her."

Pfefferkorn said nothing.

"It doesn't have to be one or the other," Paul said.

Pfefferkorn shut his eyes. He saw Carlotta fighting to save herself. He saw her beaten and thrown into a cell. He saw her forced to recite a speech. He saw her begging him to come alone. He saw her need, and her need was him.

He opened his eyes.

"When do we begin?" he said.

65.

His reeducation lasted eleven days and consisted of intensive cultural, linguistic, and tactical training. The goal was not merely to cram him with information but to give him the tools to process that information like a Zlabian would. To this end, a large staff was brought in. He was given weapons lessons (from Gretchen), acting and elocution lessons (from Canola), makeup lessons (from Benjamin), moustache lessons (from Blueblood), and so forth. Dozens more agents showed up for an hour or two to instruct him in some minor art before departing on the seaplanes that came and went round the clock. The safe house was a hive of activity, all of it centered on him and none of it with any regard for his comfort. He had never felt so important and yet so demeaned. He understood the need for his teachers to be hard on him. As a teacher himself he knew how much of what passed for education was wishy-washy navel-gazing designed to avoid, at all costs, damaging students' self-esteem. That didn't mean he enjoyed slogging through G. Stanley Hurwitz's magisterial six-volume *A Brief History of the Zlabian Conflict*. Nor did it make any more palatable the endless variations on root vegetables and goats'-milk dairy, meals meant to accustom him to Zlabian cuisine. He wasn't any less crapulous after swallowing vast quantities of *thruynichka*, the stupefying concoction made from root vegetable greens fermented in goat's whey that he would be expected to consume as part of every Zlabian social interaction. He wasn't any less sore after an hour of Sockdolager punting him around the karate studio.

Aside from the sheer stress of the routine, Pfefferkorn had to grapple with several nagging doubts. He did not doubt that his handlers were American. For one thing, they had demonstrated their power to manipulate the criminal justice system. And there were other, less overt signs. One night, for example, the safe house ran out of toilet tissue, and Gretchen commandeered a helicopter to go to Walmart. To Pfefferkorn, this incident, with its gloss of ultrasophistication overlying gross shortsightedness, embodied the Americanness of the operation. He knew he was on the same side as his native land. What he doubted, rather, was whether that was a virtuous place to be. He doubted the completeness of the information he was being given. Most of all, he doubted himself.

By far his least favorite part of the day was language class. His instructor was Vibviana, a pretty but severe West Zlabian defector. She explained that the agency had developed its methods based on developmental psychology research that pinpointed the years from birth to three as the critical period for language acquisition.

"To facilitate better, you must return please to frame of mind of young children's."

Twice a day, for two hours, Pfefferkorn became a

Zlabian. In his first lesson he assumed the role of a new-born. He submitted to being diapered and burped while Vibviana, his fictive mother, sang him lullabies and told him stories based on the Zlabian national poem, *Vassily Nabochka*. Every successive lesson advanced him through one developmental year, so that by the end of the second day he was four years old and already well acquainted with the horrors of West Zlabian childhood. His fictive family, played by a rotating cast of agents, included a beloved and mentally retarded older brother, a crone of a grandmother, and countless aunts, uncles, cousins, and goats. Everyone lived under one tiny thatched roof, so that when Vibviana suffered at the hands of Pfefferkorn's fictive father (a violent, alcoholic factory hand), Pfefferkorn was forced to sit in the corner and listen to the sounds of slaps, screaming, and broken crockery, followed by maudlin apologies and vigorous make-up sex.

It was not fun.

That was the idea, Paul said. The Zlabian psyche was steeped in abuse, degradation, and poor hygiene, and the sooner Pfefferkorn got used to it, the better.

Never before had he had so much one-on-one time with his son-in-law. In his daily policy briefings, Paul—or op com, as the other agents called him—shed his bumbling accountant's façade, revealing himself as savvy, quick, and cynical, the kind of oversmart young patriot capable of smoothly steering his country into a disastrous foreign war. He had a way of talking around the issue that inspired confidence and dread in equal measure.

"You love her," Pfefferkorn said.

Paul turned from the projection screen, which showed

a timeline charting the ramifications of the 1983 West Zlabian currency devaluation. He stared at Pfefferkorn for a moment, then switched off the laser pointer. "I thought I made that clear."

"I need to hear it again."

"I love her."

"How much."

"Well, it'll take me some time to prepare a full report."

"You proposed to her after what? Three months?"

"Five."

"And before that? How long was it in the works?"

"People get married for lots of different reasons," Paul said.

Pfefferkorn said nothing.

"I love her," Paul said, "with all of my heart."

"How do I know that?"

"How did you know it before?"

"I didn't," Pfefferkorn said.

"Then you're no worse off," Paul said. "Better, in fact, because I've shown you my hand."

Pfefferkorn said nothing.

"Don't forget Carlotta," Paul said.

"I haven't forgotten her."

"You're doing this for her."

"I know that," Pfefferkorn said.

There was a silence.

"What really happened to Bill?" Pfefferkorn asked.

"Boating accident," Paul said.

The grandfather clock chimed.

"Time for your language lesson," Paul said. "Vibviana says you're coming along nicely."

The fourteenth year of Zlabian boyhood had been an annus horribilis in which Pfefferkorn's beloved and mentally retarded older brother died of tapeworms, his pet goat was clubbed to death by an irate neighbor, he flunked his *Vassily Nabochka* qualifying exam, and he lost his virginity to an elderly prostitute who taunted him mercilessly after he ejaculated prior to entry. On the plus side, he had mastered the subjunctive.

"I feel hollow inside," Pfefferkorn said.

"That's the spirit."

66.

The night before Pfefferkorn's departure, the core members of the team threw him a graduation party. Vibviana played the accordion and sang folk songs taken from *Vassily Nabochka*. Sockdolager got thunderingly drunk and tried to kiss her. Pfefferkorn delivered him an elbow to the solar plexus that left the larger man sinking to his knees, gasping for breath. Everyone applauded and commended Pfefferkorn on the unified fluidity of his motions. Gretchen applied a sparkly gold sticker to his shirtfront. The sticker was in the shape of a shooting star and said SUPERSTAR!

The next morning he awoke to an empty house. It was his first moment of repose since his arrival, and it allowed him to reflect on the ordeal ahead. For all their efforts to prepare him, nobody, not even Paul, could predict with confidence what would happen once he crossed into West Zlabian territory. Pfefferkorn realized the hectic training schedule had served a dual purpose: first, to ready him for grueling undercover work in a burgeoning war zone, and second, to prevent him from dwelling on the fact that there was a strong chance he would not make it back alive.

He heard the drone of an approaching seaplane.

He took his wheelie bag and walked to the kitchen. He cupped his hands and drank water straight from the tap, possibly for the last time. He wiped his hands on his pants and headed down to the dock.

The seaplane nosed toward the surface of the lake, skipping twice before splashing down. As it drew near the dock, Pfefferkorn did not move to greet it. He was in no mood for air travel. He was frightened, lonely, and hungover. But these were not problems he could afford to admit. He had a mission, one demanding intestinal fortitude and stoicism. He stared hard at the sky. It was the hard stare of a man hardening himself to hard truths. He sensed changes, hard ones, taking place within his soul. He peeled the sparkly gold star from his chest and cast it, in a hard and masculine manner, into the wind. From this point on, he would have to earn his stripes. He grasped the handle of his wheelie bag and strode purposefully toward his destiny.

FOUR
дхиуобхриуо пжулобхатъ бху жпудниуиуи жлабхвуи!

(WELCOME TO WEST ZLABIA!)

67.

Like an aging actress too proud to pack up the grease-paint, the Hôtel Metropole had hobbled along bravely in the service of increasingly ill-fitting roles. The kings and potentates who had inaugurated her beds had, over the last one hundred and fifty years, been steadily supplanted by a procession of apparatchiks, spooks, journalists, and johns, and the quoined limestone façade, once smart and coquettish, was now grim with soot. Nobody had informed the staff, who continued to wear their red melton jackets with indefensible dignity, addressing without irony the haggard tarts prowling the lobby as "madame."

The desk clerk transcribed Pfefferkorn's false passport number into the registry. "It is honorable to welcome you, Monsieur Kowalczyk."

Pfefferkorn smiled somberly. At the far end of the desk, bluebottles mobbed a bowl of rotting fruit. He slung his jacket over his shoulder and swabbed his greasy forehead. If he ever wrote another thriller, he planned to make the travel scenes more realistic, with plenty of page space devoted to stale coffee and smelly upholstery. The past twenty-four hours had taken him through five different countries and as many security checkpoints. His disguise was working. At no point had he been subjected to more than a cursory inspection, and he had found it surreal to stand at a newsagent in Schiphol Airport, stroking his false moustache, gnawing a round of Edam, and reading about the manhunt still on for him, while a lady beside him reached for the rack of best sellers and selected a copy of that international blockbuster *Bloed Ogen*.

His back throbbed, he was jet-lagged, and he reeked, but he had made it.

The clerk eyed his wheelie bag. "You linger inside us for these two weeks, yes?"

"I travel light," Pfefferkorn said, sliding a ten-*ruzha* note across the marble.

The clerk bowed. In an instant the money had vanished up his sleeve. He touched a bell and three bellhops materialized. They fought like dogs over Pfefferkorn's wheelie bag until the desk clerk sent two of them packing in glum retreat.

The elevator car rose unhappily, stopping half a foot shy of the fourth floor. The bellhop jumped out and raced down the corridor, the wheelie bag bouncing wildly behind. Pfefferkorn followed, careful not to trip over the soiled ridges in the carpeting where it had pulled up from the floorboards. Radios and murmurs and oscillating fans could be heard. From the border a mile away came the stutter of automatic weapons.

Once inside the room, the bellhop made a show of adjusting the thermostat. The dial came off in his hand. He pocketed it and gave up trying to seem useful, waiting by the door until Pfefferkorn had located another ten *ruzhy*, at which point he smiled brownly and bowed his way out, leaving Pfefferkorn alone in the paralyzing heat.

68.

Pfefferkorn's time on book tour had taught him that the comfort of an American hotel room arose out of a fantasy mutually agreed upon by hotelier and guest: you were the first person to stay there. The virginal linens, antiseptic artwork, and neutral color schemes were all designed to maintain this illusion, without which it would have been difficult to sleep.

The Hôtel Metropole made no such attempt to conceal its past. To the contrary: room 44 provided a rich historical document. The ceiling, dark and malodorous, attested to thousands of cigarettes. The bedspread showed a broad archipelago of stains, chronicle of many an unsavory act. The molding was Second Empire, the furniture was Constructivist, the carpet was shag, and the curtains were missing. Soft spots in the wallpaper told of listening devices put in and ripped out. He didn't know what had caused the crimson blotch along the baseboard—it could have just as easily been the result of a rusty leak—but he suspected it had been left there as a rebuke to the chronically optimistic.

A picture of the late Dragomir Zhulk hung over the bed.

Pfefferkorn unpacked. Because the United States and West Zlabia had no formal diplomatic relations, he was traveling as a Canadian expatriate residing in the Solomon Islands. "Arthur S. Kowalczyk" was vice president of a small-time fertilizer distributor seeking bulk suppliers. His wheelie bag contained an assortment of business attire, pressed white shirts and pilled black socks. He hung up his blazer, arranged his shoes at the foot of the bed, and stowed his passport in the safe, which was a cigar box with a flimsy padlock. He stared edgily into the empty suitcase. Beneath its false bottom was a secret compartment containing two additional moustache kits. There was also a supplementary disguise: a traditional Zlabian goatherd's costume of baggy pants, a peasant shirt, and brightly painted boots with curly pointed toes and six-inch heels. These items were not illegal, per se, but they were suspicious enough to merit concealment. The illegal items were in a second secret compartment, hidden beneath a second false bottom. There he had a roll of cash the size of a soda can and an untraceable cellular phone. Possessing either of these was grounds for immediate arrest and/or expulsion. But the truly risky stuff, the stuff that would get him killed outright, no questions asked, was hidden in a third secret compartment, located underneath a third false panel. Extra precautions had been taken. What looked like a bar of lavender-scented soap was an X-ray-impervious high-density dubnium polymer surrounding a flash drive with the dummied Workbench. What looked like a bottle of designer eau de cologne was an industrial-strength solvent powerful enough to strip the polymer away. What looked like a toothbrush was a toothbrush switchblade. What looked like a stick of deodorant was a stun gun, and what looked like a tin of breath mints held fast-acting poison pills for use in the event he was captured and facing the prospect of torture.

After ensuring that everything had survived the journey, he replaced the false panels and went to take a cooling shower. The water was foul and hot, the towels abrasive. Another picture of Zhulk hung over the toilet, scowling at Pfefferkorn as he stood before the cracked bathroom mirror, pressing the moisture out of his false moustache. It was medium brown, the color of his hair in his youth. In point of fact, it closely resembled the moustache he had kept in college. There was a reason he had shaved it off: it wasn't a good look for him. Bill had the right amount of manly jowl to justify facial hair. Not him. He ran his fingers over it. It was dense, bristly, both of him and not. He appreciated the restraint Blueblood had shown in creating it.

While he waited to stop sweating, he surveyed the room's remaining amenities. There was a lamp, a bedside clock, an oscillating fan, and a painted radiator gone piebald—the last of which would be useless for the next three months, minimum. If he was still here then, God help him. He made sure it was screwed tightly off, then switched on the fan. It was dead. He picked up the rotary phone and dialed zero. The desk clerk answered with a smarmy "Monsieur?" Pfefferkorn asked for a replacement fan and was told one would be brought without delay.

A clanking started up from inside the wall, near the headboard. It was a noise he was unfortunately well acquainted with: hot water pipes coming to life. In his old apartment building it had sometimes sounded as though his neighbors were having shootouts. Why a hotel guest would possibly want hot water on a day like today, he could not venture to guess. Then it occurred to him that all the hotel's water was likely hot, whether guests wanted it that way or not. The clanking was loud and rhythmic. It made the picture of Zhulk vibrate and jump on the wall. To drown it out, Pfefferkorn aimed the remote control at the television. The screen filled with a stern young woman in an unflattering uniform, her tight hair topped with a majorette hat. She was standing in front of a paper weather map, barking the five-day forecast as she tacked up little paper suns. Her voice was even worse than the clanking, so Pfefferkorn muted her and lived with it.

In the top drawer of the nightstand he found the government-mandated copy of the West Zlabian edition of *Vassily Nabochka*. He sat down on the bed and leafed through it while he waited for his fan. The poem was familiar to him, having played a major role in his fictive life, as it did for every Zlabian. It told of the heroic quest of the disinherited Prince Vassily to find a magical root vegetable with the power to cure his ailing father, the king. The masterwork of itinerant bard Zthanizlabh of Thzazhkst, it reminded Pfefferkorn of the *Odyssey* crossed with *Lear* crossed with *Hamlet* crossed with *Oedipus Rex*, plus tundra and goats. The first two volumes of Hurwitz centered on a discussion of its history and symbolism, information essential for understanding the present state of affairs, as the Zlabian conflict traced its origins to a blood feud over the fictional protagonist's final resting place. The East Zlabians claimed Prince Vassily was "buried" in the East. The West Zlabians claimed he was "buried" in the West. Because the poem was unfinished, there was little hope of resolving the dispute. Each side staged its own parade on the day it marked as the prince's day of death. Often shots were fired or Molotov cocktails thrown across the Gyeznyuiy. And that was in times of peace. At its worst the conflict had pitted brother against brother, goat against goat. According to Hurwitz, an estimated one hundred twenty-one thousand lives had been lost over the years— an incredible number, given the size of the population as a whole.

Pfefferkorn glanced at the clock. It had been fifteen minutes and he still hadn't gotten his fan. He called the front desk again. The clerk apologized and promised it would be there shortly. Pfefferkorn hung up, picked up the poem again, and began flipping to random pages. He admired and pitied a people so fiercely devoted to their cultural heritage that they would spend four centuries slaughtering themselves over fictional burial places. Such a thing could never happen in America, because Americans lacked a sense of investment in their own history. The entire American enterprise was based on jettisoning the past in favor of the Next Big Thing. He wondered if this might make an interesting premise for a novel. The clanking died down, leaving Zhulk's picture askew. He didn't bother to fix it. It was nearing eleven a.m., time for his first appointment. He turned off the television, got dressed, and hurried downstairs.

69.

As part of Pfefferkorn's cover, meetings had been arranged with the government officials he would have needed to see had he truly been interested in exporting fertilizer. He stood among his fellow petitioners in the moldering hallway, waiting to be summoned by a squat woman more fit to guard the mouth of a cave. A one-armed Slav, his stinking greatcoat pinned at the shoulder and jangling with military decorations, whistled and smiled at the ceiling. The mewlings of a bundled child went untended by its vacant-eyed mother, eliciting clucks from a pair of babushkas fondling prayer ropes. Pfefferkorn wondered what business these folks could have with the second assistant to the deputy subminister in charge of animal waste. He had his answer when the troll lady appeared to crook a finger at him, and he gestured to the old soldier: *You first*. The Slav smiled, whistled, did not move. Nor did anyone else, and Pfefferkorn realized that he was the only one with an appointment. The rest had come inside to escape the heat.

"Comrade!" The second assistant to the deputy subminister in charge of animal waste greeted him with kisses that left wet trails in Pfefferkorn's moustache. "Sit down, yes, please, sit down! I convey to you abundance wishes for prosperity and partnership between these our two nations. Yes, sit, please! No, I insist: I am standing. I sit too long, yes? It is not conducive for buttocks. What? Yes, yes. Please, enjoy. To your health. *Thruynichka*, ah? We say: first bottle for sick, second bottle for well, next bottle for dead, four for alive again. Ha? Ha? Ha! To your health. I am please to receive application for export of waste. To your health. Unfortunately, I must report: this application is incomplete. Yes, ten thousand apologies . . . to your health. There is lacking application fee, there is lacking documentation of statement of purpose, affidavit of disloyalty unaffiliation, many else. Process requires to initiate from top. Please refrain from sadness. To your health. What? No. Expedite is impossible, impossible. What? No. Impossible. What? Shall I consult? It is not impossible." He pocketed the bribe. "To your health, ah?"

Pfefferkorn stumbled drunk into the burning noonday sun, negotiating fetid streets aswarm with dogs, cats, chickens, goats, children, factory workers, farmers, pickpockets, soldiers, and peasant women on prehistoric bicycles. Their motley faces told of centuries of invasion, subjugation, and intermarriage. Their eyes were narrow or round, ice blue or muddy. Their complexions ran the gamut from saddle brown to translucent. Their bone

structure was fine, it was rough-hewn, it was hidden
beneath clumps of flesh or tenting skin drawn tight as
a snare drum. So many faces, alike only in their fixed
expressions of distrust and resignation. So many faces,
but none the one he sought.

Carlotta, he thought, I've come for you.

One block on, a crowd had gathered to watch three
men in shirtsleeves fixing a spavined haycart, dissipating
disappointedly when the jack did not fail and nobody was
crushed to death. He turned down an unpaved alley that
opened onto a wide, potholed boulevard festooned with
posters touting the virtues of manual labor. Thatch-
roofed huts with crude goat pens and wilting garden
plots abutted Soviet-era concrete block monstrosities.
MINISTRY OF FACTS, Pfefferkorn read. MINISTRY OF MUSICAL
EDUCATION, MINISTRY OF BOOTS, MINISTRY OF LONG-CHAIN
CARBON COMPOUNDS. It was easy to identify the state's
priorities. The MINISTRY OF SECURITY was shiny and
imposing, as was the MINISTRY OF POETRY. The lobby of
the MINISTRY OF ROOT VEGETABLES was capacious enough
to house a fifteen-foot fountain. In the cracked storefront
of the vacant MINISTRY OF TRAFFIC CONTROL was a poster
memorializing the martyred Zhulk, with the slogan THE
REVOLUTION LIVES ON!

Though it was late afternoon by the time he staggered
out of his next meeting, with the auxiliary advisor to the
acting chief of the standards division of the Ministry of
Volatile Mineral Colloids, the sun was still high in the
sky, the heat as enervating as ever. Pfefferkorn eased himself down to the curb and put his head between his

knees. With respect to *thruynichka* consumption, the auxiliary advisor to the acting chief of the standards division of the Ministry of Volatile Mineral Colloids made the second assistant to the deputy subminister in charge of animal waste look like a lightweight. Pfefferkorn had no idea how he was going to find his way back to his hotel. He decided to sleep on the sidewalk. It was roughly the same temperature outside as it was in his room. No harm done, he thought. He curled up. Inside of a minute a pair of soldiers was hoisting him to his feet, demanding his papers. He produced his tourist pass. They ordered him to the Metropole and, when he started off in the wrong direction, took him by the elbows and dragged him there. He reeled across the lobby, scattering a klatsch of aged hookers and crashing into the front desk hard enough to jar the portrait of Zhulk on the wall.

The desk clerk readjusted it. "Monsieur has had a pleasant daytime, I am hopeful."

"Messages for me?" Pfefferkorn asked.

"No, please." The clerk vacuumed the money up his sleeve, handed Pfefferkorn his room key, and gestured toward the dining room. "Please, monsieur must partake of evening buffet."

Chinese businessmen were monopolizing the samovar. Eager to put something in his roiling stomach, Pfefferkorn browsed the offerings, settling on root vegetable cake with goat's-milk cream-cheese icing, cut into two-inch cubes and distributed by a dour woman wearing rubber gloves. She refused to give him more than one piece. He started to reach for cash.

"Ah, friend, no, no."

The speaker was a burly man in a grimy tweed sport-coat. In one hand he held a chipped plate piled precariously with root vegetable pierogi and smothered in a yellowish sauce. The other arm encircled a briefcase. He grinned, making three new chins. "Allow me." He spoke to the cake lady in rapid Zlabian. Pfefferkorn picked out the words for "industrious," "generosity," and "honor." The cake lady looked annoyed. All the same, she snatched Pfefferkorn's plate and added a second hunk of cake, shoving it at him as though giving up a pound of flesh.

"You must know," the man said, guiding Pfefferkorn to a corner table, "Comrade Yelena is perhaps the most duty-conscious woman in all of West Zlabia. She has been inculcated with the strictest principles. A double portion represents a desecration of all she knows."

"How'd you change her mind?" Pfefferkorn asked.

The man chuckled. "First, I instructed her that it is not proper to work without a smile. Then I reminded her that the cake ration for tourists is set at two per day, and because you were not at breakfast, you are entitled. Next, I provided examples of our benevolent Party leaders going without in order to feed the hungry. Finally, I informed her that I would in any case donate my ration to you, so that you might enjoy the full warmth of West Zlabian hospitality." The man smiled. He set his briefcase on the table, opened it, and withdrew two shot glasses, cleaning them with the corner of his coat. He uncapped a flask and poured. "To your health."

70.

Fyothor was his name, and if his clout with the cake lady and the freeness of his speech were not enough to mark him as a ranking Party member, the cell phone was. It rang continually throughout their conversation, which lasted long after the restaurant had officially closed. Pfefferkorn tried to pace himself but Fyothor kept pulling flasks from his briefcase.

"To your health. But tell me, friend, your room is acceptable to you? The Metropole is the finest our humble nation has to offer. Not up to American standards, perhaps, but comfortable enough, I hope."

"I'm not American," Pfefferkorn said.

"*Akha*, I beg forgiveness. So you said. Excuse me." Fyothor answered his phone, spoke briefly, hung up. "My apologies. To your health."

"You knew I wasn't at breakfast," Pfefferkorn said. "How."

Fyothor smiled. "I am a man whose business it is to know such things. And besides, I was there, you were not. It is elementary logic, yes?"

"What is it you do, exactly," Pfefferkorn said.

"You should ask instead what I do not do."

"All right, what don't you do."

"Nothing!" Fyothor's laughter rattled the silverware. "To your health, eh? This is the highest-quality *thruynichka*. You must be careful, friend. Most people make their own at home, it is like drinking bleach. My uncle is famous for his blend. Most of his neighbors are blind. To your health. *Akha*. Excuse me."

As Fyothor took the call, Pfefferkorn downed the rest of his cake. It tasted vile but he needed to soak up some of the alcohol—to retake the reins of his mind. A man like Fyothor could have any of a hundred different motives. He might be angling for a bribe. He might be a standard-issue Party minder. He might be secret police. He might simply be a friendly fellow, although in Pfefferkorn's estimation this was depressingly unlikely. Of greatest interest was the possibility that Fyothor was the point man Pfefferkorn was waiting for. If so, they both had to tread lightly. By law, membership in the May Twenty-sixers was illegal, making the exchange just as dangerous for them as it was for him. Should he be caught, the United States would disavow all knowledge of his existence and activities. He mentally rehearsed the identification codes.

Fyothor closed the phone. "Ten thousand apologies. This device . . . We have a word, *myutridashkha*. I believe in English you say 'both a blessing and a curse.' You understand?"

"Perfectly."

"To your health. You know, this is a word with an interesting history. It comes from a name, Myutridiya."

"The royal doctor," Pfefferkorn said.

Fyothor's mouth opened. "But yes! Friend, tell me: you know *Vassily Nabochka*?"

"Who doesn't."

"But this is wonderful! To meet a new person is rare. To meet a new person who is also a lover of poetry, this is like finding a diamond in the street. Friend, I am so joyful. To your health. But tell me: how is it that you have come to know our national poem?"

Pfefferkorn said that he was an avid reader.

Fyothor beamed. "To your health. You must know, then, the many idioms we take from the poem. We say, 'Sluggardly, like the dog Khlabva.'"

"'Happy, like the midget Juriy,'" Pfefferkorn said.

"'Redder than the fields of Rzhupsliyikh,'" Fyothor said.

"'Drunker than the farmer Olvarnkhov,'" Pfefferkorn said, raising his shot glass.

Fyothor threw back his shaggy head and roared with laughter. "Friend, you are a true Zlabian."

"To your health," Pfefferkorn said.

Fyothor uncapped a fourth flask. When he next spoke his voice was tremulous. "But you see, friend, here is the essence of our tragical national fate. Our wondrous heritage, it is also the cause of abominable bloodshed. If only the great Zthanizlabh of Thzazhkst had understood the dire consequences of leaving it in a state of incompleteness—but alas, we are doomed, doomed . . ." His phone rang. He looked at it and slid it back into his pocket. "*Akha*. Let us speak of happier things. Tell me, friend, you come for business, yes?"

It was a credit to the thoroughness of Pfefferkorn's training that, despite being sloppier than he had been since the Nixon administration, he was able to describe in pitch-perfect detail the purpose of his visit to West Zlabia, starting with his twenty-two years of experience in the fertilizer industry and ending with his visit to the auxiliary advisor to the acting chief of the standards division of the Ministry of Volatile Mineral Colloids.

Fyothor shook his head. "But friend, no! I know this man. He is a worthless fool, a lazy ignoramus whose only talent is for opening his palm. No, I insist, you must allow—" His phone rang. Again he returned it to his pocket unanswered. "My wife. Excuse me. But tell me: with whom do you meet tomorrow?"

Pfefferkorn named the functionaries he had appointments to see.

"Imbeciles, all of them. To speak with them is to spit in the ocean. You must allow me—*akha*." Fyothor checked the caller. "Excuse me. My wife, again. *Tha*. Tha. Akha, *ontheshki uithkh Dzhikhlishkuiyk, zhvikha thuy bhonyukhaya*." He snapped the phone shut and smiled sheepishly. "I regret that my presence is required at home. Thank you for a most enjoyable evening, my friend. To your health."

71.

Whoever had searched Pfefferkorn's room had made no effort to hide their work, throwing things around with such vigor that he assumed their real purpose was not to find contraband but to remind him of his vulnerability. If so, they were wasting their time. He already felt useless. He lurched about, picking up shirts, reinserting dresser drawers, smoothing the duvet. The contents of the topmost layer of his wheelie bag were dispersed, but the secret compartments had served their purpose: everything inside was untouched. With amusement he noticed that amid the chaos, the picture of Zhulk above the headboard had been straightened.

He felt in his pocket for the business card Fyothor had given him. It was printed in Cyrillic on thin paper. There was a name, a phone number, and two words. пэржюнилниуии экхжкуржубвудх. "Private tour guide." Sure, Pfefferkorn thought. He tucked the card toward the back of the room copy of *Vassily Nabochka*. He uncapped the bottle of water on his nightstand and took a long, silty pull. He felt restless. He wanted to go knocking on doors. How long before he found her?

A couple of days, at most. But his hands were tied. He had a script to follow, one both maddeningly constrictive and maddeningly vague. Contact could come at any time—tonight, tomorrow, the next day. He unbuttoned his shirt and reached for the fan.

It was still dead.

He lifted the phone and dialed.

"Monsieur?"

"Yes, this is Arthur Pfe—*Kowalczyk* in room forty-four."

"Yes, monsieur."

"I asked for a new fan."

"Yes, monsieur."

"The one I have is still broken."

"I am sorry, monsieur."

"It's very hot in here. Would you please send up another?"

"Yes, please, monsieur. Good night."

"Eh, hang on there, speedy."

"Monsieur?"

"Have there been any calls for me?"

"No, please."

"I'm expecting one, so put it through, no matter how late it is."

"Yes, please. Does monsieur require wake-up?"

"God, no."

"Good night, please, monsieur."

He hung up and went into the bathroom to splash water on his naked chest. Across the bedroom, the clanking pipes started up again, loud enough to rattle Zhulk's picture in its frame. He had no idea how he was going to sleep, unless the fan covered up the sound.

He shut off the tap and walked to the open window, stroking his moustache and letting the poisonous night air dry him as he gazed out at the squatting skyline. Somewhere out there was Carlotta. He spoke her name and the wind carried it away.

A memory came to him, unbidden. It must have been soon after Bill and Carlotta got married. Pfefferkorn had just started teaching, and he and Bill were strolling around campus.

"Promise me something, Yankel."

Pfefferkorn waved assent.

"You haven't heard what I'm asking yet." Bill waited for Pfefferkorn to pay attention, then said, "If anything ever happens to me, you'll look after Carlotta."

Pfefferkorn laughed.

"I'm not kidding," Bill said. "Promise me."

Pfefferkorn smiled at him quizzically. "What could happen to you?"

"Anything."

"Like what."

"Anything. I could get in an accident. I could have a heart attack."

"At twenty-eight."

"I won't be twenty-eight forever. Two-way deal: I'd do the same for you."

"What makes you think I'll ever get married?"

"Promise me."

"Sure, fine."

"Say it."

It wasn't like Bill to be so vehement. Pfefferkorn raised his right hand. "I, Yankel Pfefferkorn, do solemnly swear that in the event you kick the bucket, I'll look after your wife. Happy?"

"Very."

Did he have any idea then what he had been agreeing to? If he had, would he have still agreed? He decided he would have. It wasn't for Bill that he was here now.

Where was his fan?

"Yes, hello, this is Arthur Pfffkowalczyk in room forty-four. I'm still waiting for my fan."

"Yes, monsieur."

"Is it coming anytime soon?"

"Immediately, monsieur."

The clanking continued unabated. Zhulk's picture had rotated almost thirty degrees clockwise. Pfefferkorn took it down, concerned it would fall on him in the middle of the night.

One consequence of poor infrastructure was an electrical grid that functioned sporadically, and a corresponding lack of light pollution. Having lived in big cities his entire life, he was unused to such brilliant skies, and he watched, dizzily transfixed, as the clouds scudded offstage, and he was treated to a spectacular display of shooting stars.

72.

"Rise, citizens of Zlabia."

The voice was deafening, right there in the room with him, and Pfefferkorn scrambled out of bed, getting tangled up in the sheets and pitching face-first into the wall. A supernova flared inside his skull. Down he went, cracking his head a second time on the corner of the nightstand.

"Rise to productivity in the name of national greatness."

Through streamers of color and blobs of pain he saw the woman in the majorette hat. She was upside down, grainy, shouting at him in Zlabian.

"Tuesday, August ninth, will be an auspicious day for the advancement of our collective principles. You are encouraged to enjoy the weather, which will continue to be exceedingly pleasant, with an extremely comfortable high of twenty-two degrees."

He couldn't remember leaving the television on. He pulled himself to his feet and tried to switch it off, to no avail: the woman's face remained. The mute button was similarly ineffective.

"Through the generosity and wisdom of our beloved and benevolent Party leaders, the price of root vegetables remains well within reach of all citizens. . . ."

She began to list other available goods, her voice booming from the screen but also through the walls, floor, and ceiling. He raised the window sash. Loudspeakers crowned all the buildings. Down below, the street traffic had come to a complete standstill, everyone from old women shouldering wicker baskets of root vegetables to young boys driving posses of goats standing at attention. Pfefferkorn looked at the clock. It was five a.m.

"Remember to bring your allotment card to your neighborhood disbursal station."

On-screen, the woman opened a pocket-sized book. The people in the street did likewise.

"Today's reading will be the fourth stanza of the fifteenth canto."

She proceeded to read aloud a passage from *Vassily Nabochka*. The people followed along in an undertone, their collective murmur like a gathering storm. The reading ended and everyone put their personal copies away.

"Rejoice in the lofty heritage that is yours, citizens of Zlabia."

Everyone sang the national anthem.

There was a brief round of applause. Activity resumed. The woman in the majorette hat was replaced by a static image of the West Zlabian flag, backed by accordion music. Pfefferkorn hesitated before reaching to switch it off, half expecting a hand to reach through the screen and slap him on the wrist. His ears were ringing, his head pounding from hangover and impact. He was also sleep deprived. He distinctly remembered giving up on getting his fan at about one a.m. Between the heat and the pipes, he couldn't have gotten more than a few precious hours. It was a bad way to start the day. He needed his wits about him. He needed to keep his head in the game. He used the bedsheet to sponge the sweat from his body, got dressed, and went downstairs to find some coffee.

73.

He stopped at the front desk. A new clerk was on duty.

"Good morning, monsieur."

"Yes, hi, my name is Arthur. Kowalczyk. In room forty-four."

"Yes, monsieur."

"I asked last night for a fan."

"There is fan in room, monsieur."

"It's broken."

"Monsieur, I am regretful."

Pfefferkorn waited. The clerk grinned inanely. Pfefferkorn dug out a ten-*ruzha* note. The clerk took the money with the same practiced motion as his predecessor. He bowed.

"Monsieur will please to partake of breakfast buffet," he said unctuously.

Pfefferkorn stepped inside the restaurant. Intent on finding the coffee urn, he did not notice Fyothor sneaking up from behind to poke him in the ribs.

"Greetings, friend! How was your night? Yes? And how did you like our morning exhortations? Very inspiring, yes? Although, between you and me—twenty-two, my arse. Already the thermometer is pushing thirty and it's not even half past six. Twenty *ruzhy* says we hit forty by noon."

They went down the line together. There were two options: last night's pierogi and a chafing dish of gruel, both dispensed by the indomitable Yelena. There was no coffee, just sour brown tea.

"You didn't take any of the sauce," Fyothor said, waving at Pfefferkorn's plate as they took the same corner table. "The sauce is what makes the dish."

Pfefferkorn, remembering a formula from long ago, said, "Forty degrees—that's over a hundred, Fahrenheit."

"One-oh-five, I think."

Pfefferkorn groaned and pushed away his steaming bowl of gruel.

"But friend, this is delicious."

"What is it."

"We call this *bishyuinyuia khashkh*. It is like your oatmeal."

"Doesn't smell like oatmeal."

"It is made with root vegetables," Fyothor said. "And goat's milk."

"Goatmeal," Pfefferkorn said.

Fyothor laughed and thumped him on the back. "*Akha*, good one, friend. To your health."

"I'll stick with tea, thanks."

"I understand. But as our most insightful Party leaders say, let nothing go to waste." Fyothor winked and reached for Pfefferkorn's shot glass. "To your health. Surely it is fate that we meet again, yes?"

Pfefferkorn didn't know what to say to that.

"I have taken the liberty of making some phone calls on your behalf," Fyothor said.

Pfefferkorn was nonplussed. "Is that right."

"Take it from me, friend. We say: 'A man cannot cut his own hair.'"

Pfefferkorn recognized the adage as having its origin in an episode of *Vassily Nabochka* wherein the prince attempts to cut his own hair, the moral of the story being: sometimes it's better to ask for help. Although Fyothor's interference made him uneasy, Pfefferkorn saw no choice but to play along. Any sensible foreigner looking to do business in West Zlabia would be grateful for an inside track. Declining one would be the fastest way to blow his cover. And Fyothor literally kept him close at hand, taking him around the waist as they rose from the breakfast table.

"Stick with me, friend, and you will have more shit than you know what to do with."

Their first stop was the Ministry of Media Relations. Nobody said a word as they cut to the front of the line. Fyothor entered the co-sub-undersecretary's office without knocking and launched into a stirring discourse on the importance of fertilizer to the people's revolution.

Here, he said, holding up Pfefferkorn's arm, was a comrade from overseas who could do much to advance the collective principles by demonstrating to the world at large the innate superiority of West Zlabian goats, proven by science to produce waste with a nitrogen concentration higher than that of any other goats in the northern hemisphere. To substantiate this point he waved an article torn from that morning's sports section. The co-sub-undersecretary nodded, hmmed, and finally concurred that Pfefferkorn's was indeed a worthy project. He promised to write a memo to this effect. They toasted to mutual cooperation, and Fyothor and Pfefferkorn departed.

"That was fast," Pfefferkorn said. The idea that they might accomplish his stated goal troubled him, as he had no idea what to do if someone actually offered to sell him a large quantity of fertilizer.

"Akha," Fyothor said. "The man is an ass. He has forgotten us already."

A similar scene played itself out four more times before noon, as they whipped through the Ministry of Fecundity, the Ministry of Objects, the Ministry of Nautical Redistribution, and the Ministry of Resealable Barrels. Everywhere they went, Fyothor was received with kisses, and he was frequently stopped on the street by people wanting to shake his hand. Upon learning that Pfefferkorn was with him, they shook Pfefferkorn's hand as well. Pfefferkorn felt as though he was back in high school and had somehow fallen in with the star quarterback.

"You remind me of someone I used to know," Pfefferkorn said.

"Yes? This person is a friend of yours, I hope?"

"He was."

Lunch was taken standing, at a stall in the market occupying the Square of the Location of the Conclusion of the Parade of the Commemoration of the Remembrance of the Exalted Memory of the Greatness of the Sacrifices of the Magnificent Martyrs of the Glorious Revolution of the Zlabian People of the Twenty-sixth of May. The heat was ferocious, and many of the vendors had rolled up their goods and retreated to the lobby of the nearby Ministry of Flexible Ductwork. The valiant few that had not were flogging a limited assortment of diseased-looking produce. It seemed that "knobby and covered in dirt" was in season. There was no meat save goat offal that had acquired a thick carpet of flies. While Pfefferkorn wanted to disconnect these nauseating sights from his bowl of stew, there was no denying their common pungency.

On the East Zlabian side of the square was another market, this one colorful and festive. An accordion band played covers of American Top 40. There were rides. There was Bop-a-Goat. There was a petting zoo. There was a booth where you could get dressed up as a character from *Vassily Nabochka* and have your picture taken. Above all there was food. Clean booths displayed a rainbow of produce, lacquered pastries, satiny chocolates, fresh fish on ice. Pfefferkorn stared at a sign in Cyrillic for a long time before deciphering it as "funnel cake." It was an awesome display of plenty, making it all the more baffling that the entire scene was devoid of patrons. Indeed, this seemed to be the case as far as he could see into East

Zlabia: aside from the accordion band, the vendors, and roving packs of well-equipped soldiers, the place had the eerie tranquility of a film set. Here, no teeming masses filled the sidewalks. Luxury cars were parked but nobody was driving. There were cafés, teahouses, bistros, boutiques—all deserted. The picture was so bizarre that Pfefferkorn was unconsciously drawn forward.

"Turn away, please?"

Fyothor had spoken with uncharacteristic urgency and without looking up from his own bowl of stew. It was then that Pfefferkorn noticed a ragtag group of West Zlabian soldiers observing them.

"Come," Fyothor said, discarding his half-finished stew. "We will be late."

74.

In fact, they were nowhere near late. Fyothor's line-jumping had given them three hours to kill before their next appointment, so he had decided to add in a few extra stops.

"You are a tourist," he said, kneading Pfefferkorn's shoulders tenderly. "You must *tour*."

At the interactive section of the Museum of Goats,

Pfefferkorn managed to eke out a half cup of milk. He was proud of himself until he saw the bucket-plus produced by a four-year-old girl with huge, callused hands. At the Museum of Peace he read an account of the Cold War exactly the opposite of the one he knew. At the Museum of Concrete he learned about the building of the museum itself. By dinnertime, he was ready for cake.

His room had once again been tossed.

The picture of Zhulk had been straightened.

The fan was still kaput.

"Yes hello, this is Arthur Kowalczyk in room forty-four. Where's my fan?"

"Monsieur, fan is in room."

"The one I have is broken, so either you didn't replace it like I asked or somebody's been buying off the back of the truck."

"Monsieur, I am sorry."

"I don't want apologies. I want a new fan."

The pipes began to bang.

"Hello?" Pfefferkorn said. "Are you there?"

"Yes, monsieur."

"I'm tired of calling down. Please send me a fan. A working one. Right away."

He hung up before the clerk could reply. He moved around the room, restoring it to order, stripping off his clothes as he went. The banging was getting louder. He began to question his original hypothesis. For one thing, he was fairly certain that what made hot water pipes clank was the temperature differential between the water and the pipe. Hot water caused the cold metal to expand, which in turn caused the characteristic ticking. But it was so hot in West Zlabia that he couldn't imagine the differential to be more than a few degrees: not enough to produce sound, and certainly not enough to produce the ear-splitting racket he was hearing. Another reason to doubt the hypothesis was that in his experience, clanking pipes tended to speed up and then taper off. The noise coming through his wall was following a different pattern. It was steady and insistent, more indicative of, say, the feral urgency of a headboard knocking against plaster. It would be just his luck, wouldn't it, to be stuck next to a honeymooning couple.

He waited for the fan to be delivered, and when it wasn't, he called again.

"Immediately, monsieur," the desk clerk said.

The clanking kept on going. Zhulk's photo was jumping all over the place. Pfefferkorn stood on the bed and took it down. Then he pounded angrily on the wall.

"It's late," he said.

The clanking ceased.

At midnight he gave up waiting. He threw back the duvet and lay on the sheet, basking in the silence, aware that five a.m. was just around the bend.

75.

The next morning, following the forecast and public reading, he went straight to the front desk. The clerk from the first day was back on duty. Pfefferkorn made sure to tip him in advance.

"Monsieur will to partake of breakfast buffet."

"In a minute. First things first. I need to change rooms, please."

"Monsieur, there is problem?"

"Several. I've asked for a new fan at least ten times. How hard could that possibly be? Apparently very hard. So I'd like a new room."

"Monsieur—"

"And the couple next door to me is making a tremendous amount of noise. They sound like a pair of over-sexed gorillas."

"Monsieur, I am regretful. This is impossible."

"What is?"

"Rooms cannot be exchanged."

"Why not?"

"Monsieur, there is no availability."

Pfefferkorn looked at the back wall, where they hung the keys. "What are you talking about? I can see for myself there aren't more than ten guests in the whole place."

"Monsieur, reassignment of rooms requires six months' notice."

"You can't be serious."

The clerk bowed.

Pfefferkorn took out a ten-*ruzha* note. It disappeared up the clerk's sleeve but the clerk did not otherwise move. Pfefferkorn gave him another ten *ruzhy*. Still nothing. He gave him ten more and then he threw up his hands and walked across the lobby to the restaurant.

"Friend, good morning. But what is the matter?"

Pfefferkorn explained.

"Akha," Fyothor said, knitting his brows, "yes."

"It's really true that I can't get another room for six months?"

"That would be soon, friend."

"Jesus."

"Have no fear," Fyothor said. "Today we are going to have some real fun."

"I can't wait."

They made the rounds. Meeting after meeting ended identically: with promises of memos, sweltering embraces, and *thruynichka*. Between appointments they took in the sights. There were more museums, more memorials. Virtually every street corner featured a sign commemorating some momentous event of the people's revolution. On the few unclaimed corners, metal plaques had been set into the earth:

THIS SPOT RESERVED FOR
FUTURE HISTORICAL EVENTS.

They stood before a seedy-looking building.

HERE THE PEOPLE'S REVOLUTION FOREVER IMPROVED
THE LOT OF THE ZLABIAN WOMAN

They entered the strip club and sat down. A waitress pecked Fyothor on the cheek and set down a bottle of *thruynichka*. Techno music beat relentlessly.

"You enjoy breasts?" Fyothor shouted.

"As much as the next fellow," Pfefferkorn shouted back.

"I come here every day," Fyothor shouted.

Pfefferkorn nodded.

"It is different from America, yes?" Fyothor shouted.

"I'm not American," Pfefferkorn shouted back.

It was different: both the patrons and the strippers were in equal states of undress.

"This is our collective principle of equality," Fyothor shouted. "Every article of clothing the woman removes, the man must do the same. Fair, yes?" He tucked a five-*ruzha* note inside the G-string of a writhing woman and started unbuttoning his shirt. "To your health."

The highlight of any West Zlabian vacation was a visit to Prince Vassily's grave. Pfefferkorn, expecting grandeur, was surprised by the spot's humility. Tucked in among a busy thoroughfare was a small brick plaza, at the center of which stood a raggedy tree.

HERE LIES IN ETERNAL SLUMBER

THE GREAT HERO

FATHER AND REDEEMER OF THE

GLORIOUS ZLABIAN PEOPLE

PRINCE VASSILY

"HOW LIKE A ROOT VEGETABLE SWELLS MY HEART

TO GAZE UPON THY COUNTENANCE

HOW LIKE AN ORPHANED KID GOAT DOES IT BLEAT

FOR THY LOSS"

(canto cxx)

Fyothor bowed his head. Pfefferkorn did likewise.

"Next month we celebrate the fifteen-hundredth anniversary of the poem. The festivities will be unforgettable." Fyothor smiled slyly. "Perhaps you will extend your stay, yes?"

"One day at a time," Pfefferkorn said.

En route to the Ministry of Double Taxation they passed a throng of people waiting to enter a dilapidated wooden shack.

"The home of our dearly departed leader," Fyothor said.

Pfefferkorn tried to appear appropriately respectful.

"Come," Fyothor said, and began bushwhacking to the front of the line.

The interior of the hut was easily twenty degrees hotter than it was outside. The furniture had been cordoned off and easels set up with photographs of Dragomir Zhulk orating, scowling, saluting. People used clunky

Soviet-era twin-lens reflex cameras to photograph the desk, still set with Zhulk's fountain pen, datebook, and a dented tin mug with an inch of tea left at the bottom. A spotlit glass case housed his well-used copy of *Vassily Nabochka*. Soldiers lined the perimeter of the room, using their Kalashnikovs to jab at the visitors and hasten their circuit around the rope protecting the room's centerpiece: a burlap-lined coffin, inside which Zhulk's embalmed body lay in state. Pfefferkorn blinked the sweat out of his eyes and stared. He felt himself going tingly and light-headed. Here was a man he had killed.

A soldier shoved him with the butt of his gun and told him to move along.

Out in the street, Fyothor was adamant. "Enough death for one day," he said.

They skipped their meeting and went back to the strip club.

The schedule repeated itself for several days running. Following a restless night spent sweating into his sheets, banging the wall, and plugging his ears with toilet tissue, Pfefferkorn would be shouted awake at dawn. The woman in the majorette hat would declare that the weather would be pleasant beyond compare, that the price of root vegetables had reached an all-time low, that miraculous advances had been made by the Ministry of Science, that the East Zlabian aggressors had been repelled and were cowering in fear. It was unclear to Pfefferkorn whom these lies were intended to fool. Still, he began to enjoy the pageantry of it. He read along from *Vassily Nabochka*. He sang the anthem lustily while he shaved around his moustache. He had just about forgotten it was fake.

Having established himself as a friend of Fyothor's, Yelena took more of a shine to him. She never gave him more than his ration, but she did it with a hockey linesman's gappy smile.

He spent close to every waking moment with Fyothor. It was clear enough to Pfefferkorn that he was being watched, but as he didn't see what he could do about it, he tried to spin it for the best.

"You know all these people and you can't get me a new hotel room?"

"Some things are beyond even my power, friend."

In the evenings they would dine together in the restaurant, talking about literature and polishing off several bottles of *thruynichka*. Then Fyothor would head home to his wife and Pfefferkorn would stop by the front desk to check for messages. The clerk would say there were no messages. Pfefferkorn would ask for a new fan. The clerk would promise it immediately.

Up the ancient elevator Pfefferkorn went, down the whispering hallway, past mumbling rooms, rooms full of ghosts, rooms more men had entered than left.

Stretched out on his bed, listening to the honeymooners getting to work, he reflected on the similarities between spying and writing. Both called for stepping into an imagined world and residing there with conviction, nearly to the point of self-delusion. Both were jobs that outsiders thought of as exotic but that were in practice quite tedious. Both tested one's ability to withstand loneliness, although Pfefferkorn decided that in this respect, spying was harder, because it demanded that the spy resist, at every moment and with all his power, the human instinct to trust. One of life's minor consolations was the presumption that you could ask most strangers most questions and get an honest answer most of the time. Not always, of course, but often enough. Absent that, conversation became an exhausting, depressing labor, more so in the face of the sort of unflagging cheer Fyothor threw at him. Pfefferkorn felt like he was being forced to stand on one foot for hours on end. He thought of all the faceless men and women doing their duties in hotel rooms the world over. He admired them. He felt for them. He wished them well. Their loneliness was his, and his theirs.

And he thought of Bill. In reevaluating their relationship Pfefferkorn had seen himself as the survivor of a house fire, returning to pick through the ash. There might be one or two scraps of authentic friendship, but they were buried under so much falsehood that it seemed wiser and less pathetic to let them go. But perhaps Paul had been right when he said that it didn't have to be one or the other. Now that Pfefferkorn was a spy, he understood. He remembered Bill's copy of his novel, the dense scribblings in the margins. What else could that be but love? He was almost afraid to accept this, because if Bill truly had loved him, the pain he must have endured in deceiving Pfefferkorn all these years was unimaginable. Heroic, even.

The clanking got louder.

Pfefferkorn turned on the television and put the volume way up.

There were three channels. Channel one was the flag. Channel two aired round-the-clock footage of Party rallies and speeches. For entertainment, it was hard to beat channel three. Pfefferkorn watched a soap opera about goatherds. He watched the news, anchored by the woman in the majorette hat. Like the rest of West Zlabia, he was waiting for the game show that came on at nine. The national curriculum included poetic composition, and teachers nominated their best students to appear before a panel of celebrity judges, who would then proceed to tear the poem apart mercilessly, reducing the student to tears and bringing burning shame upon him, his family, and their entire neighborhood. To be humiliated in this way was considered a great honor, and *The Poem, It Is Bad!* was the second most popular show on West Zlabian TV, its ratings topped only by those of the show that followed, a live broadcast of the teacher being flogged.

76.

"Rise, citizens of Zlabia. . . ."

Pfefferkorn opened the dresser. The day's itinerary included a visit to a goat farm on the outskirts of town, which seemed as good an occasion as any to use his one polo shirt. Still coursing with sweat, he unwrapped his towel and pressed it to his face. When he took the towel away from his face he saw that his moustache had come off in his hands.

There was no cause for panic. He had been in West Zlabia for a week, and the epoxy was supposed to last ten to twelve days. Constant perspiration had likely hastened its dissolution. He picked the old moustache out of the folds of his towel and flushed it down the toilet. He put his wheelie bag on the bed, pried up the first false bottom, removed one of the moustache kits, tore it open, and dumped its contents across the bedspread. Swatches of fake hair in a wild multitude of sizes, shapes, colors, and textures spilled out. It looked like a caterpillar pride parade. He selected two pinkie-length pieces in a medium brown and carried them into the bathroom along with the thimble-sized tube of adhesive and the instruction sheet.

Superficial identity alteration package (male)

1. Choose the part which is sorted appropriately of the hairpiece at size.
2. In order to meet to the most desirable size, carve the hairpiece
3. Solicit moisture with the surface area of the face where the hairpiece will have in application.
4. Using the cotton stick, solicit Mult-E-Bond™ in verso of the hairpiece to receive the influence which ties on with moisture.
5 Solicit the hairpiece, maintain for thrity second..
6. You look so good!

He didn't remember the process being quite so esoteric. Then again, Blueblood had been there to help. Flummoxed, he turned the page over.

MADE IN INDONESIA

There was a knock at the front door.

"Good morning, friend!"

What was Fyothor doing here? Breakfast didn't start for another half hour. Pfefferkorn poked his head out. "Just a minute," he called.

He ducked back into the bathroom. He uncapped the tube of adhesive, squeezed a dollop onto his fingertip, and put his finger to his lip, instantly fusing the two surfaces together.

77.

It was ugly. His left middle finger was stuck to his upper lip midway between the left corner of his mouth and his philtrum. The angle of contact was particularly grievous. Had the finger been pressed down at twelve o'clock, he might have been able to pass off the pose as one of contemplation. As it was, the finger was between nine and ten o'clock, making it look like he was about to excavate a booger. He dashed to the bed and combed through the pieces of facial hair.

Next door the banging started up, steady as a metronome.

"Really?" he yelled. "Now?"

"What?" Fyothor called.

"Nothing."

He found what he was looking for: the enclosed Q-tip, or what the instructions called a "cotton stick." In his haste, he had forgotten all about it. Knowing where he had gone wrong didn't get him any closer to fixing the problem, though. At present he was holding his own face, and Fyothor was tapping at the door, and the lovebirds were going at it like a pumpjack.

"I apologize for the rude awakening," Fyothor called, "but today we must stick to the schedule."

"I'll be right there." Pfefferkorn raced back to the bathroom, threw on the hot water, and stuck his head under the tap, without effect. Despairingly he stood up, wet all over again. There was a way to dissolve the epoxy, he knew. Blueblood had told him. The banging was driving him crazy and making it hard to concentrate.

"I recommend closed-toe shoes," Fyothor called.

"Right-o," Pfefferkorn called.

He remembered: a solution of salt water, twenty-two percent by weight. Simple enough, except that he had yet to see a saltshaker (or any normal condiment, for that matter) anywhere in West Zlabia. A bit of ketchup would do wonders for root vegetable hash, he thought. Then he told himself to focus. He needed salt water. He could cry.

He dug deep for the saddest memories he had. He thought of his father. He thought of all his failures. It was no use. Shortly after his life had taken a turn for the better, he had worked to put his misery behind him. Instead he imagined awful things that might yet happen. He pictured Carlotta in her cell. He pictured himself getting treated for cancer. With distaste, he pictured his daughter . . . but his brain refused to go there, and his eyes remained dry as toast.

"The driver is waiting. We can still beat the traffic."

"On my way."

He tugged at his lip again. He was stuck fast, his options dwindling. What distinguished men like Harry Shagreen and Dick Stapp, he thought, was their monomania. They did whatever it took—anything at all—for failure was not an option. He gripped his left wrist with his right hand, took a deep breath, and yanked as hard as he could, spinning himself around and landing in the shower with a crash.

"Friend? Is everything all right?"

"Fine," Pfefferkorn said weakly. He had been somewhat successful. His finger did feel looser. He climbed out of the shower, took hold of his hand, and braced himself for another go.

In retrospect he would not be able to decide which was worse: the pain or the wet, ripping sound. It took all his willpower not to scream. He bent over, silently heaving, his eyes finally (and pointlessly) blurring, blood dripping from his lip onto the tiles. He wasn't finished, either. The very tip of his finger was still attached. With a grunt he pulled it free. He wadded toilet tissue against his bleeding face.

"The early goat gets the peels," Fyothor called.

Pfefferkorn used the Q-tip to apply a fresh coat of adhesive. It stung going on, and he realized he had smeared an assuredly toxic substance directly into his bloodstream. The epoxy worked like a chemical cauterization, coagulating the blood on contact. With trembling hands, he pressed the two matching pieces of moustache to his lip. He held them in place for a ten count, then tested each side with a gentle tug. The right side was fine. The left side yodeled with pain, but it, too, remained secure.

He ran to the bed, swept the spilled moustaches into the wheelie bag, replaced the first false panel, zipped the bag up, and threw on his clothes. By now Fyothor was pounding loud enough to compete with the pipes.

"Must I break down the door?"

"Ha ha ha ha ha."

Pfefferkorn ran back to the bathroom for one final mirror check and recoiled.

He had glued his moustache on upside down. Instead of following the downward curve of his upper lip, it shot upward, like a set of surprised eyebrows. Seeing this did in fact surprise him, and when his actual eyebrows went up, he seemed to have two sets of surprised eyebrows, one above his eyes and the other above his lip. "I didn't expect this," the top of his face seemed to be saying. "Me neither," the bottom half seemed to be agreeing, "*any* of it." He tried to bring his moustache back into alignment by frowning, hard. It worked, sort of. Assuming he could keep it up all day long, Fyothor might not notice anything amiss.

"I am counting to three. One."

Still frowning, Pfefferkorn ran from the bathroom.

"Two—"

Frowning, he threw open the door. Fyothor was waiting, smiling, his big hand raised with two fingers up. Pfefferkorn then saw himself in his mind's eye, frowning and staring back fearfully. It wasn't very convincing. As if to confirm this, Fyothor's smile faltered—the tiniest flicker imaginable, but more than enough for Pfefferkorn to know that the jig was up. His cover was blown. He was a dead man. With any luck he could get to his weapons. He was reasonably adept with the toothbrush knife. The deodorant stun gun was neater but more cumbersome, as it entailed the added step of removing the cap. He wasn't sure it would work on a man of Fyothor's girth, either. He decided to go with the knife, cleanup be damned. As he had been trained to do, he visualized himself diving to the floor, rolling to the closet, grabbing the bag, opening the zipper, flinging aside the first false panel, flinging aside the second false panel, flinging aside the third false panel, seizing the toothbrush, flicking open the blade, driving it home. It was a lot to contend with. Still frowning, he started to move backward. Fyothor smiled wider and took him firmly by the arm.

"We will be late," he said, drawing him toward the elevator.

78.

Frowning for hours at a stretch was more physically taxing than Pfefferkorn would have guessed. As they squelched through the goat stalls, ankle-deep in muck, his face pulsed hotly with exertion. He was distracted, too, by something that had escaped earlier notice: the pad of his left index finger was totally smooth, having gained a thin new layer of skin, grafted there from his upper lip. In theory he could commit a crime without leaving prints, provided he just used that one finger. Fleetingly he wondered if this might make an interesting premise, not for a novel, perhaps, but for a screenplay. Then he refocused on frowning.

At the end of the tour, he received a parting gift, three vials of nutrient-rich animal waste.

He and Fyothor stood under a tree by the side of the road, waiting for the driver to return and take them back to town. On another day, Pfefferkorn might have found the smell of hay and the clang of neck bells relaxing. Still frowning, he remarked upon the resemblance between the farm's interim ancillary director of droppings and the tertiary auditor-adjutant of the Ministry of Gas-Emitting Semisolids, with whom they had met the previous day.

"Cousins," Fyothor said.

Pfefferkorn raised his eyebrows—his real ones—at this frank admission of nepotism.

"We are all related. Geography is destiny, yes?" Fyothor gestured to the steep hills that bounded the Zlabian valley, cupping its inhabitants in uncomfortably close proximity. "In this light, our tragic history appears even more tragic. We harm no one but ourselves."

Pfefferkorn, still frowning, nodded.

"As I said, it is a rare honor to meet someone new." Fyothor patted Pfefferkorn's shoulder and left his hand there, as though Pfefferkorn were a wayward child. Pfefferkorn's heart hiccuped. Before he could think of something to say, the troika appeared in a slowly churning cloud of dust. It came to a halt and they climbed aboard. Fyothor murmured to the driver and handed him some notes. The driver nodded. Rather than execute a three-point turn to take them back toward the city center, he cracked his whip and the troika began to inch forward.

Pfefferkorn's frown was now genuine. "Where are we going?"

"It is a lovely day, yes?" Fyothor said. "Let us enjoy it."

They rumbled alongside fields amok with clover. Sunlight enameled the languishing carcasses of Soviet tractors. Soon the space between farmhouses lengthened, as pitted asphalt turned to dried, rutted mud, and the whirr of insects rose high enough that Fyothor had to bellow to be heard. Pfefferkorn wasn't listening. The thought of being outnumbered and outweighed, with only his fists and feet for weapons, had him in such a state that for a moment he neglected to frown. He felt the ends of his moustache turning skyward and brought them back down.

They came to a fork in the road. A corroded sign indicated three kilometers to the ruined nuclear reactor. The driver took the other, unmarked road. Pfefferkorn stirred.

"It is not far," Fyothor said.

Up ahead, a line of trees demarcated the northern edge of the Lykhabvo Forest, off-limits to tourists and locals alike as part of the exclusion zone. Fyothor had the driver pull over. He handed him a few more notes and told him to wait.

"Come," Fyothor said, putting his arm around Pfefferkorn's waist and marching him into the woods.

79.

The effects of high-dose radiation were evident all around them. Oaks and maples bore asymmetrical leaves the size of guitars. Psychedelic ferns genuflected in the breeze. Nine-toed squirrels with patchy fur scampered

over boulders blackened by lichen. Beneath the smells
Pfefferkorn associated with a normal forest (sweet decay-
ing vegetation, savory sunlit rock) lay an unnatural,
chemical base note. He could get cancer just by being
here. But that concern was overridden by a more pressing
one. He and Fyothor were alone.

"Pretty, yes?"

Pfefferkorn, frowning, did not reply. He was trying to
figure out why Fyothor had left the troika driver behind.
If two men went into the forest and only one emerged,
that demanded an explanation—unless it was the expected
outcome. So the driver had to be in on it. But then why
trade four arms for two? The answer must be that Fyothor didn't consider Pfefferkorn dangerous. This had to
be counted as an advantage, albeit a slight one that might
not hold much longer. The sooner he acted, the better.
He spied a half-buried stone with a sharp edge. He visualized himself diving to the ground, rolling toward the
stone, prying it up, and using it—all before Fyothor had
a chance to react. Too many potential snafus, he decided.
He didn't know how big the hidden part of the rock was.
It might not come up easily or at all. He passed. They
walked on, following a widening creek. Fyothor, his hand
around Pfefferkorn's waist, was talking about the hard-
ships he had endured growing up, a large family and a
tiny hut. There was no word for privacy in Zlabian, did
Pfefferkorn know that? Pfefferkorn, still frowning,
scanned the forest floor. It was spongy with mutant foliage, pine needles as long as pool cues curling in piles.
There were countless broken branches, any one of which
would have made a decent club had he stopped to pick it

up. He waited for his training to kick in. Yet his body was rubbery and accepting as Fyothor urged him on. Muscle memory, Pfefferkorn shouted to himself. Solar plexus! Pressure points! It was awful, being jostled along toward death like a rag doll.

The creek fed a murky pond. At long last Fyothor released him and walked to the water's edge, standing with his back turned, looking out. Now or never, Pfefferkorn thought. He crouched noiselessly and pulled a stone from the mud. It made a sucking sound but Fyothor did not notice. He was talking about coming to this spot as a boy, pouring out his troubles to the fish and the trees. He had not visited in years but he felt happy to be here now with Pfefferkorn, his friend. Sockdolager had said that the right place to inflict blunt-force trauma was at the temple, with its abundance of blood vessels and nerves. The important thing was to commit. A pulled punch was worse than no punch. Pfefferkorn rolled the stone in his hand. All the moisture in his mouth seemed to have been redirected to his palms. He was thinking of his one experience inflicting violence on another living being. His old apartment had mice. Usually they were clever enough to skirt the glue traps he put out, but one evening while reading he heard a series of frenzied squeaks. He went to the kitchen and found a mouse stuck by its hind legs. It was trying to pull itself across the linoleum by its front paws. He had given up on ever catching any mice and so had no plan for what to do if he did. He'd heard of people drowning them in a bucket of water. To him that sounded sadistic. He gave it some thought, then picked up the trap by the other end and

put it in a shopping bag. He tied the bag shut and took it
down to the street. The bag twitched and squeaked. He
untied the handles and looked inside. The mouse was
going berserk, like it knew what was coming. Pfefferkorn
thought of removing it and setting it free but he was
afraid of ripping its legs off. So he just looked at it for a
long minute as it shrieked and clawed at the plastic. At
times like that he wished he had become an electrician or
a bus driver. Real men did not stand around, staring
dumbly into a shopping bag. They knew what to do. But
did the job make the man or vice versa? He retied the
bag, lifted it high in the air, and smashed it against the
curb. There was a crunching sound but he could still feel
the mouse squirming. He smashed the bag again. The
squirming stopped. He gave the bag one more whack
and dropped it in the sidewalk bin before running
upstairs to take a shower. Then as now his whole body
shook. He broke the problem down into steps. He visualized. The problem with visualization was that, done well,
it made the task ahead more concrete and divisible but
also intensely tangible and gruesome. He was feeling the
stinging reverberation in his palm as the rock made contact with Fyothor's skull. He was seeing the bloom of
blood and hearing a sound like a fistful of potato chips
being crushed. He swallowed back acid and tightened his
grip. He supposed he had killed plenty of spiders in his
day, too, but they didn't count. He stepped forward.
Fyothor turned and saw what was happening and smiled
knowingly and said "Ah yes" and with breathtaking
speed his hand darted out and snatched the stone away.
Pfefferkorn wheeled backward and dove to the ground,

rolling with his arms clamped around his head for protection. He ended up crouched behind a log, poised and ready for action. But Fyothor was not charging him or taking out a gun. He was staring at him in unadulterated confusion. Pfefferkorn stared back. There was a silence as they stared at each other. Fyothor shrugged and wound up and sent the stone skimming across the pond. It bounced three times before sailing into the bushes on the far bank. He picked up another stone and offered it to Pfefferkorn. "Your turn."

Pfefferkorn did not move.

Fyothor shrugged again and skimmed the second stone. *"Akha,"* he said. "Very poor. When I was young . . . *pip, pip, pip,* seven times or more." He extended his arm along the imaginary trajectory. Then he addressed Pfefferkorn with a look of concern. "How is your lip?"

The back of Pfefferkorn's neck prickled.

"To continue making that face for so long must be tiring. Certainly, there is no need to perform on my account." Fyothor smiled faintly. "I can see the glue where it pushes out."

Pfefferkorn said nothing.

"There have been others like you, before. None of them have survived."

There were no other rocks within easy reach.

"You have secrets. I understand. Who among us does not? Who among us does not suffer because of them?"

There were no broken branches, either.

"You may speak freely. There are no listening devices here, I can assure you." Fyothor paused expectantly. "Very well. This is something I understand, to be afraid to speak. We Zlabians understand it too well. But you must believe me, friend: the burden does not get lighter with time. It gets heavier. I know, because I am fifty-five years old and my own burdens are so heavy that often I feel I cannot go on. I think, sometimes, that I would like to sit down forever, to let the dust and the cobwebs cover me over. I might become a little mountain. I would like this very much. Mountains feel nothing, yes? Because I know that change will not come for me. I know this. Perhaps, though, if I become a mountain, others will climb upon me and stand upon my shoulders, and from there they will look into the future."

There was a silence.

"No listening devices," Pfefferkorn said.

"None."

"How can you be sure?"

"I am sure."

There was a silence.

"A tour guide," Pfefferkorn said.

"In my spare time."

"And in the rest of your time."

Fyothor bowed. "I am but a humble servant of the Party."

"Serving in what capacity."

"Executive director for electronic monitoring," Fyothor said. He bowed again. "Ministry of Surveillance."

There was a silence.

"I see why you're so popular," Pfefferkorn said.

"I have thousands of friends," Fyothor said. "Not one of them likes me."

He looked out at the water.

"I know how it feels to live with your tongue pressing at the back of your teeth. I believe, friend, that my form of service to the state was not an accident but the work of a God with a sense of humor. Yes? The man with secrets, he lives by destroying others through their secrets. This is a constant punishment for me." He looked at Pfefferkorn. "Please speak."

"And say what."

But Fyothor did not answer. He turned away again.

"It would be easy for me to turn you in," he said. "I could have done it at any time."

Pfefferkorn said nothing.

"Do you believe I would do such a thing?"

There was a silence.

"I don't know," Pfefferkorn said.

Fyothor bowed his head. "You cannot know how sorry I am to hear that."

There was a silence.

"What do you want from me?" Pfefferkorn asked.

"Give me hope," Fyothor said.

There was a silence.

"How," Pfefferkorn said.

"Tell me it would be better for me elsewhere."

Pfefferkorn said nothing.

"Tell me about America," Fyothor said.

There was a long silence.

"I wouldn't know anything about that," Pfefferkorn said.

Fyothor's shoulders sagged. He went ashen. It was as if his soul had been siphoned off.

"Of course not," he said. "My apologies."

Silence.

The cell phone squawked. Pfefferkorn flinched but Fyothor did not move. The phone rang six times and stopped. Then it started up again. Wearily Fyothor reached into his pocket.

"*Tha*. Okay. Okay. *Tha*." He closed the phone. "I regret that my wife requires my presence at home." His voice had taken on a new quality, a listless formality. "My apologies."

He bowed and turned and walked back into the forest.

A moment later Pfefferkorn followed, trailing at a slight distance.

They remained silent throughout the long, bumpy ride back to town, and when they got stuck in traffic, three blocks from the hotel, Fyothor instructed the driver to take Pfefferkorn the rest of the way and started to slide out of the seat.

"What about you," Pfefferkorn said.

Fyothor shrugged. "I can walk."

"Oh," Pfefferkorn said. "Well, then, I guess I'll see you tomorrow."

"Tomorrow, I am sorry, I have appointments I must keep."

It was such an obvious lie that Pfefferkorn saw no point in arguing.

"All right," he said. "Another time, then."

"Yes, another time."

"Thank you," Pfefferkorn said. "Thank you very much."

Fyothor did not reply. He lowered himself to the sidewalk and walked off without a backward glance, weaving through the crowds and soon becoming lost to sight.

80.

The restaurant was quiet, unoccupied except for one drunk colonel and Yelena. She did a double take as Pfefferkorn approached the buffet, his plate out for the last remaining pierogi. Aware of her staring at his moustache, he frowned decisively, took his sorry dinner, and dragged himself to the corner booth. He sat down in a daze and began breaking the pierogi into tiny pieces to make it last longer. In a world where nobody could be trusted, he had done the right thing. He had followed his orders. Believe no one. Deny everything. In a world where nobody could be trusted, certain events followed logically. He had rejected the overtures of a powerful man, who would now feel vulnerable for having made those overtures, and furious at having had them rejected. In a world where nobody could be trusted, payback would be forthcoming. Pfefferkorn knew he ought to be afraid. He ought to be in his room right now, throwing all his things in a bag and formulating plan B. In a world where nobody could be trusted, a van was being started up somewhere across town. In a world where nobody could be trusted, that van would pull out of an underground parking garage and head for the Metropole. Its occupants would be heavies in leather jackets. They would file out of the van and into the hotel lobby. They would enter the restaurant and grab Pfefferkorn in full view of everyone and drag him out to the van and toss him in back and hog-tie him and imprison him in a dank basement and strap him down and visit upon him unspeakable bodily desecrations. In a world where nobody could be trusted, the only reasonable choice was to run. In a world where nobody could be trusted, the clock was ticking, the sand was falling, the die had been irretrievably cast.

Who in the world wanted to live in a world where nobody could be trusted?

In place of fear he felt a profound sense of loss. A stranger had come to him, desperate for hope, and he had looked away, because those were his orders. A world where nobody could be trusted was a miserable world. He felt the loneliness of the spy, and he felt anger. He had done what needed doing and he hated himself for it. The squalidness of the room, previously obscured by Fyothor's vitality, seethed forth. The walls crawled with vermin. The carpet festered with more. The table was sticky and gouged. It was not the same table it had been for the last week. Before it had been *their* table. Now it was *his*, and it disgusted him. He pushed the pierogi away. He hated his handlers. He hated everything about this mission. If he had any sense at all that he was getting closer to Carlotta, he might have consoled himself. But nothing was happening. It was like he was the lead role in some insipid student-written play. He felt his humanity leaching out into the stuffy night air. He swirled his teacup and stared dejectedly into the vortex. His mouth hurt from frowning all day. He had been doing his best to obey Paul's instructions. He had been focused, he had not let emotions cloud his judgment, he had kept his eyes on the prize. Now he gave himself over to wallowing. He let melancholy and frustration wash over him. He missed Carlotta. He missed his daughter. He didn't care what his country needed. He just wanted to go home.

Across the restaurant, the colonel's head hit the table with a thunk, interrupting Pfefferkorn's gloomy reverie. Loud snoring commenced. The kitchen doors swung wide and Yelena emerged holding a doggie bag, its neck rolled tightly and stapled shut.

"Hungry," she said in English, holding the bag out.

Apparently Fyothor's lecture on providing for the needy had taken root. Pfefferkorn was touched. Though he had no appetite, for politeness's sake, he thanked her and moved to accept.

She moved the bag out of reach. "Hungry," she said again.

The colonel snorted and shifted. Yelena glanced at him, then at Pfefferkorn, her eyes imploring.

Hungry.

A gear clicked.

Pfefferkorn remembered.

"I am satisfied, thank you," he said. He spoke automatically, his voice rising. "But perhaps I will take this for later."

"Later," Yelena said. She left the doggie bag on his table and went about tidying up.

He tucked the bag under his arm and made his way carefully across the lobby. The desk clerk saw him and called out, "No messages, monsieur."

But Pfefferkorn already knew this. He skipped the elevator, taking the stairs two at a time.

81.

He locked himself in the bathroom and put the doggie bag on the counter, wiggling his fingers in anticipation. He pried open the staple and unrolled the bag. Inside was a foam box. He took it out and opened the lid. Inside was a napkin tied like a hobo's bundle. Delicately he undid the knot and pulled back the edges, ready for an electronic key or a microchip. That was what he expected, anyway, and he blinked in disbelief at a pale wad of doughy pastry. No, he thought. No, no. He'd practiced the exchange with the training staff until it was hardwired in his brain. *Hungry. I am satisfied, thank you, but perhaps I will take this for later. Later.* That was the code, word for word. This had to be it. Why else would Yelena refuse to hand over the bag until he reciprocated? Why had she picked tonight, of all nights, unless it was because Fyothor's absence permitted her to act unobserved? But then where was his microchip? He prodded the dumpling. He'd been fed one like it at the safe house. To him it had tasted just as bland as any other example of Zlabian cuisine, but Paul said it was considered a delicacy. *Pya-*something. *Pyatshellalikhuiy.* "Little parcel."

At once the answer hit him and he felt incredibly thick. He broke the dumpling open and began to pick through its contents. He was looking for a microchip. He was looking for an ear transmitter. He found neither. He found bits of diced root vegetable and gray flecks of herb suspended in a starchy goo. He flattened the exterior dough and held the pieces up, hoping beyond hope for instructions written on their insides. But he found nothing. It was a dumpling and nothing more. Disappointed, he moved to throw it away, pausing as his stomach let out a growl. He'd eaten nothing today and a week in West Zlabia had taught him never to turn down food. He stuffed a piece of the dumpling in his mouth and carried the rest to bed, switching on the television in time to catch the theme song to *The Poem, It Is Bad!*

It was an interesting episode. The student poet had reinterpreted the one hundred tenth canto of *Vassily Nabochka*, popularly known as the "Love Song of the Prince," in which the protagonist reflects on what he has forsaken in order to undertake his quest: the love of a beautiful maiden—a moment pregnant with irony, as the reader has been privy to scenes showing the maiden to be a nasty piece of work, poisoning the king and plotting to do the same to the prince upon his return. Pfefferkorn groped on the nightstand for the room copy so he could follow along for comparison. He opened to the back of the book and Fyothor's business card fell out onto his chest. He picked it up and stared at it regretfully. The name, the number. Private tour guide. After a moment he took it to the bathroom and tore it into dozens of tiny pieces and flushed them down the toilet. He watched them spin and disappear. He got back into bed.

The student poet had taken liberties with rhyme and meter, but his boldest stroke was spicing the prince's tone with cynicism. While this choice diminished the dramatic irony somewhat, it gave nuance to a character who often came across as a Goody Two-shoes. Pfefferkorn approved. A little edge went a long way. A character didn't have to go around like Dick Stapp or Harry Shagreen, pulverizing fingers and snapping vertebrae at the slightest provocation, to be interesting. He put the last piece of *pyatshellalikhuiy* in his mouth and wiped his palms on the bedspread. How anything so dense and gluey could be a delicacy escaped him. He yawned. It was only twenty after nine but he felt sleepy. The panel of judges was going ballistic. They seemed to feel that the national poem made a bad platform for experimentation, and they laid on a critique so vicious that the camera zoomed in to show a spreading stain near the student's crotch. Pfefferkorn disapproved. Never had he let a workshop get so out of hand. The closing theme played. Another yawn came on, a huge one that sucked all the air from the room. He got up to use the bathroom but his feet missed the floor somehow and he ended up flat on his face on the carpet. He waited for himself to stand up. New theme music played. Stand up, he told himself. His body wouldn't listen. His arms said to leave them alone. So did his legs. It was as if he had four surly teenagers for limbs. He knew how to deal with that. He had raised a daughter. He pretended not to care. It was going fine until he noticed the room dimming. On-screen a teacher was being flogged. He saw her at the end of a narrow, shrinking tunnel. Her screams came tumbling toward him across an abyss. It was thankless work, teaching.

Moments before he blacked out, he remembered why *pyatshellalikhuiy* were so treasured. The recipe called for wheat flour, a rarity in West Zlabia. Practically the only way to get some was to smuggle it across the border from the east, a crime that carried the death penalty. As he heard the fading sound of a key in the door, he was thinking that it wasn't worth the risk.

82.

He awoke in darkness. His hands and feet were bound. His mouth was full of cloth. His groin was clammy. He felt forward momentum in his bowels and rattling in his joints. He heard the modulating pitch of a shifting trans- mission. The heat was suffocating and the air suffused with mildew. He could state with confidence that he was tied up in the trunk of a car. Hysteria clutched at him. His throat started to close up. He bucked and thrashed around and ended up banging his head hard enough to subdue himself. He commanded himself to be rational. What would Dick Stapp do? He would lie still and con- serve energy. What about Harry Shagreen? He would count turns. Pfefferkorn lay still, conserving his energy and counting turns. He determined that his right shoul- der was up against the rear of the trunk. Hence pressure on top of his head meant a right turn. Pressure on the soles of his shoes meant left. He soon became attuned to changes in the elevation: the rightward jolt that indicated uphill, the gentler leftward yaw for down. They drove for what seemed like hours, making what seemed like a thousand turns. The car had rotten suspension. It hit a pothole and he was tossed against the roof of the trunk, landing painfully and losing count. The third time it happened he gave up counting and gave in to despair. All the turns in the world would tell him nothing if he didn't know the starting point and what direction they had set out in. Nor did he have any idea how long he'd been passed out. He knew nothing, nothing at all, and to be confronted by his ignorance sparked a new fit of rage. He thrashed and bucked and rolled and kicked and screamed and gnawed at his gag, rivers of spit running down his neck.

The car slowed.

It stopped.

Doors opened.

Humid night air kissed him.

He put up no fight as they removed the blindfold. The orange glow of a highway sodium vapor lamp haloed four faces. A fifth face appeared, close enough to eclipse the light. The fifth face had two crinkly eye sockets, two thin bloodless lips, a bulbous pate like an overfilled balloon. It smiled, showing unnaturally even teeth. Pfefferkorn could tell they were dentures.

"Oh, for God's sake," he said, or tried to say. He was still gagged.

"Hush," Lucian Savory said.

He shut the trunk.

FIVE
дхиуобхриуо пжулобхатъ бху
вхожтъиуочнуиуи жлабхвуи!

(WELCOME TO
EAST ZLABIA!)

83.

"You look good," Savory said. "Have you lost weight?"

Pfefferkorn couldn't answer. He was still gagged. The henchmen—he'd never before had occasion to use the word, and despite his abject state he could appreciate its aptness, for the four apes dragging him across the parking garage and into the elevator carried an unmistakable air of henchiness about them—smirked.

"The hell happened to your face, anyway? You look like Salvador Dalí with a cattle prod up his ass."

The elevator doors closed and they began to rise.

Savory sniffed. He frowned. "Christ," he said. "You pissed your pants, didn't you."

Pfefferkorn grunted.

"Give him yours," Savory said.

One of the henchmen unhesitatingly removed his fatigue pants. The other three stripped Pfefferkorn from the waist down. Two of them lifted him like an infant while the third slid the dry fatigues on. The donor remained standing in his underwear.

"Don't get too comfortable," Savory said. It was unclear whom he was addressing.

The car went up, up, up.

"Here's some advice, free of charge," Savory said. "Try not to look so damned sullen. He hates that."

Pfefferkorn was unaware of looking sullen. He wanted to grunt "Who's 'he'?" but the elevator dinged and the doors opened onto the grandest living room he had ever seen—it made the de Vallées' house look like a Motel 6—and he knew the answer.

The henchmen carried him through an ornate wooden door and into a maze of corridors lined by armed guards.

"Don't slouch," Savory said. "Posture's a big deal to him. Don't fidget or stare. Speak only when spoken to. And if he offers you a drink, take it."

The final door was made of steel. Savory swiped a keycard and pressed a code. A moment later there was a click, and Pfefferkorn was brought inside.

84.

None of the photographs Pfefferkorn had seen did justice to Lord High President Kliment Thithyich in the flesh. A photo failed to convey the way his hands made toys of everyday objects. It failed to capture the voice that came at Pfefferkorn like a gale wind. It did not account for his fondness for air quotes.

"The real problem with Communism has nothing to do with 'civil rights,' or the gulag, or breadlines. It's got nothing to do with 'history' or 'destiny' or anything like that. It's got nothing to do with Stalin, and it's certainly got nothing to do with Dragomir Zhulk, who, politics aside, I thought quite highly of. We are 'family,' after all, not close but eleventh cousins or something like that. Spend enough time jousting with a bloke of his capabilities, and you're bound to develop a measure of respect, if not for the content of his thoughts then for the way they're phrased. Understand: I'm not saying I approve. The man was a bona fide 'head case,' and the methods they use over there are just too too much. You've never had to experience scrotal electroshock, but let me tell you, from what I've heard, it's the very 'definition' of unlovely. So, yes, a raving sociopath he may have been, but there's no denying he was good with the old rhetoric, and I admired him for it. Nor am I ashamed to admit that I've learned a few things about rallying the 'people' and whatnot from watching him work. So it's not a 'vendetta' or anything like that. People have this image of me as 'ruthless,' 'sadistic,' 'incapable of forgiving the tiniest slight,' what have you. I'm not in a position to say whether there's any merit to that. What I can tell you with perfect honesty is that my pet peeves have nothing to do with my reasoned opinion on the matter. I'm a rather 'left-brained' sort of fellow, you see, and I've given this a lot of thought. You might call it my 'life's work.' In that sense, I suppose it is personal, insofar as I was born poor—and I'm not using that term the way Americans do, saying 'poor' when what you really mean is 'not rich.' You lot have no concept of what it is to go without the basics. Take an uneducated black from the Deep South in 1955 and drop him down with just the change in his pocket in the middle of the Gyeznyuiy and he's going to be bathing in goat's milk and wiping himself with silk. Here, being poor *means* something. My father toiled nineteen and a half hours a day in the fields. My mother's hands were perpetually bloody from scrubbing dishes and poking herself with knitting needles. She did that habitually, stab herself. Not just knitting needles, anything within reach: diaper pins, rusty bolts, sharpened root vegetables. I never quite got what she was trying to 'tell me,' mutilating herself like that, but I'm fairly certain it had to do with not being able to afford to go to the movies. There I was, a 'barefoot boy,' asking myself: 'Why? Why must it be this way?' Years passed before I understood that the answer is in our 'cultural DNA.' It's the same answer to my original question. What's the real problem with Communism? And why are we as a people so susceptible to it? Two sides of the same coin. Want to guess? No? I'll tell you why. Because the average Zlabian, like Dragomir, and like the Communist system in general, doesn't know how to have any goddamned *fun*."

The sumptuous wingback chair to which Pfefferkorn was cuffed had been specially modified for that purpose, with two thick iron hoops drilled into its arms, and ankle chains that prevented him from lifting his feet more than six inches off the ground. The lord high president was not thus constrained. His custom-made size-twenty-two goatskin boots landed on his George II desk with a mighty crash.

"That's all people really want," he said, shifting his seismic bulk and sipping from a generous pour of fifty-five-year-old single malt scotch. "To enjoy themselves. And why shouldn't they? But that's not the way the Zlabian thinks. It's always 'suffering this,' 'shame that.' Or it was, once upon a time. I've done my damnedest to change that around here. It's much more about psychology than economics. Take that TV show they love, the one with the crying poets. I'm proud to say that on our side of the boulevard, it wouldn't fly. Now, we want winners."

Savory, standing by the jukebox, nodded. The ten security guards did not move a muscle.

Thithyich fished an extra-long Marlboro out of the carton in his coat pocket. He pressed a button on his desk and an eight-foot jet of flame roared from the wall, narrowly missing his face and incinerating the cigarette by half. He dragged, blew, tapped a diamond-studded ashtray shaped like a roulette wheel. "We as a people have had it rough. No argument there. At some point, though, you have to take responsibility for yourself. That's the beauty of a free market: it has no memory, neither for your successes nor for your failures. Merciless, but in a way also very forgiving. God, I'm peckish. Where are they?"

On cue, the door opened and fifteen bikini-clad women with global breasts bore in sterling-silver trays laden with food. They set them on the sideboard, kissed the president on the cheek, and left. Pfefferkorn could smell smoked fish and freshly made blini. One of the security guards loaded up a plate and placed it in Pfefferkorn's lap. A second guard kept his rifle trained on Pfefferkorn while a third removed his gag and unlocked his hands. Thithyich watched him eat with a placid smile.

"Good, isn't it? Better than 'root vegetable this,' 'goat milk that.'"

"Thank you," Pfefferkorn said. He didn't see any sense in antagonizing the man.

"My pleasure. Drink?"

Pfefferkorn would have accepted even if Savory hadn't told him to.

"This is the stuff," Thithyich said, pouring. He held the tumbler out and a guard took it and held it under Pfefferkorn's nose so Pfefferkorn could appreciate the aroma.

"Peaty," the president said. "Yet smooth."

Pfefferkorn nodded.

"Cin cin," the president said.

Compared to *thruynichka*, the scotch went down like cream.

"Try the gravlax," Thithyich said. "It's house cured."

"Delicious," Pfefferkorn said.

"I'm so glad. A little more, perhaps?"

Pfefferkorn handed the guard his empty plate. "Thank you," he said, although he was feeling rather craven for taking seconds.

Thithyich stubbed out his cigarette. "And your trip? I hope it wasn't too hard."

POTBOILER 267

Pfefferkorn shook his head.

"Lucian went easy on you, I hope."

Out of the corner of his eye, Pfefferkorn saw Savory smiling at him in a threatening way.

"I feel like I'm on vacation," Pfefferkorn said.

A guard handed Pfefferkorn a new plate. There was caviar and crème fraîche and capers and delicate matjes herring in a light tomato sauce.

"Well, good, good. It's a matter of principle that you be comfortable and entertained." Thithyich took out another cigarette and stuck it between his lips. "Everyone deserves a taste of what this world has to offer." He summoned the jet of flame and sucked in smoke. "Not least those soon to depart it."

85.

Pfefferkorn paused, an unchewed piece of herring in his mouth. He swallowed it down whole and wiped red sauce from his lips. "Beg pardon?"

Savory was grinning.

"You're going to kill me?" Pfefferkorn said.

"You can't honestly be surprised," Thithyich said.

"Not after all the inconvenience you've caused me. It was no simple matter, kidnapping Carlotta de Vallée, and for you to start running around, playing the 'hero'—"

"Hold on," Pfefferkorn said.

Everyone winced.

There was a long silence.

The president smiled.

"Please," he said. "Go right ahead."

"I—eh. Eh. I thought the May Twenty-sixers kidnapped Carlotta."

"They did."

"But you just said you kidnapped her."

"Indeed."

"I'm sorry," Pfefferkorn said. "I don't follow."

"I am the May Twenty-sixers," Thithyich said. "I created them out of whole cloth. Remember, I'm trying to provoke a war here. What better way to do that than to fan the flames of revanchism? The May Twenty-sixers' raison d'être is to reunify greater Zlabia under true collectivist rule by any means necessary. It's expressly stated in their manifesto, which I wrote in the bathtub. Lucian, the relevant part, please, from the preamble."

Savory pressed keys on his smartphone and read aloud. " 'Our raison d'être is to reunify greater Zlabia under true collectivist rule by any means necessary.' "

"What have you done with her?" Pfefferkorn asked.

"She's being held at May Twenty-sixer headquarters in West Zlabia," Thithyich said.

"*West* Zlabia."

"Naturally. If I put the headquarters here, it would be rather obvious who was 'pulling the strings,' mm? I give my orders through an intermediary. Besides, nothing lends a fake West Zlabian counter-counter-revolutionary movement verisimilitude like having it staffed by genuine West Zlabian counter-counter-revolutionaries. Fabulously committed bunch, they are. Trained from birth to embrace fervent dedication to unattainable goals. God bless the Communist school system."

"You're barking up the wrong tree, provoking a war," Pfefferkorn said. "The U.S. won't get involved."

"Bosh. They'd much rather that than the alternative, which is that the West Zlabians give the gas up for pennies on the dollar to the Chinese."

"It didn't work the first time," Pfefferkorn said.

"What first time?"

"When you faked your own assassination attempt."

"That's what your people told you."

Pfefferkorn nodded.

"And you believed them."

Pfefferkorn nodded again.

"Do you have any idea how much it hurts to get shot in the buttocks?"

"No," Pfefferkorn admitted.

"If you did, you'd know that that's utter claptrap. I never shot myself."

"Then who did?"

"You did. Well, your government, really. They're the ones who planted the book for you."

Pfefferkorn was confused. "Which book."

Thithyich looked at Savory.

"*Blood Eyes*," Savory said.

"That's the one," Thithyich said. "Smashing title."

"Thank you," Savory said.

"That's impossible," Pfefferkorn said. "*Blood Eyes* had a dummy code."

"My buttocks beg to differ," Thithyich said.

"But they're your allies."

"My buttocks?"

"The U.S."

" 'On paper,' perhaps, but you know as well as I do how much that's worth."

"You just said they would support you in the event of an invasion."

"Certainly."

"Now you're telling me they tried to kill you."

"Yes."

"That doesn't strike you as contradictory?"

Thithyich shrugged. "Politics."

"I don't know why I should believe you."

"What reason do I have to lie?"

"What reason did *they* have to lie?"

"Plenty. They were indoctrinating you. It wouldn't have done to admit that they engage in covert acts of cold-blooded political murder, now, would it? They much prefer that people think of them as the 'good guys.' In any event, Lucian intercepted the code shortly before it came off, and I was able to escape with minor injuries. But the whole experience set me thinking. You lot have been meddling with our affairs for nigh on forty years. High time for a taste of your own medicine, don't you reckon? Hence . . . what's it again?"

"*Blood Night*," Savory supplied.

"That's the one," Thithyich said. "Bang-on title."

"Thank you," Savory said.

"Let me get this straight," Pfefferkorn said. "You got Savory to get me to get my publisher to get American secret operatives to kill Dragomir Zhulk."

"Yes, yes, yes, and no."

"No to which part."

"The last bit. About killing Zhulk. I'm afraid you've been misinformed. *Blood*—damn it, I'm at sixes and sevens, here."

"*Night*," Savory said.

"Bang-on. *Blood*, et cetera, the second one—*that* contained a dummy code."

Pfefferkorn stared. "A dummy code."

"Well, we couldn't possibly plant a real code. We don't have the Workbench."

"But why would you give me a dummy code?"

"To disrupt the pattern of transmission and create confusion."

"Then who killed Zhulk?"

"Made to guess, I'd say it was your government as well. They're not big fans of his."

"But how? According to you, *Blood Night* was dummied."

"My goodness, man, you're not the only blockbuster novelist out there. The order to kill Dragomir could have been in any one of a dozen beach reads."

Pfefferkorn massaged his temples.

"Take your time," Thithyich said kindly. "It's very complicated. More caviar?"

"No, thanks," Pfefferkorn said. "Why did you have the May Twenty-sixers kidnap Carlotta?"

"Well, the idea was that getting ahold of the Workbench—or I should say, rather, a dummied version of the Workbench, because it should be obvious to anyone who gives it five seconds of thought that your government would never give them the *real* Workbench, although thankfully we can count on our friends across the border *not* to give it five seconds of thought—would give the May Twenty-sixer rank and file enough confidence to support a preemptive strike against me, and that's all the excuse I need to steamroll them."

"My understanding was that you could steamroll them right now," Pfefferkorn said.

"True. But it's better if they move first. Nobody likes a bully. And it's nice to have the support of the international community. It's very 'in,' geopolitically speaking. Anyway, so far, so good. I've had my intermediary suggest that a good time to invade would be right after their fifteen-hundredth anniversary festival. You know, swept along by a 'tide' of nationalist fervor and so forth. Fingers crossed, we should be able to get things into full swing by the first week of October."

"I still don't see why you have to kill me."

"You didn't let me finish what I was saying. One of the hallmarks of a successful businessman is his ability to assimilate new information and make creative use of adversity. Don't feel bad about being caught. No way you could've anticipated it, because while I knew you were in town, of course, it never occurred to me to pick you up until Sunday. I made what you Americans call a 'game-time decision.'" Thithyich stubbed out his cigarette. "Getting shot was uncomfortable enough, but the damage from a public-relations point of view has been much worse. In my universe, you see, the most valuable asset is respect. I can't take what people say about me lightly. I can't have people saying, 'Thithyich is vulnerable, he's gone soft. . . .' It's bad for business. What's bad for my business is bad for the economy and therefore bad for the whole country. People know I've been shot. They know no one has been punished. It's created all sorts of stickiness vis-à-vis my 'ruthless' image. Really, I've been terribly put out. I've gone so far as to hire a consulting firm, which ought to tell you a lot, because normally I hate that sort of thing. The groupthink makes my skin crawl. I have to say, though, I was impressed with the clarity of their findings, and while I'm sure you won't be thrilled with their recommendations, they were unequivocal: the best way for me to revive my 'bloodthirsty' persona, or whatever, is to demonstrate that I'm just as capable of lashing out with indiscriminate violence as I ever was. They project a five-to-ten-point bump with a public execution. But here's the interesting twist: executing a famous or prominent person gives an extra two to three points. I suppose it has to do with perceptions of power and so forth, i.e., 'a famous person is powerful, therefore the person who kills the famous person is perforce more powerful.'"

"I'm not famous," Pfefferkorn said. "I'm not prominent."

"My dear sir, you most certainly are. At the moment, you're the hottest writer around."

"Nobody cares about writers," Pfefferkorn said.

"Zlabians do," Thithyich said. "Literature has been

powering our ethnic strife for some four centuries. Ah—
ah—please. No whining. I understand why you'd find
these conclusions disagreeable, but data are data, *n'est-ce
pas*? It's nothing 'personal.' So, right. I do hope you can
manage to enjoy yourself a bit today, because tomorrow
you will be shot, publicly. Apologies for the short notice.
Have a pleasant day."

86.

Pfefferkorn was driven to death row in a metallic purple
limousine. They took the scenic route. Savory rode along
to point out East Zlabia's many attractions. Old Town
had been restored to its former glory, with brand-new
artificially weathered cobblestones and new cornices and
gargoyles for the cathedral. Everything was nightmar-
ishly quaint. There was nobody strolling. Nobody was
throwing coins into the fountains. The limo cruised past
lush public parks filled with blemish-free flowers. Nobody
was sunbathing. Nobody was tossing the Frisbee around.
They passed the opera house, the museum of modern
art, ZlabiDisney, the shopping district—all empty. It was
as if a neutron bomb had fallen, leaving a perfect stillness, perfectly chilling.

Just as Pfefferkorn was about to ask where everybody was, the limo turned the corner onto what could be described only as the Las Vegas Strip unfettered by good taste. The chauffeur slowed to five miles per hour, allowing Pfefferkorn to drink it all in. He counted eleven separate casinos. There was an *Oliver Twist*–themed one. There was a Genghis Khan–themed one. There was a Las Vegas–themed one, its frontage occupied by a one-eighth scale model of the Strip. Next door was a casino whose theme was the very street they were driving on, its frontage occupied by a one-eighth scale model of everything around them, including a one-eighth scale model of the Las Vegas–themed casino complete with a one-sixty-fourth scale model of the Las Vegas Strip and adjacent to a one-eighth scale model of the casino on which the model was located that in turn featured a one-sixty-fourth scale model of the street they were driving on that in turn featured a one-five-hundred-twelfth scale model of the casino on which the model of the model was located. Pfefferkorn assumed there were further models embedded in that model. He wasn't close enough to tell, and his sight line was then blocked by a seventy-foot-high LED marquee touting an upcoming performance by a 1970s rock supergroup he had thought defunct.

It was a lively scene, made more so by the presence of what appeared to be the entire population of East Zlabia. For the most part they looked like their cousins across the border, except more obese. They were snacking and sipping soft drinks, pushing strollers and leaving junky compact cars at any of the myriad valet stands. Outside the Amazon jungle–themed casino, they applauded and snapped pictures as a team of pink dolphins broke the hypnotic blue of an artificial lake to execute a precisely choreographed midair pas de deux.

The largest casino was at the end of the street. It had a *Vassily Nabochka* theme. A massive gold statue of the prince stood out front. He was holding a root vegetable in one hand and a sword in the other. Though the iconography made it clear who he was, his face had been cast to resemble Kliment Thithyich's.

The limo pulled up. Valets rushed to greet it. Pfefferkorn was escorted inside at gunpoint and guided through a bleeping, blooping field of slot machines to the shopping promenade. Savory led the way. They entered a men's haberdashery done up in dark wood and brass railings. Pfefferkorn was handed a binder of sample fabrics and made to stand on a wooden box. A tailor appeared and began taking his measurements.

"Pick a good one," Savory said. "It'll be in the photos."

Pfefferkorn selected an understated blue. The tailor nodded approvingly and rushed off.

In the meantime Pfefferkorn was taken to the spa. He got a hot-stone massage at gunpoint. He swam a few laps in the saltwater pool, also at gunpoint. His moustache came off, revealing a semi-hardened scab. He left the moustache floating on the surface of the water.

Back to the haberdashery they went. He stood up on the box for a fitting. The tailor slashed at him with chalk.

"Have you ever had a suit made before?" Savory asked.

Pfefferkorn shook his head. "I've never had a hot-stone massage, either."

"First time for everything."

The tailor promised the finished product by morning.

Their last stop was the casino courtyard, wherein a magnificent black granite plaza surrounded a runty tree.

HERE LIES IN ETERNAL SLUMBER

THE GREAT HERO

FATHER AND REDEEMER OF THE

GLORIOUS ZLABIAN PEOPLE

PRINCE VASSILY

"HOW LIKE A ROOT VEGETABLE SWELLS MY HEART

TO GAZE UPON THY COUNTENANCE

HOW LIKE AN ORPHANED KID GOAT DOES IT BLEAT

FOR THY LOSS"

(canto cxx)

Pfefferkorn and Savory bowed their heads.

"All right," Savory said. "Party's over."

They got into an elevator. One of the guards pushed the button for the thirteenth floor. Beside it was a little placard.

13: EXECUTIVE LEVEL / HONEYMOON SUITE / DEATH ROW

87.

Pfefferkorn's death-row cell featured movies on demand, a bidet, multizone climate control, and seven-hundred-thread-count bedding. For a man about to be publicly shot, he didn't feel afraid. Nor was he angry, at least not at Thithyich, who after all was a barbaric, unhinged autocrat acting on the advice of an expensive American consulting firm. Mostly he was disappointed in himself. He had failed the mission, and by extension Carlotta, his daughter, and the free world.

This was the part of the story where he applied his ingenuity to escape from a life-threatening situation. Now that he was in such a situation, he appreciated how asinine a trope it was. In real life, evil captors did not forget to lock the door. They didn't accidentally leave out an assortment of parts that cleverly combined to form a working crossbow. Lying on his comfy sheets, he ruminated on the phrase "action hero." It didn't mean merely that the hero underwent a series of exciting events. It meant that the hero was active—that is, he *did* something. But what could an action hero do when there was nothing doable? Did the fact that he wasn't attempting to escape mean that he wasn't a hero, or that the concept of action heroism was inherently far-fetched? He decided it was both. He might not be able to escape, but he doubted that anyone else could, either. Still, his passivity did make him feel guilty, as though it was morally incumbent upon him to fight back. He could kill himself. That would show Thithyich. His first thought was to hang himself with his bedsheet, but the walls of the cell were made of a smooth plaster inhospitable to nooses. He examined the bedframe, hoping to take it apart and use a piece to slit his wrists. The screws were tight, meant to resist just that sort of mayhem. The television was set into the wall and covered with a thick layer of Plexiglas. The minibar held pretzels, Baked! Lay's, SunChips, golden raisins, two ingots of Toblerone, six-ounce cartons of orange and cranberry juice, cans of Coke and Diet Coke, and plastic mini-bottles of scotch and vodka. With luck he might be able to snack himself to death, but more probably he would go to his fate with heartburn. Suicide was out.

He rummaged around in the desk. Beneath a leather-bound copy of the East Zlabian edition of *Vassily Nabochka* he found a small pad of paper with the casino insignia at the top. A golf pencil had rolled to the back of the drawer. He sat down and started to write.

It was a purely symbolic form of resistance—he did not expect anything he wrote to leave the room—but he felt compelled to give it his all. *Sweetheart* he began. He used metaphors, he used similes, he made allusions. He stopped and reread. Overall, the tone was self-conscious, as though he were trying too hard to ingratiate himself to an audience of strangers. He threw the page away and started over, beginning with a story from his own childhood. He wrote for an hour before going back to assess his progress. Again, it was all wrong. It wasn't about her or how he felt about her. He tried again and again. Nothing worked. A significant pile of paper accumulated on the floor of the cell. Soon enough he ran out. He banged on the cell bars until the guard came. He asked for more paper. It was brought. He wrote through that whole pad, and when he still failed to express himself adequately, he called for and was brought a third pad. His pencil snapped. He still hadn't written anything he could live with. He decided to stop. Then he changed his mind. Then he changed it back. It was four forty-eight in the morning. He could no longer think clearly. It was coming now, fear. He curled up on the floor and held himself. He wasn't ready to give up on life. He still had so much to do. He wanted to see his daughter happy in her new house. He wanted to see her children. He wanted to hold Carlotta one more time. Would he ever feel ready to die? Could a man know that he had accomplished as much as he ever would? He believed he had more in him. He always would. He could be on death's door and still he would be reaching. No matter what the world said, he would always believe that the best of him was yet to come.

The cell door slid open. A guard wheeled in a room-service cart. He paused briefly to stare at Pfefferkorn, lying fetal on the floor. Then he set the cart up and left.

Gradually the light in the room increased. The cell turned pink and purple and gold. The sun was a herald.

The day was catching up with him. Nothing could stop it. Pfefferkorn sat up. He was going to die today. Suddenly he felt ravenous. He attacked the food. There were croissants, half a grapefruit, Danish, coffee, a panoply of fancy jams and jellies, and an egg-white timbale in the shape of a Calabi-Yau manifold.

Everything was delicious.

The bathroom was stocked. Pfefferkorn took a shower. He shaved with an electric wet/dry shaver. He brushed his teeth and rinsed his mouth with mouthwash. He applied talcum powder and swabbed out his nose and ears. A card on the sink informed him that in order to protect the environment, a towel back on the rack would be reused, while a towel on the floor would be replaced. He dropped all the towels on the floor, including the clean ones.

His new clothes had arrived while he was showering. Everything had been laid out for him on the bed. In addition to the suit there were fresh socks and broadcloth boxers, a bright white shirt and a canary yellow necktie. Pfefferkorn pulled the pins from the shirt and put it on. The polished cotton felt good against his skin. He took the suit out of its garment bag and stepped into the pants. They fit perfectly, enough so that he didn't need the crocodile-skin belt. He put it on anyway. The soles of the penny loafers were slippery, so he scuffed them up with a disposable emery board from the bathroom. He tied the tie, taking time to get the knot right. He held up the jacket. The lining was burgundy. The label read дэус экс мачина. He shrugged the jacket on and tugged it straight. It was snug but not overly so. He folded the white handkerchief and tucked it neatly in the lapel pocket. He went back to the bathroom and reordered his hair in the mirror. He put some petroleum jelly on his upper left lip. Except for the scab, he didn't look too bad, and even that looked better than it had the day before. He examined himself in profile. He buttoned the suit and felt something poke him in the ribs. He patted himself down. He unbuttoned his suit. He reached into the left inside pocket and took out a piece of paper. He unfolded it. He read it. It was a list of instructions on how to escape.

88.

Pfefferkorn escaped.

89.

Stumbling from the freight elevator in the casino's parking garage, his hair wild and his shirt torn, he saw the Town Car with the tinted windows. Two men were waiting by the rear of the car. One was blond and the other was bald. They were both dressed in black. Pfefferkorn sprinted toward them and got into the popped trunk.

The ride this time was more comfortable than it had been coming into East Zlabia. For one thing, the Lincoln's trunk was roomier. Also, he wasn't tied up or gagged. All the same, he had no idea who his rescuers were or where he was going. He decided to be positive and assume that the Americans had come to exfiltrate him. He bumped along. He felt the road deteriorating, as if they were headed into the countryside. He counted turns. He waited patiently. The ride went on and on. The stuffiness was like a scarf being drawn tight around his neck. He felt his brand-new suit becoming soaked with sweat. He felt the old familiar hysteria. He flailed and pounded the roof of the trunk.

The car slowed.

It stopped.

Doors opened.

The trunk swung open. Pfefferkorn blinked up at the two men in black. The blond man was holding a wad of cloth. There was also a third person. He must have been waiting in the backseat of the car when Pfefferkorn got in.

"You have got to be kidding me," Pfefferkorn said.

"Hush," Savory said.

The blond man pressed the cloth into Pfefferkorn's face.

SIX
дхиуобхриуо пжулобхатъ
(обвхратъниуо) бху
жпудниуиуи жлабхвуи!

(WELCOME [BACK]
TO WEST ZLABIA!)

90.

Pfefferkorn fought off his attackers in a series of fluid motions, landing blows to their solar plexuses that left them sinking to their knees, gasping for breath. He heard the satisfying crunch of bone as Lucian Savory's bulbous forehead caved under a fearsome barrage of elbows and karate chops. He grabbed Savory around the neck and wrung him like a chicken on the eve of Yom Kippur. It felt wonderful. Savory turned five different shades of blue. It was beautiful. Pfefferkorn closed his eyes and reveled in the feel of the old man's pulse fading beneath his fingers. He kept compressing Savory's neck, smaller and smaller, until it seemed as though he had squeezed all the blood and bone and neck meat out of the way and was clutching empty skin. He opened his eyes. He was wringing his pillow wrathfully. All the stuffing had been forced out to the sides. He released it and fell back, panting.

His new cell was spartan and chilly. It was made of solid concrete, painted lint gray. He was lying on a mattress on the floor. The mattress was narrow and sharp with twigs. The blanket covering him was made of a coarse goat hair. There was a formidable steel desk. There was a wooden desk chair. A drain was set into the floor near the toilet. There was no bidet. The ceiling was high. There were no windows. A fluorescent tube provided the light.

He kicked off the blanket. His custom-made suit was gone, replaced by thick woolen trousers and a scratchy T-shirt. Instead of his penny loafers he wore straw slippers. There was a leg cuff around his left ankle. It was connected to a heavy chain. The chain ran across the floor and attached at the other end to the foot of the desk.

"Sir, good morning."

The man standing outside his cell was bald and sunken-cheeked. He wore an austere suit and steel-rimmed glasses, and his voice—clipped but clear, accented but precise—marked him as a man of worrisome efficiency. His eyes were black and cold, like twin camera lenses, or a chocolate-covered Eskimo. He bowed deeply.

"Sir, it is an honor to make your acquaintance," Dragomir Zhulk, the dead prime minister of West Zlabia, said.

91.

"You are surprised. Sir, this is understandable. I, the individual, am dead, or so you have been led to believe. It would be surprising to most people, even a man of your powerful imaginative gifts. Sir, pertinent background information will ameliorate the expression of wonderment that I, the individual, observe in your face."

Dragomir Zhulk's version of events differed drastically from both Kliment Thithyich's and the Americans'. According to Zhulk, the Party had been running the show all along. Everything that happened—from the publication of *Blood Eyes* to Pfefferkorn's recent stint on death row—was designed either to advance Party aims or to underscore the inherent incompetence and inferiority of the capitalist system.

The Party, he said, had planted the assassination code in *Blood Eyes*, thus exploiting the capitalist system by tricking it into killing Kliment Thithyich, who after all was himself a tool of the capitalist system. That the assassination had failed proved nothing, because anything the capitalist system did must by definition fail, and so while the superficial objective—namely, Thithyich's death—had not

been achieved, the underlying ideological objective—
namely, a demonstration of the inherent incompetence
and inferiority of the capitalist system—had.

"QED," Zhulk said.

Blood Night was also the Party's handiwork. It contained a dummy code designed to disrupt the capitalist
system's transmission sequence, thereby creating confusion. The Party had then carried out the assassination of
a man dressed up to look like Zhulk.

"The reason for this is self-evident," Zhulk said. "The
Party wished to give the appearance that I, the individual, was dead. This has enabled me, the individual, to
engage in covert activities free from capitalist scrutiny.
The comrade who volunteered his life for this purpose
has been accorded appropriate honor in death."

As for the May Twenty-sixers, the movement was not
a splinter group at all but a top-secret elite unit of the
Party, whose ostensible illegality was an ingenious ruse
designed to exploit the inferior intellect of capitalist
aggressors. "You object: 'Kliment Thithyich has informed me that he is the leader of this movement.' Sir,
this is incorrect. The ruse he claims as his own is in fact
a counter-ruse. The Party has allowed him to believe
this, so that the Party may obtain information about his
nefarious capitalist designs. Sir, do not be fooled. Many
of his most trusted agents in truth work to advance the
cause of the Party, including the man you know as Lucian
Savory. Sir, everything has gone according to the plan.
Soon national destiny shall be achieved in accordance
with the principle stated in the preamble to the manifesto of the movement of the glorious revolution of the

Twenty-sixth of May, which I, the individual, humbly penned at a desk provided by the Party, namely, the reunification of greater Zlabia under true collectivist rule by any means necessary. Sir, it is for this purpose that your government has sent you. QED."

"I don't have it," Pfefferkorn said, or cut in, or interjected, or managed to say.

"Sir?"

"I don't have it. The Workbench. I don't know where it is. It was in my suitcase but I lost it when I was kidnapped."

"Sir, you have been misinformed."

"I don't have it. You may as well kill me and get it over with."

"Sir, you are mistaken. There is no Workbench."

"At least let Carlotta go. She's of no further use to you."

"Sir, you are not listening." Zhulk began to pace agitatedly in front of the bars. "Your government has misled you. This is not surprising, for the capitalist system is inherently depraved. It is rapacious and bellicose, an abhorrent monster of gluttonous imperialism gorged on materialism and overconsumption. The terms of the deal, sir, do not include carpentry. The terms of the deal, sir, concern you."

"Me?"

"Sir, yes." Zhulk plunged his hand inside his coat and withdrew a small hardcover book. He held it up for Pfefferkorn to see, like a hopeful suitor bearing flowers.

The book was covered in a protective plastic wrapper. The jacket was blue with yellow lettering and a drawing of a tree. Pfefferkorn's own copy, back on the mantel in his apartment, was in far worse shape, and he needed a moment to fully recognize the thing in Zhulk's hands as a mint-condition first edition of his first and only novel, *Shade of the Colossus*.

The prime minister smiled shyly. He bowed.

"I, the individual," he said, "am such a very big fan."

92.

"As a child I dreamed of becoming a writer. My father did not approve. 'These are not the ambitions of a man,' he told me. He liked to beat me with a rake, or sometimes a trellis. When he was in a bad mood, he would pick up my infant sister and use her to beat me. He called this 'saving time.' Often I prayed for his death. Yet when it came I was heartbroken. Who can understand love?"

He sounded far away. Pfefferkorn noticed that he had dropped the "I, the individual."

"Alas, I did not become a writer. I became a scientist. I subjugated myself for the sake of serving the Party. Literature was not needed; nuclear power was needed. Still, my greatest pleasure was reading. While a student in Moscow I happened to come upon your book. Sir, I was captivated. I was captured. I was ensnared and entranced. This story of a young man whose father ridicules his attempts to find meaning in art—this story was *my* story. Hungrily I awaited the sequel. I wrote letters. I was informed that no such book existed. Sir, I was bereft. Long after my return home, I grieved. I grieved more than I was to grieve the loss of my first wife, who I regret to say was unloyal to the Party and required removal. Sir, I made further inquiries. Concomitant with my increasing authority within the Party I ordered an overseas investigation. Sir, I was disappointed to learn of your struggles. Here we find the clearest condemnation of the capitalist system. A writer of your extraordinary gifts should be honored and extolled. Instead he languishes in obscurity. Sir, tell me: is this just? The answer must be no.

"Sir, I then resolved to correct this injustice.

"Patiently I worked, and the will of the Party dictated that I should rise to my present position, allowing me to fulfill this resolution of so many years. Sir, I must tell you that I have come to rescue you. Do not thank me. Sir, you will admit the essential baseness of the American capitalist system, a system so ignoble that it would fritter away its greatest living artistic treasure in exchange for partial access under favorable terms to our natural gas field. Be not surprised that your government has betrayed you. The capitalist system is incapable of recognizing true value.

"Sir, the Zlabian people are different.

"Sir, the Zlabian people are by nature symbolic. They are aesthetic. They are poetic. Hence reunification is not strictly a matter of correct economic and military policy.

It cannot be achieved merely by collectivizing root vegetable production. It cannot be won with guns and bombs alone. True reunification requires that we overcome the conflict which has long rent us asunder. Sir, there are no accidents. Sir, you have been rescued so that you may realize your fullest potential and in doing so enable the Zlabian people to realize ours. Sir, it is with a most vital, historical task that I, the individual, now charge you. Sir, you must beat the rhythm to which our great army will march to victory. You must apply the healing balm that will then seal the wounds of ages. You must sing the songs that will reconcile divided families. It is you, sir, who will bring our glorious people together. Others have tried before and failed. But sir, others were not the author of a great novel. It is you, sir, who will fulfill our national destiny. It is you. Sir, you must take up your pen. You must finish *Vassily Nabochka*."

93.

"I think you've got the wrong guy," Pfefferkorn said.

"Sir, this is incorrect."

"Trust me. I'm a lousy poet."

"Sir, your novel contains any number of passages of

such surpassing beauty as to cause aches in the joints and chest."

"Take an aspirin," Pfefferkorn said.

Zhulk smiled. "What wit," he said. "Surely you will exceed all expectations."

"Where's Carlotta? What have you done with her?"

"Sir, the question is not convenient."

"Is she here? Where am I?"

"Sir, this is a place of maximum quietude, encouraging to literary pursuits."

"I won't do it. I refuse."

"Sir, your reaction is understandable. The task of completing the great poem would daunt even the most capable writer."

"It has nothing to do with the poem. I don't care about the poem."

"Denial is understandable."

"It's not even that good. Do you know that? It's long and boring. All that tundra?"

"Sir, this attitude is not convenient."

"Convenient for whom?"

"Sir—"

"All right. All right. Answer me this: it's your national goddamned poem, right? Then how can a non-Zlabian finish it?"

"Sir, this observation is understandable. I, the individual, was given pause by the same concern. However, the problem has been removed. A thorough investigation has been done into the matter by the Ministry of Genealogy, and conclusive proof adduced showing the presence of one C. Pfefferkorn, chair maker, in the royal census of

1331. Additionally, your physiognomy is suggestive of native origins."

Pfefferkorn stared. "You're out of your fucking mind."

"Sir, this is incorrect."

"I'm Jewish."

"Sir, this is immaterial."

"My whole family is. Ashkenazi Jews from Germany."

"Sir, this is incorrect."

"And Poland. I think. But—but—look, I know for a fact that there is no Zlabian in me."

"Sir, this is incorrect."

"I'm not going to argue with you about this."

"It is the will of the Party that the work be completed in advance of the festival to commemorate the poem's fifteen-hundredth anniversary."

"Hang on a second," Pfefferkorn said. "That's next month."

Zhulk bowed. "I, the individual, leave you to great thoughts."

He walked away.

"Wait a minute," Pfefferkorn yelled.

A door opened, closed.

Pfefferkorn lunged for the bars. The chain around his ankle bit, jerking his leg out from under him. He fell, hitting his head on the floor.

Silence.

He lay there for a while, contemplating this latest turn of events. Then he got up. He grasped the chain and leaned back with all his might. The desk did not budge.

He walked out the length of the chain and paced out his maximum circumference. It encompassed the toilet and the mattress. Other than that, he was going nowhere.

94.

Zhulk returned not long after. He was not alone. The surroundings would seem to preclude maid service, but sure enough, the woman following him was dressed in a black polyester dress, a limp white headband, and a white apron gone gray with numerous launderings. The dress had seen better days. Its seams were puckered. The maid herself was a stout, sallow creature, with swollen calves and a broad, flat backside. Her eyes were droopy. The backs of her hands were flaky from washing dishes. She was carrying a tray of food. She seemed unhappy to be there. Pfefferkorn could more or less see the rain cloud over her head. She unlocked the cell door, crossed to the desk, put the tray down, and started to walk out.

Zhulk clucked his tongue at her. She paused and turned to face Pfefferkorn.

Pfefferkorn had never imagined how much venom could be packed into a single curtsy.

She stepped out of the cell. Zhulk spoke harshly to her and she trudged out of sight. A moment later, a door opened and closed.

Zhulk gestured to the food. "Sir, please."

Pfefferkorn peered at the tray. Its contents confirmed that he was back in West Zlabia. There was a charred puck of root vegetable hash, a cup of brown tea, and a small pat of goat's-milk butter, whose barnyardy aroma caused him to retch.

"I'll pass," he said.

"Sir, this is unacceptable. Food represents labor, and labor represents the will of the Party, and what the Party wills cannot be denied."

"I'm not hungry."

"Sir, this is incorrect. Article eleven of the principles of the glorious revolution dictates that nothing exists except for that which is necessary. Sir, I, the individual, have already eaten my lunch. Hence the need for this food cannot reasonably be ascribed to me, the individual. Therefore you, sir, must have need of this food. If you did not, then the food would exist without its being necessary, and clearly this cannot be true, for the principle just stated. Therefore, either this food is an illusion or you must need it. But this food is not an illusion. Sir, it is plainly there. Therefore you must need it. QED."

Pfefferkorn, mindful of the phrase "scrotal electroshock," sat down in the wooden desk chair. He picked up the puck of hash. He spread the butter across it and shoved the whole thing into his mouth. It tasted like scarcity. He got it down as fast as he could and chased it with the tea. He sat back, wishing he had something to chase the tea with. His chest hurt. It was too much food to take in at once and he could feel its mass exfoliating the interior of his gullet. He had a premonition that he would soon be tasting it in reverse.

"Sir, the Party salutes you," Zhulk said.

A door opened and closed. The maid staggered into view, pushing a wheelbarrow full of books and papers. Zhulk held open the cell bars for her and she carted the wheelbarrow in. She set it down near the desk and began unloading it.

"Sir, you will find these items inspiring."

The books were old and musty, with broken spines and dangling covers. There were a lot of them, and the maid was perspiring lightly by the time she finished. She took the empty tray, curtsied to Pfefferkorn, and exited the cell.

"Sir, it is the intention of the Party to provide you with all that you require, within reason. Please state any additional needs and they will be seen to."

There was a silence.

"I could use a shower," Pfefferkorn said.

"Very good," Zhulk said. He spoke harshly to the maid, who trudged off again. "My wife will accommodate this request as soon as possible."

"Your wife?"

"A proud and humble servant of the Party," Zhulk said. "No different from any other comrade of the revolution."

"Right," Pfefferkorn said.

Zhulk bowed. "If there is nothing further, sir, I, the individual, shall leave you to great thoughts."

95.

He had been given eleven reams of writing paper, an assortment of the finest West Zlabian leakproof ballpoint pens, four different linear English translations each of the West Zlabian edition of *Vassily Nabochka*, a compendium of errata, a Zlabian-English dictionary, a Zlabian rhyming dictionary, a Zlabian thesaurus, the complete *Encyclopædia Zlabica*, a bundle of maps as thick as a phone book, a copy of the Party writings, D. M. Piilyar-zhkhyuiy's seventeen-volume history of the Zlabian peoples, an anthology of Marxist literary criticism, and reprints of Zhulk's speeches dating back to 1987. There were several photo albums filled with picture postcards of the local countryside. There was a calendar, a freebie distributed by the Ministry of Sexual Sanitation. Each month highlighted another venereal disease. Zhulk had circled three days in red. The first was that day's date. Pfefferkorn counted twelve more days of chlamydia before the clap rolled around and the countdown to the festival began. The thirteenth was opening night, and the Friday prior was labeled **final deadline** in Zlabian.

Twenty-two days.

He tossed the calendar down and picked up a plastic-wrapped copy of the East Zlabian *Pyelikhyuin*. He couldn't understand why Zhulk would provide him access to capitalist media. He tore open the plastic and unfolded the paper.

EXTREMELY FAMOUS

AND VERY PROMINENT

AUTHOR EXECUTED

According to the article, the mood at the Kasino Nabochka had been uplifting. The Cirque du Soleil theater had been filled to capacity with people eager for the first public execution in more than a year. Face value of a ticket was US$74.95, but scalpers had been asking as much as four hundred a pop. The festivities kicked off with a rousing speech by Lord High President Kliment Thithyich. He promised the same bloody fate to anyone who dared cross him. Next there had been a dance performance by his entourage. In honor of the proceedings, the ladies wore special black "Grim Reaper" miniskirts and twirled neon sickles. The president had then decreed a weeklong reprieve from interest on all gambling debts owed to him. Seeing as how most of the populace was cripplingly in hock, this announcement elicited enthusiastic cheers. A T-shirt cannon was fired, and at last, the execution got under way. Notorious American hack thriller writer and international fugitive from justice A. S. Peppers was brought out hooded and handcuffed. He was made to kneel. The president asked if he had any last words. Peppers shook his hooded head, and the president made a joke about not having such a big vocabulary after all. Laughter and jeers flew at the condemned man. Thirteen sharpshooters took up positions. They raised their rifles. At the president's command, they fired. Peppers's bullet-riddled body was removed, the T-shirt cannon brought out once more, and accordion music played.

Pfefferkorn supposed that, for PR purposes, it was almost as good to kill a faceless A. S. Peppers as it was to kill the real him. He also understood why Zhulk wanted him to read the article. In the eyes of the world, A. S. Peppers, Arthur Pfefferkorn, and Arthur Kowalczyk no longer existed. Nobody would come looking for him. However terrible this realization was, it was not nearly as terrible as knowing that someone had died solely because he happened to be about Pfefferkorn's height.

A door opened and closed. Zhulk's wife appeared shlepping a massive, sloshing bucket, a burlap sack slung over her shoulder. She put the bucket in the crook of her arm and fought to get the keys out of her apron without setting her burdens down, all the while doing an uncomfortable little dance. Pfefferkorn recognized the feeling. He remembered doing similar things on early mornings, thirty years ago: trying to bottle-feed his infant daughter with one hand, for example, and make coffee with the other. Zhulk's wife succeeded in getting the right key into the lock. The cell door swung open. She left it ajar, brushing past him as she carried the sack and the bucket across the room. As long as he was chained up, there was no danger of his making a break for it. At the same time, he found her indifference to her own safety peculiar. He could have severed her carotid with one of his leakproof pens. He could have jammed his fingers into her eye sockets and popped out her eyeballs. Harry Shagreen and Dick Stapp had done that on more than one occasion. He could have strangled her. The chain tethering him to the desk looked long enough for him to gather the slack off the floor and get it around her neck. Yet she didn't hesitate to bend over with her back turned. Was he that unintimidating?

She set the bucket and the sack down. She straightened up, winded, her hand pressed to the small of her back.

"Thank you," he said.

She curtsied.

"You don't need to do that," he said.

She glared at the floor.

"Really," he said. "I mean it."

She looked up, meeting his eyes for a fraction of a moment. Then she turned and left.

Inside the burlap sack were a towel, a washcloth, and a hunk of rancid soap. The towel and the washcloth were identical to the ones at the Hôtel Metropole. He took off his clothes, leaving the left leg of the woolen pants and the left leg of his underwear strung along the chain. He stood over the floor drain and sluiced himself with water from the bucket. For a moment he allowed himself to fantasize that the soap was a high-density dubnium polymer, and that it would split open, revealing a weapon or a key. But it turned to lather in his hands.

96.

Pfefferkorn got to work.

It wasn't easy. To begin with, he really was a lousy poet. He'd given up on the form sometime in high school. Moreover, the structure of *Vassily Nabochka* was extraordinarily demanding. Each canto was ninety-nine lines long, broken into nine stanzas of eleven lines of trochaic hendecameter apiece, adhering to a rhyme scheme of ABACADACABA, with triple internal rhymes on lines one, two, five, seven, ten, and eleven. What made the Zlabian language so tricky to master was its use of gendered, neuter, and hermaphroditic forms as well as a system of declension that had been mutating continuously since the days of Zthanizlabh of Thzazhkst. Add in several thousand textual variants, and a state of affairs resulted whereby a seemingly simple sentence—"Verily he loved him, for he was his beloved since days of yore"— could also be rendered "Verily she did love him, for she was his lover since long ago," "Verily they did love each other, for he was his uncle since many a time," or "Not necessarily false was her love for it, for he had not fondled it since Tuesday." Pfefferkorn could all too easily see how this sort of muddiness would give rise to violence. It also accounted for the poem's sustained popularity, for *Vassily Nabochka* possessed a quality essential to great literature, one that ensured it could be read by every successive generation and appreciated anew: it was meaningless.

Another major obstacle he faced was that Zhulk kept turning up to chat. Once or twice a day, as Pfefferkorn was getting ready to take another failed run at the thing, he would hear bony knuckles touching the bars. The prime minister wanted to know: was Pfefferkorn comfortable? Did he require more paper, more pens, more books? Was there something else, Zhulk asked, he or his wife could do to ease the maestro's toil? These questions were but a prelude to the interrogation that inevitably followed, for Zhulk was unduly obsessed with Pfefferkorn's creative process. When did the maestro like to write? Early in the morning? Late at night? After a large meal? A small meal? No meal at all? What about beverages? What role did carbonation play? Did he get his best ideas standing, sitting, or lying down? Was writing like pushing a boulder? Rowing a boat? Climbing a ladder? Netting a butterfly?

All of the above, Pfefferkorn said.

There was only so much poetry he could produce per day. The rest of the time he was profoundly bored. Other than Zhulk, he saw only Zhulk's wife, and she resisted all his attempts at conversation. Mostly he was alone. The fluorescent tube never shut off. The lack of sunlight was disorienting. It warped his sense of time and made him drowsy. He dozed. He did push-ups, sit-ups, jumping jacks, and squats. He jogged in place, the chain rattling noisily against the floor. He projected maps of the world onto the cracks in the ceiling. He used the finest West Zlabian leakproof pens, all of them hemorrhaging ink, to play the cell bars like a xylophone. He marked off the days on his venereal disease calendar. The clap was rapidly approaching. He pressed his ears to the wall, hoping to catch a hint of the outside world. The temperature in the cell led him to conclude that he was far underground. He imagined what the rest of the prison looked like. He envisioned rows and rows of press-ganged authors, all of them laboring to complete the poem. *There have been others like you. None of them have survived.* It was like the world's worst writers' retreat.

On the seventh day of his captivity Pfefferkorn looked up from his desk to find Zhulk standing outside the cell, rocking back and forth on his heels. His hands were clasped behind his back. He started to speak, decided against it, and without further ado hurled a ball of paper through the bars. It bounced and landed at Pfefferkorn's feet.

Pfefferkorn uncrumpled four handwritten pages, covered in crabbed script and marred by strike-throughs and carets. He looked at Zhulk uneasily.

Zhulk bowed. "Sir, you are the first to read it."

Pfefferkorn read Zhulk's own take on the final canto of *Vassily Nabochka*. In it, the king died before the antidote got to him, and a grief-stricken Prince Vassily repudiated the throne, deeding the royal lands over to the people and going to live as a commoner, tilling the fields and herding goats, finding redemption in manual labor before dying peacefully beneath a runty tree in the meadows of West Zlabia. It was the worst kind of agit-prop: heavy-handed, impatient, and artless. The turns were improbable, the imagery fuzzy, and the characters reductive.

"Wonderful," Pfefferkorn said in his writing-workshop voice.

Zhulk frowned. "It cannot be."

"It is. Frankly, I don't know why you need me at all."

"It is putrid, disgusting, an offense to eye and ear alike. Please, you must say so."

"It's not, it's very . . . evocative."

Zhulk threw himself to his knees. He began to keen and pull at his hair.

"Don't be so hard on yourself," Pfefferkorn said.

Zhulk moaned.

"I'm not saying it doesn't stand to benefit from a little editing. But for a first draft—"

With a howl Zhulk sprang to his feet. He grabbed the bars and shook them like a madman. *"It is bad,"* he yelled, "and you must *say* it is bad."

There was a silence.

"It's . . . bad," Pfefferkorn said.

"How bad."

". . . very."

"Use adjectives."

". . . sickening?"

"Yes."

"And, and—and juvenile."

"Yes . . ."

"It's repetitive," Pfefferkorn said. "Pointless."

"Yes, yes . . ."

"Trite, bland, rambling, overwritten. Poor in conception, worse in execution, just bad, bad, bad. Its only virtue," Pfefferkorn said, finding his groove, "is that it's short."

Zhulk honked pleasurably.

"The person who wrote this ending," Pfefferkorn said, "deserves to be punished."

"How."

"How should he be pu—eh, well—"

"Spare nothing."

"He should, uh—beaten?"

"Oh yes."

"And—shamed."

"*Yes.*"

"He should . . . be forced to wear a bell around his neck so people can know he's coming and run away."

"Truly, he should," Zhulk said. "Truly, his is a dead soul, and the ending reflects that."

"You said it," Pfefferkorn said.

"Yes, maestro. But tell me: if the ending seems bad now, how much worse will it seem when the maestro's ending is revealed? And how much more glorious will the maestro's ending be? Speak, maestro: *how glorious will the ending be?*"

There was a silence.

"Pretty darn glorious, I guess," Pfefferkorn said.

Zhulk stood back, starry-eyed. "The suspense is killing me, the individual."

Pfefferkorn did not share his patron's optimism. Ninety-nine lines in twenty-two days equaled four and a half lines per day. By day eleven, the halfway point, he was still stuck on line nine. He knew exactly what was happening to him. He'd gone through it before, only this time there would be no salvation. He was at the mercy of a villain crueler than any Dick Stapp or Harry Shagreen had ever faced: crushing self-doubt. And he was beginning to understand the word "deadline" in a whole new way.

97.

Late at night, unable to sleep, Pfefferkorn wrote unsendable letters.

He wrote to Bill. He described his earliest memories of their friendship. He remembered their eighth-grade teacher, Ms. Flatt, who everyone had a crush on. He remembered taking the wheel of Bill's Camaro, only to get pulled over for speeding. He had counted off the officer's steps in the sideview mirror while Bill fumbled with the glove box, trying to hide an open can of beer. After the cop had ticketed them and sped off they heard dripping. The glove box was leaking into the footwell. He couldn't believe what they'd gotten away with. Could Bill? Times were simpler then, weren't they? Weren't they. He asked if Bill had ever read any of the books he had recommended. He admitted that he hadn't finished some of them himself. He reminisced about breaking into the university boathouse and stealing a flatbed cart of equipment. The next day they had stood in the quad among the crowd, watching the crew team try to get their oars down out of the trees. He painted pictures of all-nighters at the literary magazine, the two of them hunched over a drafting board, working the monthly puzzle of text, image, and advertisement. He wrote fondly of their basement apartment. He still savored the cheap, greasy meals they had shared. He wrote that Bill was a true gentleman. He confessed that he had been jealous of Bill, but that his jealousy had its origin in admiration. He wrote that once, in the thick of a fight, his ex-wife had told him he was half the man Bill was. He had been so furious that he hadn't returned Bill's calls for months. He apologized for punishing Bill for someone else's sins. He wrote that he still thought of Bill's first story. It had been better than he had been willing to cop to at the time. He wrote that, clandestine government activities aside, Bill surely would have made it as a writer. He wrote that their friendship was precious to him, no matter what else had been going on behind the scenes, and he regretted that he hadn't come out to California while Bill was still alive. He hoped it was all right that he had slept with Carlotta. He wrote that he believed Bill would have given them his blessing, because that was the kind of person Bill was. He wrote that he wished he himself could be more generous. He wrote that he was working on it.

He wrote to Carlotta. He wrote that he had loved her from that first moment. He wrote that he had been afraid of her. It was this fear that had caused him to stand idly by as she fell into the arms of another man. He described a habit he had: at the end of a long writing session, when he would go back to read aloud what he'd put down that day, he would pretend that she was sitting in front of him. He would read to her, watching her facial expressions in his mind, listening to her laughter or gasps. That was how he knew something was right, if the Carlotta in his mind liked it. He had done this every day of his writing life, even when he was married. He had done it while writing his novel. Originally, he confessed, he had patterned the novel's love interest after her, but he had worried that she would know and that that would be the end of seeing her, and he wanted her in his life one way or the other, any way he could have her. So he changed the book. It had been a mistake, he wrote, because everything he knew about romantic love came from her, so in writing away from her, he was writing falsely. It was a costly decision, in that it had informed everything since. He had not written a word of truth until now. He was happy she had married Bill, for Bill had provided her a life he never could have. And he was happy she had reentered his life at a moment when they could give to each other unselfishly. He wrote that he enjoyed making love to her. They had lived long enough to know what that act did and did not mean. He wrote that he didn't care if she was a spy. It was sexy, actually. Nor did he regret coming to rescue her. He was sorry only that he had botched it so badly.

He wrote to his daughter. He wrote about the unreal spectacle of her arrival into the world. The change that took place within him felt physical. He felt it: felt his heart ripen. Like anything ripe, it was swollen and delicate and prone to split. In one instant the world went from a place of no consequence to an endless series of life-and-death decisions. Everything mattered. Her face was slightly smushed and he worried. The nurses gave her supplementary oxygen and he worried. He put her in the car seat and worried. The worry burned underneath him and distilled him to his essence. Joy was real joy and fear was real fear and anger was real anger and happiness was the real thing. He revisited the coffee-colored sofa, the one that had springs exploding out of it before they finally got rid of it, and he told her that once upon a time it hadn't been a wreck but a nice new piece of furniture that he liked to sit on with her in his arms, the sun coming up blue, her warm little head squirreled against his bare chest, her lips pursing and sucking in her sleep. Those hours had seemed endless then, but now he cherished them as the last moments he had had her all to himself. He wrote about the first time he accidentally pricked her foot while pinning on her diaper. She had barely bled and she hadn't made a peep but it destroyed him to see what he could do to her if he wasn't careful. He wrote that he was sorry. He wrote that it was silly of him to have insisted on cloth diapers. He wrote about how he had studied her as a child, collecting her every gesture and feature. He wished he had taken the time to write more of them down. He remembered her first day of school. She had thrown up from anxiety. He'd made her go anyway. At the time he had wondered if he was making a mistake, but in retrospect it seemed like the right thing to do. He wrote that he was glad he hadn't gotten everything wrong. He wrote of the triumph he felt at her triumphs, the agony of her disappointments. He remembered soccer practice and dance practice. He remembered father-daughter dances. He apologized that he had never danced at these dances, and that they'd always ended up standing on the side of the gym. He remembered the first time a boy broke her heart. He wrote that it was the first time in his life that he had honestly wanted to hit someone. He apologized that he had sometimes been angry at her for no reason other than that she made him acutely aware of his own shortcomings. He remembered the look on her face during those few months, long ago, when he was making progress on his lame attempt at a mystery novel. He had seen that she was happy, and he knew that her happiness came from thinking that *he* was happy. That kind of generosity made her special. She could be as smart and as beautiful as anybody in the world—she was that smart, she was that beautiful—but nothing made him prouder than her decency. He couldn't take too much credit for that. She had always been that way, even as a baby. Some people were born pure, and somehow, in defiance of all the odds, she was one of them. He wrote that he was glad she had found someone who could take care of her. She deserved the best. She always had. Her wedding was the best investment he had ever made. He apologized that he had not articulated his feelings more clearly and more often. He had never had the right words. He still wasn't sure he did, but it was better to try than to remain silent. In all his years, he wrote, he had produced nothing of value save her. She was his life's work. He considered himself a successful man. He wrote that he loved her, and he signed it *your father*.

98.

With less than forty-eight hours left until his deadline, Pfefferkorn stood up from the desk and cricked his neck. A few days earlier, he had struck upon the idea of using the last chapter of *Shade of the Colossus* as a model for the ending of *Vassily Nabochka*. It was either the best idea or the worst idea he'd ever had, and since he had nothing to lose—at that point he'd come to a complete standstill—and since Zhulk liked the novel well enough, he had made up his mind to give it his all. Nonstop toil had pushed the total to more than seventy lines. So far he had the beleaguered and road-weary prince coming to his dying father's bed, magical root vegetable antidote in hand. Then followed an internal monologue worthy of Hamlet, as the prince debated whether to give the antidote or to let the old man slip away peacefully. In the end the prince dropped the antidote into a chamber pot. These events were meant to correspond to the novel's young artist pulling the plug on his father. To be on the safe side, he'd also thrown in some flattering references to Communism. With the remaining two dozen lines, he planned to have the prince ascend to "a most bitter throne." He had thought of the phrase the day before and, liking the sound of it, had jotted it down in the margin. In Zlabian it was slightly less mellifluous: *zhumyuiy gorkhiy dhrun*. He thought it worked all right. He couldn't tell. He was under pressure and he felt himself losing perspective.

A door opened and closed. It was Zhulk's wife, come with dinner. As usual, her carriage was leaden and her face a mask of gloom. As usual, she left the cell door ajar and set the tray down on an empty corner of the desk.

As usual, he thanked her.

As usual, she curtsied.

"You really don't need to do that," he said, as usual.

As usual, she started out.

"I know it's none of my business," he said, "but you don't seem very happy."

For nineteen days she had ignored him, so for her to pause and stare at him was more than a bit unsettling.

"I'm just saying," he said.

She said nothing.

"I'm sorry," he said. "I shouldn't have said anything."

There was a silence. She looked at the pages on the desk, then at him for permission. He didn't think he had any real choice in the matter. He stood back. "Please."

She picked up the pages. Her lips moved slightly as she read. Her brow furrowed. She finished and put the pages facedown on the desk.

"It's terrible," she said.

Pfefferkorn was too shocked by the sound of her voice to reply.

"I don't understand," she said. "Why would Prince Vassily withhold the antidote?"

"Well," he said, "well, but, well." He paused. She was watching him in her moonfaced way, waiting for an answer. "Well, look. Look. Think about it. The king has disinherited him. He's bound to have some resentment over that." He paused again. "A lot of resentment."

"So he lets his father die?"

"It's the whole kingdom. It's a big deal."

She shook her head. "Makes no sense."

"Don't you think you're being a tad literal?"

"How so?"

"I mean, it's not necessarily the case that he's letting him *die*."

She picked up the pages again. "'Lifeblood hotly overbrimmed his bristly wizened nostrils like a glist'ning ruddy fountain,'" she read, "'Rendering his kingly spirit unto heavens slightly cloudy with a chance of showers.'"

She looked at him.

"You're missing the point," he said.

"Am I?"

"Completely."

"Okay, what's the point?"

"The important thing is not whether the king lives or dies. I mean of course that's important, in a, a, a *plot* sense, but, first of all, I could change that in about five seconds, and anyway, the crucial part, thematically, is showing that the *prince* is conflicted."

"About what?"

"Lots of things," Pfefferkorn said. "He's got mixed emotions."

Zhulk's wife was shaking her head. "No."

"Why not?"

"Prince Vassily is not that kind of character."

"What kind, nuanced?"

"The prince's moral purity, and therefore a large part of his appeal, rests on his ability to set aside his feelings and do what's right. Why else would he start out on the quest, if he didn't intend to give his father the antidote? It makes no sense at all."

"But isn't it more interesting if at the last moment he has doubts?"

"It's inconsistent with the rest of the poem."

"I asked if it was interesting," he said.

"I know," she said, "and I told you: it's inconsistent. It doesn't matter whether it's interesting. That's not the right criterion. You're working in someone else's style. You have to accept the constraints handed to you." She nosed at the page. "You've also got all sorts of fancy words in there that don't belong."

"Well, look," Pfefferkorn said, snatching the pages from her, "you said you didn't understand it, so maybe you ought to keep your opinions to yourself, thank you very much."

She said nothing. He remembered that she was still the prime minister's wife.

"I'm sorry," he said. "It's just that I'm sensitive about people reading work in progress."

"You've only got a couple of days left."

"I'm aware of that," he said. He shuffled the pages anxiously. "Do you, eh, have any suggestions for where to go from here?"

"I'm not a writer," she said. "I just know what I like."

He tried to hide his disappointment. "Well. I appreciate the constructive criticism."

She nodded.

He hesitated before asking what she thought her husband would think.

She shrugged. "He'll love it."

Pfefferkorn relaxed. "Really?"

"Dragomir's not a very tough critic. Certainly not as tough as I am. And he's primed to think anything you do is genius."

"Well," Pfefferkorn said, "that's good."

"It won't matter," she said. "He's still going to kill you before the festival."

". . . really."

She nodded.

"I . . . wasn't aware of that."

"He thinks it's more dramatic that way. Living writers lack a certain romance."

". . . mm."

"You'll be making him very happy," she said. "He's dreamed of this his entire life."

Pfefferkorn said nothing.

"What's that?" she asked.

He followed her gaze to the desk. The letters he had written were stacked up where he had left them.

"May I?" she asked.

His first instinct was to say no.

"Knock yourself out," he said.

While Zhulk's wife read the letters, Pfefferkorn for the hundredth time contemplated assaulting her. If it was true that Zhulk was going to kill him soon, this might be one of his last chances to escape. He did the visualization. Grab the chain, wrap it around her neck, pull it tight, put a knee into her back. His heart began to pound. His palms were sweaty. He readied himself. He didn't move. He couldn't. All that training, he thought. What a waste.

She finished reading and looked up. Her cheeks were wet and her eyes red-rimmed. She folded the letters neatly and put them back on the desk.

"You're a good writer when you want to be," she said.

There was a silence.

"Thank you," he said.

"You're welcome."

There was a silence.

"Of course I'm unhappy," she said.

He said nothing.

"I can't have children," she said.

There was a silence.

"I'm so sorry," Pfefferkorn said.

She wiped her eyes on her apron. She began to laugh. It was a dirty, strident sound, full of disappointment and expecting more to come. She clutched the apron in her fist. "Can you believe he makes me wear this."

Pfefferkorn smiled.

"I'm the wife of the goddamned prime minister." She shook her head and laughed again and looked at him. She stepped forward. He could smell the same rancid soap she brought him to bathe with. He could smell cheap cosmetics. Her lips were chapped and parted. She leaned in as if to kiss him. His body tensed.

"Come with me," she said, "if you want to live."

99.

The chain had prevented him from seeing too far beyond the cell bars. He didn't know what to expect when he stepped through the door. What he saw underwhelmed him. It was an ordinary concrete hallway, about eight feet long. At the far end was a plain wooden door.

"What about the guards?" he whispered.

"There are no guards," she said.

She opened the wooden door. It wasn't locked. On the other side was a square concrete antechamber. In front of him was a spiral staircase—nothing glamorous, just a narrow twist of steel ascending through a shaft bored in the ceiling. To his right were two more wooden doors. To his left was a third. It was a far cry from the dystopian holding pen he had envisioned.

"What about the alarm?" he whispered.

"There's no alarm. And you don't have to whisper."

She opened the first of the doors on her right. It was a storage room, about ten feet on a side. Utilitarian wire shelving lined three walls. Pfefferkorn saw packs of one-ply toilet tissue, stacks of Hôtel Metropole linens, a carton of soap, more reams of writing paper, more boxes of pens. A crepey white jumpsuit hung from a hook. The wheelbarrow was propped in the corner. Zhulk's wife got down on her knees, reached under one of the bottom shelves, and dragged out his wheelie bag. She stood it upright and invited him to take possession of it.

Pfefferkorn opened the bag. Incredibly, its contents were untouched. He looked at Zhulk's wife. She shrugged.

"Dragomir doesn't like to throw anything away," she said.

She covered her eyes while he changed into the Zlabian goatherd's outfit. It was comfortable, with the exception of the six-inch heels, which felt too unstable for a prison break. He kicked them off and put the straw slippers back on. He presented himself for inspection.

"Close enough," she said.

He put the deodorant stun gun in one pocket and the toothbrush switchblade in the other. In his back pockets he put the dubnium polymer soap and the designer eau de cologne solvent. He tucked the roll of cash and the untraceable cell phone into his socks. He put his false passport in his underwear. "Don't forget these," she said, handing him his unsendable letters and his unfinished ending to *Vassily Nabochka*. He slid them in along with the soap. He was trying to decide what to do with the tin of breath mints when she put out her hand.

"These aren't what you think they are," he said.

She took the tin and dropped it into her apron pocket. "I know what they are," she said.

He looked at her.

"Hurry," she said. "We don't have much time."

The adjacent room was a galley kitchen. On the counter was a wicker basket filled with root vegetables, a crusty box grater, and a stack of unwashed trays. She made him drink two cups of tea. Then she sat him on a stool while she opened up the spare moustache kit and read through the instructions.

"Don't forget the Q-tip," he said.

"I can read," she said.

She used up most of the tube of adhesive and all of the swatches. She polished a spatula on her apron and held it up so he could see his reflection.

He had a moustache to rival Blueblood's.

They returned to the storage room. She handed him the white jumpsuit, which he now saw wasn't a jumpsuit but a hazmat suit. He started to unzip it. She stopped him.

"Do you need to pee?"

He thought. "Probably not a bad idea."

The room across the antechamber mirrored his almost exactly, with a mattress, a toilet, and a floor drain. Instead of books, the desk held a sorry assortment of cosmetics and a plastic comb tangled with hair the same color as Zhulk's wife's. The pillow was dented and shiny, the blanket rumpled.

She had been living next door to him the entire time.

He used the toilet and went back out to the antechamber. She held the hazmat suit open. He stepped into it. It was a roomy one-size-fits-all. He pulled his arms through the sleeves.

"Where's your husband?" he asked.

She smiled sourly. "The penthouse at the Metropole." She zipped him up and sealed him in with Velcro. "He's busy with festival planning. He won't be back until tomorrow morning." She zipped the hood on. The interior of the suit smelled like her. "That's your deadline," she said, pressing the Velcro around his neck. "From this point on, you're on your own."

"I understand," he said. His voice boomed inside the suit. "Thank you."

She nodded. "Good luck."

He started for the stairs. He paused and turned back.

"What's going to happen to you?" he asked.

The same sour smile came across her face. She reached into the apron for the breath mints. She rattled the tin. If she swallowed one, she would be dead in three minutes.

"I'll be minty fresh," she said.

100.

He must have been a mile underground. As he rose, so did the ambient temperature. Breathability, he discovered, was not one of a hazmat suit's selling points. Soon his peasant shirt was sticking to his chest and the viewing panel had fogged up. His thighs quivered with every step. His pockets felt like they were loaded with birdshot. The shaft was claustrophobic and dim. He imagined Zhulk's wife doing the same climb carrying stacks of books, crates of root vegetables, re-ups of towels. He gritted his teeth and pressed onward.

The stairwell ended unceremoniously at a metal ladder bolted to the wall. Pfefferkorn climbed up and heaved against a trapdoor. It fell open with a clang. He poked his head up into a circular concrete chamber lit by bare yellow bulbs. At the center of the room stood a ten-foot tank that had burst open to resemble an enormous, rust-colored orchid. Oily puddles disclosed an uneven floor. Everything bore the universal three-petaled symbol for radiation. A series of pictorial placards ran along the wall. The first showed a smiling stick figure touching the tank. The next showed the stick figure down on one stick knee, proposing to a female stick figure. The third showed the stick-figure man standing by nervously as his stick-figure wife (her legs in stick-figure stirrups) bayed, a stick-figure midwife urging her on. The fourth placard completed the cautionary tale: the stick-figure couple's faces contorted in stick-figure horror as they received a stick-figure baby with three eyes and both sets of genitals.

He found the exit. It was unlocked, as he knew it would be. He stepped onto a small concrete apron. The sun was going down. There were no dogs, no razor wire, no watchtowers, no arc lights, no cameras. Instead, extending in every direction for half a mile, was a vast lake of toxic goo. It was thick, sticky, and antifreeze green. It glowed faintly. Anyone wanting to come in or out of the building would have to cross it. He couldn't smell it but he reckoned that the background smell from the forest multiplied by a billion was a decent approximation. He felt his prostate curling up and trying to hide. The hazmat suit didn't much reassure him. It was one thing to know and another to do. He sighted the perimeter fence and stepped off the apron, sinking in up to his knees. He was glad he'd ditched the heels.

As he waded along, he glanced back at the ruined reactor. Cylindrical, flared at the top and bottom, the building looked like some overblown dessert sauced with lime coulis. A jagged crack ran up its side. It was identical to other nuclear reactors he had seen pictures of, only far smaller. The smallest in the world, he thought, remembering Zhulk's obituary.

He reached the fence in thirty minutes. The goo had thinned enough that he could feel solid earth. He walked parallel to the fence for another twenty minutes and came to an abandoned checkpoint, the barrier arm replaced by a chain welded to the bent fencepost. He ducked underneath and was free.

Just off the dirt driveway was a three-sided wooden shower stall, like those at the beach for washing off sand. A sign read диигужутзиуннииуии пункхтъ. Decontamination station. He looked down at an ordinary garden hose connected to a pipe rising from the ground. He rinsed the goo off, unzipped the suit, and stepped out of it carefully, leaving it puddled in the stall. He hurried down the driveway to the main road. He walked for a while—he wanted to put some distance between himself and the reactor—then stopped and scanned in all directions. He saw dewy moonlit fields. All was quiet, not even a bleat. He took out the cell phone. He was getting one bar, barely. He moved around until it fixed. He closed his eyes and pictured the card. He opened his eyes and dialed.

"*Tha,*" Fyothor said.

"It's me," Pfefferkorn said.

There was a scratchy silence.

"Where are you?" Fyothor said.

"About five or six kilometers outside the city, I think."

"Has anyone seen you?"

"No."

"You are alone?"

"Yes."

Pfefferkorn heard the phone's mouthpiece muffled. Fyothor spoke to someone. The reply was inaudible. Fyothor came back on. He recited an address.

"It is near the waterfront district."

"I'll find it."

"Come quickly," Fyothor said and hung up.

Pfefferkorn took a good look at the stars. He might never see them again. In a world where nobody could be trusted, he had just committed a fatal error. He refused to live in that world. He put the phone back in his pocket and walked on.

101.

Fyothor lived on the eleventh floor of a hideous concrete-block tower. The elevator was out of service. The stairwell was slick with urine and sown with condom wrappers. Pfefferkorn's legs were still sore from climbing out of the reactor and the long hike back to town. He relied heavily on the handrail.

Fyothor had told him to head straight to the end of the corridor. It was a sensible instruction, because most of the apartments were missing numbers. The prevailing hush amplified his knock. The door opened a crack. A hairy arm beckoned him in.

Pfefferkorn stepped into the entry hall. A sack-eyed Fyothor stood re-cinching his bathrobe. Through a doorless frame was the kitchen: a closet with a hot plate and a hand sink. A wooden drying rack nailed to the wall held four plastic plates. There was no refrigerator. It didn't look like enough for a family to get by on. Down the hall was a darkened room.

"After you," Fyothor said.

Pfefferkorn groped his way forward. His nose picked up a briny, masculine smell. He could hardly see. The room's shades were drawn against the moonlight. He stopped short. Fyothor bumped into him from behind. He reached past Pfefferkorn and switched on the light.

Pfefferkorn cringed at the bright blast. Then his eyes opened and he was disappointed to learn that he indeed lived in a world where nobody could be trusted. The person waiting for them was not Fyothor's wife. If Fyothor even had a wife. And if Fyothor was even his real name. The person waiting for them was six foot five. He—for it was a he, very much so—was muscular and mean looking, with a jet-black goatee and tattoos on his hands and neck. He wore a leather motorcycle jacket and black leather boots, and he was making a growly noise not unlike a garbage disposal. Pfefferkorn sank to his knees, gasping for breath. Nobody had hit him yet, but his mind seemed to know what was coming, and it was determined not to be awake when it came.

102.

"Ahn dbhiguyietzha."

"Dyiuzhtbhithelnyuio?"

"P'myemyiu."

"Friend. Friend. Are you all right? Can you hear me?"

Pfefferkorn opened his eyes. Fyothor and the man in the motorcycle jacket were standing over him, fretting. Contrary to expectation, he was not back in his cell but in the selfsame living room, laid out on a mushy sofa. He tried to sit up. They restrained him gently.

"Please, friend, rest. You had a bad fall. You went down like a sack of root vegetables. We thought you had a heart attack."

Down the hall a kettle whistled. The man in the motorcycle jacket growled and left.

Pfefferkorn palpated himself. He was not tied up, and aside from a sore head, he did not seem to be injured.

"Akha," Fyothor said. He grunted as he sat down in a plastic chair. "I apologize. It was not my intention to disturb you. I assumed that you, as a foreigner, would be more accustomed to such things. But perhaps I am

wrong." He sighed and rubbed his face, then smiled tiredly. "Well, friend. My secret is now yours."

Pfefferkorn, coming around, pointed to his ear and then to the wall.

Fyothor shook his head. "Not here. Besides, it is not them I worry about. It is my neighbors, friends, family. Jaromir's mother is old. It would kill her to find out."

Jaromir brought three steaming mugs of tea. He handed them out and sat on the floor near Fyothor. Fyothor laid his hand comfortably on Jaromir's brawny shoulder. Jaromir's hand went up to meet it. Their fingers laced and stayed that way as Pfefferkorn told them what he needed to do. He finished talking and fell silent and then he waited for a response. Fyothor's eyes were focused on an imaginary point in the distance. Jaromir was likewise expressionless. Pfefferkorn feared that he had asked too much. He was betting the chance to save his life and Carlotta's life against all of their lives, and he was getting poor odds. Action heroism was not a rational undertaking. He was far too preoccupied to wonder if that might make an interesting premise for a novel.

Suddenly Fyothor pushed himself out of the chair and went into the next room. A moment later he could be heard talking on the phone. Pfefferkorn offered Jaromir an apologetic smile.

"Sorry to disturb you like this," Pfefferkorn said.

Jaromir growled and waved him off.

"Have you been together a long time?" Pfefferkorn asked.

Jaromir held up all ten fingers, then one more.

"Wow," Pfefferkorn said. "That's just great. Mazel tov."

Jaromir smiled.

"And, eh. What is it you do?"

Jaromir growled as he searched for the word. He smiled and snapped his fingers. "Semen," he said.

Fyothor came back with a slip of paper. "She is here."

Pfefferkorn looked at the address.

"This is the Metropole," he said.

Fyothor nodded.

Pfefferkorn looked at the room number. It was four higher than his old room number.

"Be at the harbor no later than three," Fyothor said. "Jaromir sails at dawn."

Pfefferkorn looked at Jaromir. "Ah," he said. "Right. *Sea*man."

"He told you this?" Fyothor chided Jaromir in Zlabian. "He is the captain."

Jaromir shrugged modestly.

Pfefferkorn shook Jaromir's hand and thanked them both. Fyothor embraced him and walked him to the door. Before he let him out, he said, "Tell me, friend. Is it true that in America men can walk down the street together, free of shame?"

Pfefferkorn looked him in the eye. "I'm not American," he said. "But that's what I've heard."

103.

The night was gauzy and moist. At that hour there were few pedestrians other than soldiers. Preparations for the festival were coming along. The sidewalks had been swept. Bright banners rippled and snapped. Aluminum barricades lined the parade route. Pfefferkorn guessed that there would be a good deal more pomp than usual, owing to the momentous nature of the anniversary. To avoid attracting attention, he stuck to side streets and kept a medium pace. He put his head down, his hands in his pockets, and his faith in his moustache.

Typically during the day there was a line of troikas waiting outside the Metropole, but now he found the block deserted except for a lone soldier lighting a cigarette. The solider glanced at Pfefferkorn incuriously before taking his first drag and looking off in another direction. As Pfefferkorn approached the hotel's glass doors he spied the night clerk engrossed in a magazine. He decided to go for it. He crossed the lobby, making a beeline for the elevator. He was almost there when the clerk called out in Zlabian. "Excuse me."

Pfefferkorn froze.

The clerk ordered him to turn around.

Pfefferkorn put on an indignant face and marched to the desk. *"Uiy muyiegho lyubvimogo uimzhtvyienno otzhtalyiy zhtarzhyegoh bvrudhu ghlizhtiy,"* he snapped.

The clerk was understandably startled by this outburst. Pfefferkorn would have been startled, too, by a comprehensively moustachioed man in a goatherd's outfit yelling at him that his beloved and mentally retarded older brother had tapeworms.

"Tapeworms," Pfefferkorn repeated, for emphasis. Then he yelled that he had been waiting for an oscillating fan for more than a week. He slammed his fist on the desk as he said this. The clerk jumped. Then, with enormous contempt, as if he couldn't stand to deal with such an imbecile any longer, Pfefferkorn reached into his left sock and whipped out the roll of cash. He peeled off a fifty-*ruzha* note and dangled it in front of the clerk's face, as if to say, *I can bribe you right out here in the open and no one can do anything about it. So how important must I be? Very important, that's right. So don't mess with me.* That was his intention. It was equally possible that the message was *Take this money and shut up.* In any event, the clerk plucked the bill and gave him a timid smile. "Monsieur," he said.

104.

Pfefferkorn's finger hovered over the button for the penthouse. He told himself that he had more than enough on his plate as it was. He chafed, knowing he would have to let Dragomir Zhulk live to plot another day. He punched the button for the fourth floor.

As the car labored upward, he visualized what he was about to do. The Metropole was old and quirky enough for every room to be done up differently. Certain constants would hold, though. There would be an entry hall with a closet on one side and a bathroom door on the other. There would be a bed. There would be a dresser. There would be a television on top of the dresser. There would be a nightstand, a telephone, a clock, a radiator, and a lamp. There would be an oscillating fan, although the likelihood of its functioning would be low.

The elevator ground to a halt. The doors parted. He crept down the hall.

There would be Carlotta. That was important to keep in mind. He couldn't come storming in like a maniac, striking at everything that moved. He had to be deadly but precise. If the room was anything like the one he'd stayed in, it could fit four comfortably. This being West Zlabia, he had to count on things being less than optimally comfortable. He steeled himself to fight ten men. They would be armed. They would have shoot-to-kill orders. His motions would have to be unified and fluid. He would go for the solar plexus.

He passed his old room. He passed 46, home of the noisy honeymooners. He came to number 48 and stopped. She had been no more than forty feet away the entire time.

He checked that he was alone.

He was alone.

He uncapped the deodorant stun gun and held it in his left hand. Not too tight, not too loose. He snicked open the toothbrush switchblade and held it in his right hand. Not too tight, not too loose. He reviewed Sockdolager's advice. Let the weapons become an extension of your own body. Don't pull punches. Commit. He held up the butt end of the toothbrush and tapped the door three times. There was silence, then footsteps, and then the door opened.

105.

The door opened.

"What the fuck?" Lucian Savory asked, or started to ask. He hadn't gotten any further than "What the f—" when Pfefferkorn jammed the stun gun into his withered gut and fired. Savory's knees folded and he went down like a sack of root vegetables, his bulbous head hitting the carpet. In one fluid motion Pfefferkorn sprang over him and rolled into the room, coming to his feet in a defensive crouch, whirling and ducking and weaving and jabbing with the knife and snapping off nasty eighty-thousand-volt crackles. "Hah!" he said. "Heh!" He dashed from end to end, a cyclone of lethality destroying everything in its path, meeting no opposition. He paused to assess the damage. Aside from Savory, who was an inert heap, the room was empty. He had completely subdued the finishings, though. He had mauled the curtains, lamed the lamp, annihilated the radiator, obliterated the fan, and electrocuted the duvet.

Carlotta was nowhere to be seen.

But then he saw that he had missed something. The

room was mostly the same as his, but there was one key difference. There was an extra door, the kind that connects two adjacent rooms. It connected room 48 to room 46, home of the honeymooners.

He opened the door. The corresponding handleless door was ajar. He pushed it all the way open with his foot and stepped through the doorway and there she was, tied down to the bed, a moon-shaped scar in the wallpaper corresponding to the top of the headboard that she had been rocking back and forth for weeks, slamming the wood into the wall and producing a rhythmic banging that was not hot water pipes or overzealous lovers but a frightened woman's desperate bid to attract the attention of whoever it was in room 44, not forty feet away but less than the same number of inches.

He ran forward to free her. She raised her head up off the pillow and stared at him uncomprehendingly as he used the knife to cut the ropes on her wrists. He cut the ropes holding her ankles and then he turned toward her with open arms but instead of kisses and pent-up passion he was met by a stinging right hook to the jaw that knocked him off the bed and onto the floor. He tried to sit up and with a primal scream she came flying off the bed and her knee smashed into his jaw and his teeth snapped shut like a mousetrap and he tasted blood and the knife pinwheeled out of his hand and embedded itself in the wall. He managed to scrabble backward and turn onto all fours and crawl away from her. She let him get as far as the doorway connecting room 46 to room 48 and then she kicked him in the rear, sending him sprawling on his stomach. She fell atop him with her knees in his kidneys and began punching him in the back of the head. She was deceptively strong and unfathomably vicious. He tried to roll over and she began belting him in the side of the head instead. He covered his head with his arms and she gave up punching him and started choking him. A remote part of his brain observed that she had absorbed her training well—much better than he had. Good girl, he thought. He also felt vaguely ashamed and made a note never to pick a fight with her. He grabbed her wrists and wrenched them from his throat and she screamed and started clawing at his eyes. It took both his hands to control one of hers, and with her free hand she grabbed his moustaches and began yanking on them hard enough to start tearing the glue. He realized then what was happening. She didn't recognize him. He was dressed like a goatherd and he had more facial hair than the East German women's gymnastic team. "Carlotta," he cried. "Stop." She didn't hear him. She just kept on screaming and pulling at his moustaches and punching him in the mouth. "Stop," he yelled. But she was berserk, lost in some kind of hateful hypnotic trance. He had no choice. He made a fist and walloped her on the side of the head hard enough to stun her. He wriggled out from under her and scrambled for the shredded curtain and hid behind it like a sorority girl caught in the shower.

"It's me," he yelled. His mouth was full of blood. *"Art."*

She stopped screaming and looked at him. She was shaking.

He spat. "It's me."

She trembled and stared. Her fists were still tight little bloodless rocks. He said her name. Her face was pale and varnished with sweat. Her roots had grown out. She was thinner than he ever remembered seeing her. "It's me," he said. Her fists unclenched and fell, and her hands hung limp at her sides. "It's me," he said. Her trembling peaked and began to subside. She said his name. He nodded. She said it again. He nodded again and put out a tentative hand. She said his name a third time and then he stepped all the way toward her without fear or hesitation, taking her in his arms and pressing her humming body close to his and kissing her like the California state bar exam, long and hard.

106.

He retrieved the knife. He wiped the plaster from the blade and closed it.

"How many others?" he asked.

"One. He went outside for a cigarette."

"I saw him. He was just lighting up when I got here." He spat blood and drew the back of his hand across his mouth. "We'll have to find another way out."

She glanced at Savory's body. "What about him?"

Pfefferkorn knelt and took Savory's pulse at both wrist and neck. He looked at Carlotta and shook his head.

"Don't beat yourself up about it," Carlotta said. "He *was* a hundred."

Pfefferkorn expected to feel guilt, like he had standing in Dragomir Zhulk's hut, staring at the prime minister's waxwork "corpse." He expected to feel disgust: unlike Zhulk, Savory really was dead, and he had died directly at Pfefferkorn's hands, not via a middleman. He expected to feel fear. Any minute now the soldier would be coming back to the room, and they had at most a few hours before the manhunt for them began. He did not feel any of these emotions. Nor did he feel satisfaction, empowerment, or righteous fury. He felt nothing, nothing at all. He had become, irrevocably and without fanfare, a hard man hardened to hard truths.

"Closet," he said.

They dragged the body into the closet and covered it with the spare blanket.

"It'll do," he said. His mouth was filling up with blood again. He spat, hard.

"Arthur."

He looked at her.

"You came for me," she said.

He set his jaw and took her by the hand. "Let's move."

107.

The service elevator let them out in the kitchen. They raced through a dark, steamy labyrinth of prep tables and swinging plastic strips. There were large walk-in coolers full of goat dairy and racks of unbaked pierogi on sheet trays. The whole place stank of garbage and bleach. The first exterior door they found was locked. He kicked it. It held firm.

"What now?" Carlotta asked.

Before he could answer, there was a noise. They turned to see a largish shadow moving toward them across the kitchen tiles. The shadow belonged to a largish person smiling menacingly and swinging a largish chef's knife in lazy figure eights.

"Hungry," Yelena said.

"Not in the least," Pfefferkorn said.

He pulled Carlotta to safety behind him and flicked open his toothbrush.

108.

"Really, Arthur, that was very impressive."

They were running.

"Brutal," Carlotta said. "But impressive."

Somewhere not too far away, a siren began to wail.

"You damn near took her head off," she said.

"Keep your voice down," he said.

They had no trouble at all finding the right ship. It dominated the harbor, a weathered twenty-five-thousand-ton handy-size freighter with *Тъедж* in red letters along the starboard side. Jaromir was waiting for them by the gangplank. He blinked at their bloody clothes, then ushered them down into the cargo hold. There were hundreds of wooden crates, stacked eight high atop wooden pallets. They squeezed their way to the back of the hold, where Jaromir had cleared out a space and laid down a blanket. There was a bucket of water. He told them to keep quiet. He would let them know when they had reached the safety of international waters.

They waited. Pfefferkorn's legs were cramping and it was hard for him to sit still. Carlotta massaged him and used the bucket to wash the blood from his face and hands. He couldn't be sure whose blood it was, his or Yelena's. Both, he assumed. He watched it come off impassively. Time ticked by. The sounds of a busy ship trickled down through the ventilation system: forklifts and winches, hydraulics and pistons. The engine began to churn and the whole ship juddered. Home free, he thought. Then he heard barking.

"They're searching for us," Carlotta whispered.

He nodded. He uncapped the stun gun and handed it to her. He opened the knife. The barking got louder and nearer and more insistent. There was a shrill metallic squeal as the cargo hold's doors were hauled open. They could hear Jaromir arguing vociferously with a man in Zlabian. The dogs were going crazy, their barks echoing. Pfefferkorn could sense them straining in his direction. They could smell him. He thought fast and pulled the designer eau de cologne solvent out of his back pocket. It was amber and viscous, just like real designer eau de cologne. He had no idea if it was disguised to smell like anything, but he didn't think twice. He pulled Carlotta out of the way, held the bottle out at arm's length, and spritzed the side of a crate. A heady base note of sandalwood and musk, overlaid with ylang-ylang and bergamot, filled the air.

The effect was instantaneous, in more ways than one. The barks turned to whimpers. Pfefferkorn could hear the handler fighting to keep the dogs there, without success. They broke free and ran, and the handler's voice faded as he chased after them. Right away the doors to the cargo hold slammed shut.

They were safe.

Except they weren't.

"Arthur," Carlotta said.

She pointed.

He looked.

The solvent was rapidly eating its way through the crate, the wood dissolving before their eyes. There was a creak and a spray of splinters. Pfefferkorn processed this information just fast enough to throw himself on top of Carlotta and tent his back. The bottom crate collapsed and the seven stacked atop it crashed inward on him, each one loaded with more than fifty-five kilograms of the world's finest-quality root vegetables.

109.

He awoke with his leg bound in a crude splint. His arms and torso were taped up. His head was bandaged tightly. His skin burned with fever. He looked around. He was in a tiny cabin, surrounded by metal canisters and mason jars. He was in the ship's infirmary.

"My hero."

An uninjured Carlotta smiled at him from the foot of his cot.

110.

She and Jaromir nursed him as best they could, feeding him soup and expired blister packets of Soviet-era antibiotics and keeping watch as he slipped in and out of delirious dreams. Eventually he awoke lucid enough to ask for a full serving of root vegetable hash and strong enough to get it down.

"Good?" she asked.

"Revolting," he said. He twisted to set the plate aside and winced at his broken ribs.

"Poor baby," she said.

"What about you?"

"What about me."

"Are you okay?"

"You're asking me that?"

"I mean, did they hurt you."

She shrugged. "They roughed me up a bit in the beginning, but on the whole I was treated very well."

"No funny business," he said.

"Funn—oh." She shuddered. "No, nothing like that."

"Good," he said. "I needed to know that first."

"Before what."

"Before this."

They made love. It was unsanitary, precarious, acrobatic, and transcendent.

Afterward she lay in his arms, lightly stroking his head.

"It was *trés* sweet of you to come rescue me," she said. "Stupid, but sweet."

"That's my motto."

"How in the world did you find me?"

He told her everything. It took a while.

"That's rather complicated," she said.

"I'm still having trouble figuring out who was telling the truth."

"Possibly everybody, in parts."

"They sent me in knowing I would fail," he said. "I was a pawn."

"Welcome to the club."

"Didn't they care about getting you back?"

She shrugged.

"You could have died."

"I suppose."

"You don't seem too bothered by that possibility," he said.

"We're all going to die, at some point."

"That's an awfully forgiving line to take on folks who, as far as I can see, have shown no concern for you."

"You don't become a beekeeper if you're not ready to get stung," she said. "And let's be fair. I've had a comfortable life, courtesy of them. Everything's a compromise."

"How long have you been a spy?" he asked.

"Never ask a lady that."

"Was it Bill's idea?"

She laughed. "I was the one who recruited him."

"Did you love him?"

"Enough."

"What about me."

"I've always loved you, Arthur."

They made love.

"Sorry we're not galloping off across the misty moors," he said.

"It'll do."

"I'm still looking into that beefcake for your birthday."

She smiled. "I can't wait."

They made love.

"Where are we going?" he asked.

"Tomorrow is Casablanca, last stop on this side of the Atlantic before we cross. Once you get to Havana the first thing you need to do is check yourself into a hospital."

He nodded.

"Promise me you will."

"Of course," he said, "but I'll be fine, as long as you're with me."

"That's what I mean," she said.

He didn't understand.

Then he did.

"No," he said.

"It's too dangerous for me to stay with you, Arthur. And it's too dangerous for you to stay with me."

"Carlotta. Please."

"I've worked with these people for thirty years. I know how they think. They hate loose ends."

"I'm not a loose end."

"To them you are. You know too much. Not to mention that if Zhulk *was* telling the truth, he's bound to renege on the gas, now that you're gone. That's an enormous setback for our side. They're going to be mad. Someone's got to be blamed, and you'll make an ideal scapegoat."

There was a silence.

" 'Our side'?" he said.

"I'm sorry, Arthur."

He felt the hardness coming on.

"Go someplace far away," she said. "Start over."

"I don't want to start over."

She put her hand on his. "I'm sorry."

They lay without speaking, listening to the ocean beat against the side of the ship.

"Whatever you do," he said, "please don't tell me I'm like a moth drawn to a flame."

"All right, I won't tell you that."

The waves raged like war.

"Make love to me again," she said.

He turned his head on the pillow. Her eyes were full of pain. He kissed them shut. Then he closed his own eyes and did his duty.

111.

They stood on deck, watching the rising sun gild the medina, listening to the muezzin's fading wail as it yielded to the plashing of *floukas* in the harbor. Pfefferkorn was leaning on the railing to take the weight off his broken leg. Carlotta had her arm around his waist.

"I'll miss you more than you know," she said.

"I'll know," he said.

She started for the gangplank.

"Carlotta."

She turned around.

"Read it at your leisure," he said.

She tucked the letter into her coat, kissed his cheek, and walked away.

Pfefferkorn tracked her slender form as it moved along the waterfront. She was headed to the American embassy. There she would make contact with the local field agent. She would report that the West Zlabians had released her in the wake of Pfefferkorn's execution at the hands of the East Zlabians. He would be gone before anyone thought to start hunting for him.

Jaromir helped him back down to the infirmary. He tucked Pfefferkorn into bed and handed him a tepid mug of *thruynichka*.

"To your health," Jaromir said.

Pfefferkorn took a long pull. It burned.

SEVEN DEUS EX MACHINA

112.

The *mercado* was of a piece with the rest of the village, sleepy, low-slung, and salt-eaten. Life began before dawn with the arrival of fishermen offloading buckets of wriggling squid and fraying sacks of shrimp. At half past five the produce trucks pulled up, and by nine all but the sickliest foodstuffs were gone. Toward midafternoon the people rose from their siesta, yawning men jellied by drink, heavy-bosomed women shooing half-naked children with incongruously ancient Indian faces, boys doing battle over a scabby, wheezing *fútbol* until once again drawn homeward by the sweet smell of stewed pork.

Pfefferkorn, a wide-brimmed straw hat on his head, moved among the stalls, squeezing tomatoes. No longer did he feel petty for demanding a discount of a few pesos. Bargaining was not merely tolerated but appreciated, a dance that helped to freshen an otherwise tiresome courtship. He handed the six ripest to the vendor, who placed them on the scale and announced a total weight of eleven kilograms. *Es ridículo*, Pfefferkorn replied. Never in the history of agriculture had tomatoes weighed so much, he said. He would complain to the *alcalde*, he would inform the padre, he would get his axe (he owned no axe), he would pay a certain amount (he swung the bills, axe-like) and not a centavo more. The vendor replied that he would be reduced to poverty, that he was already giving Pfefferkorn a discount, and who did he think he was, gringo, talking to him like this? After several more thrusts and parries, they agreed upon the same price they had the day before and shook hands.

Christmas was on the horizon, the streets awash with the remains of the previous evening's *mercado*. Pfefferkorn took his bags of food and walked to the post office, which was also the sewer department, pest control, and Western Union. The lone clerk swapped out the sign on the wall depending on who came through the door and for what purpose. As soon as he saw Pfefferkorn, he replaced ALCANTARILLADOS with CORREOS and began digging through a jumble of parcels, jostling the gimpy desk and setting its little plastic nativity scene aquiver, so that the animals and magi appeared to line-dance.

"It came yesterday. . . . Don't you get headaches? . . . Sign here. . . . Thank you."

Pfefferkorn tended to forget what he had ordered by the time it arrived, which made tearing into the brown paper more exciting—a surprise to himself, from himself. To prolong his pleasure, he strolled down the *avenida*. He sat in the *zócalo*, passing the time of day with the elderly men feeding the birds. A woman in a serape striped like a TV test pattern sold him fritters drenched in jaggery syrup, a seasonal specialty. He ate one and felt as though he had been kicked by a mule. He shifted the package under his other arm and headed toward the rectory.

113.

Some thirty-eight months prior, the *Тьедж* had put
ashore in Havana. While the rest of the crew stormed the
city to carouse, Jaromir got Pfefferkorn into a taxi and
rode with him to the nearest hospital. They checked him
in under a false name. He was shown to the medical-
tourism ward. He was given X-rays. His leg was rebroken
and reset. Jaromir stayed at his side for four more days.
Before he left, Pfefferkorn offered to pay him, but he
waved it off, growling. He was fine, he said. He was taking back tobacco and sugar, several hundred pounds of
which were undeclared and would be sold on the Tuni-
sian black market. Pfefferkorn should keep his money.

The hospital discharged him with crutches, a bottle of
painkillers, and instructions to reappear in five weeks.
He holed up in a cheap hotel and watched baseball. He
watched Venezuelan sitcoms. He watched a dubbed episode of *The Poem, It Is Bad!* For practice, he spoke back
to the screen. He hadn't used Spanish since high school,
when he and Bill had been conversation partners.

After the cast came off he spent another month
rebuilding his strength. He took long, slow walks. He

resumed his regimen of push-ups and sit-ups. He sat in the Plaza de la Catedral, eating *croquetas* and listening to the street musicians. He felt the nightly thump of the cannon at the Castilla de San Carlos de la Cabaña. He did a lot of thinking.

He took a taxi to a secluded beach about thirty minutes east of the city. He paid the driver to wait for him. He walked along the sand, his pockets swinging. The tide was far out. He knelt and dug a hole with his hands. He took out the dubnium polymer soap and dropped it into the hole. He took out the designer eau de cologne solvent and aimed the nozzle at the soap and spritzed it three times. The soap began to bubble and dissolve. The solvent was far less effective on the soap than it had been on the wooden crate. He spritzed again and watched the polymer fizz. He kept on spritzing until there was nothing left in the hole except a tuft of foam. At no point did he see anything resembling a flash drive. Which meant that he had been the real bait in the deal with Zhulk. Which meant that Paul had lied, at least about that, and that Carlotta was right. He could never go home.

He had the taxi driver take him to the Malecón. He walked along the esplanade, shielding his eyes and gazing northward toward Key West. It was too far away for him to actually see it, but he pretended he could.

114.

He moved on.

He boarded a propeller plane to Cancún. He spent the night in a motel and caught the first bus out of town. He got off the bus in a random village and walked around. He spent the night in a motel and got back on a different bus. He did the same thing the next day, and the next. Rarely did he stay in one place for more than twenty-four hours. He ate when he was hungry and slept when he was tired. He let his beard grow. It came in everywhere except for the strip of scar tissue on his upper left lip.

One evening while walking from the bus station in some no-name rural hamlet he heard the sound of a struggle and went to investigate. Down a trash-strewn alley, a pair of thugs was robbing an old woman at knife-point. Pfefferkorn flexed his arms. His healed leg was still stiff. It impaired his mobility a hair. On the other hand, he was leaner and stronger than he had been in years. He was all sinew and muscle and bone.

The old woman was crying, being jerked about as she clung to her handbag.

Pfefferkorn whistled.

The thugs looked up, looked at each other, and smiled. One of them told the other to wait and then he advanced on Pfefferkorn, the knife glinting in the moonlight.

Pfefferkorn left him sinking to his knees, gasping for breath.

The other thug ran.

Pfefferkorn scooped up the old woman in his arms and carried her three blocks to her home. She was still crying, now with gratitude. She blessed him and kissed his cheeks.

"*De nada,*" he said.

The next morning, he moved on.

115.

The places he visited all had the same markets, plazas, and cathedrals. They all had the same murals of Hidalgo or Zapata or Pancho Villa. They were all too provincial and remote to get foreign newspaper service, and so he had to wait until he reached Mexico City to get to an Internet café and catch up on the latest developments in the Zlabian valley.

What had happened depended on whose account you chose to believe. According to the West Zlabian state-run news agency, the festival celebrating the fifteen-hundredth anniversary of *Vassily Nabochka* had been an unmitigated success. Copies of the newly completed poem were distributed to every citizen, and the resulting swell of patriotism provoked the jealousy of the East Zlabian capitalist aggressors, who then invaded. According to the East Zlabian *Pyelikhyuin*, the release of the controversial new ending had sent waves of anger through a West Zlabian populace already brimming with discontentment. The rumblings grew in strength and ferocity until they erupted into riots. Violence spilled across the Gyeznyuiy, at which point it became incumbent upon Lord High President Thithyich to breach the median and reestablish order. According to CNN, the chaos was total. Everybody was killing everybody. Neighboring governments, fearing errant shells and a flood of refugees, had begged the world powers to intervene. The White House had petitioned Congress to authorize the use of troops. In theory, the peacekeeping force was to be multilateral, but ninety percent of the boots and all of the strategic command were American. Within twenty-four hours they had put the entire valley on lockdown. The president of the United States had issued a statement that there would be a complete withdrawal as soon as feasible. He refused to set a timetable, calling that a "prescription for disappointment." Nor would he comment on what would happen to the West Zlabian gas field.

Pfefferkorn reread the words "newly completed poem" several times.

He tried looking for a copy of it online but found nothing.

Back at his motel, he reread his unfinished ending to *Vassily Nabochka*. A few months' distance enabled him to admit that Zhulk's wife had been right on the money. It was terrible.

That night he went out for a walk. He passed a pimp slapping around a prostitute, threatening to cut her tongue out.

Pfefferkorn whistled.

116.

He used public phones.

He dared not try more than once every few months. He didn't know who was monitoring the line. He also worried that overdoing it would lead her to stop picking up calls from strange Mexican numbers. On balance he preferred the answering machine. His sole aim was to hear her voice, if only for a second, and it was less painful to get a recording than to listen to her asking *Hello? Hello?* without being able to respond.

117.

He liked to tell himself that he had chosen to settle in the seaside village because of its pleasant weather, or because reaching the Pacific implied some sort of finality. The truth was he had simply run out of money. At that point he had been on the road for more than a year, and he was tired: tired of the smell of diesel, of falling asleep sitting up, of waking up and having to ask his seatmate where he was. He was tired of dispensing vigilante justice. It had been fun for a while—he had been blessed more than a hooker having an allergy attack inside a confessional— but on the whole, the country was so saturated with corruption that he wasn't doing much except gratifying his own ego.

The focal point of every Mexican village was an overlarge church, and his was no exception. Among other tasks, Pfefferkorn swept up, shined the pews, did the shopping, and helped prepare meals. He had become reasonably handy. If a lightbulb got stuck and broke off, he could get it out with a raw potato. If a chair went wobbly, he could screw the leg back on.

His chief duty was maintaining the belfry. He shooed

away the birds and bats. He scaled off the guano. He oiled the hinges. He re-rigged the ropes. It was hard work, but later he would be reading or walking and he would hear the hour peal. What busy people heard as a single sustained note was to the patient listener a densely woven cloak of tones and overtones. Knowing that he had contributed in some small way to its beauty gave him a sense of accomplishment, one that lingered long after the ringing had died.

For his efforts he received a few pesos, two meals a day, and the right to sleep out back in a converted coal shed. It measured six by nine, with a packed dirt floor and a screened window that kept out most of the larger insects. He fell asleep to the sough of the ocean and woke to the mad babble of chickens running free in the yard. The gulls and pelicans that perched along the rear fence made an odd, bobbing skyline. Summers he slept nude. In winter the padre loaned him extra blankets, and Fray Manuel spread a tarp across the tin roof. Just in case, as soon as the clouds started to darken, they disconnected the extension cord. For this reason Pfefferkorn kept a flashlight on hand. His spare shirt hung on a nail. Obeying the rebukes of his ancestors, he had surreptitiously taken down the crucifix. There was enough space for a cot and—on the floor, along the wall—his growing library.

On the first of the month, he wired money to an independent bookseller in San Diego. A few weeks later, he received in return a parcel addressed to "Arturo Pimienta." The postage alone ate up most of his spending money. He didn't mind. What else did he need it for?

Four paperbacks per order made for a nice, unhurried pace. One would be a classic novel he'd always meant to read but had never gotten around to. The second book was the seller's choice. She leaned toward contemporary fiction that had received favorable reviews in certain publications of repute. The third and fourth books varied. Biographies, history, and popular science were his favorites. This month, with Christmas coming, he had chosen a thriller for Fray Manuel, who liked to work on his English, and Graham Greene's *The Power and the Glory*, which he planned to reread before giving it to the padre.

He put the food away in the rectory kitchen and retired to his shed. He hung up his hat, kicked off his shoes, and sat on the cot with the package in his lap, combing his fingers through his beard. He wasn't ready to part with the delicious feeling of anticipation. He spanned the package with his hand. It was bulkier than usual, owing to the presence of a fifth book, a hardcover.

He had a ritual. He began with the cover. If there was an image, he analyzed it as one might a work of art: framing, perspective, dynamics. If the design was abstract, he contemplated the effect of its color scheme on his mood. Did it match the contents? He would have to wait and see. Next he read the flap copy, sleuthing out hidden meanings. He read the blurbs aloud, warmly dismissing their extravagant comparisons. He flipped to the front matter, starting with the Library of Congress information. He admired its tidy divisions. He read the author biography, stitching together names, institutions, cities, and accolades. The omissions spoke loudest. If a writer had graduated from a prestigious university, and this, ten years on, was her first novel, Pfefferkorn inferred that the intervening decade had been full of rejection. Other writers claimed advanced degrees, as if to explain why it had taken them so long. Still others made a fetish of their struggles, boasting of time spent driving taxis, delivering pizzas, working as short-order cooks or process servers. All wanted it to seem as though writing had been their destiny. Pfefferkorn understood the impulse and pardoned it.

He studied the photo, picturing the author buttering toast or waiting at the doctor's office. He imagined what he or she would be like as a brother, a sister, a lover, a teacher, a friend. He imagined the author calling his agent and pitching a half-formed story that made no sense outside of his mind. He imagined the frustration the author felt when he understood, yet again, that his mind was not synonymous with anyone else's, and that to tell his story he would have to sit down and write and rewrite and work and rework. And the frustration that came with knowing that the story would never come out quite the way he had envisioned it. Writing was impossible. It was easy to think of books as products, made in a factory, churned out by some gigantic machine. Pfefferkorn knew better. Books came from people. People were imperfect. It was their imperfections that made their books worth reading. And in committing those imperfections to paper, they became omnipotent. A book was a soft machine that made a god of its builder. It was impossible and yet it happened every single day.

Writing is impossible, Pfefferkorn thought, reading more impossible still. To read truly—to read bravely—to read with compassion and without fear—did anyone? Could anyone? There were too many ways to understand, too much emptiness between word and mind, an infinite chasm of misplaced sympathies.

118.

The hardcover had red library binding stamped with gold lettering. Breaking with tradition, he turned straight to the last page.

He wanted to feel disappointed, but disappointment entails the possibility of surprise, and he had formed in advance a fairly clear notion of what to expect. In the final, unattributed canto of the revised West Zlabian People's Press edition of *Vassily Nabochka*, the king died before the antidote got to him, and a grief-stricken Prince Vassily repudiated the throne, deeding the royal lands over to the people and going to live as a commoner, tilling the fields and herding goats, finding redemption in manual labor before dying peacefully beneath a runty tree in the meadows of West Zlabia. It was the worst kind of agitprop: heavy-handed, impatient, and artless. The turns were improbable, the imagery fuzzy, and the characters reductive.

Pfefferkorn laughed until he cried.

119.

Three days before Christmas he made a pilgrimage. The bus dropped him at a dusty intersection in a village thirty miles south. He visited the market and the plaza. He admired the murals. He noted with pride that the church bell was not as fine as the one he tended.

He checked to make sure he was not being watched.

He entered a bodega and found the pay phone at the back.

He put in his phone card.

He dialed.

It rang once.

It rang twice.

They had it set to answer after the fourth ring.

It rang a third time.

"Hello?"

Pfefferkorn's heart pitched. It felt as though he were breathing through a drinking straw.

"Hello," his daughter said again. She sounded harassed. He wondered if she had had a bad day. He wanted to console her. It'll be all right, he wanted to say. Let me help you. But he could not say that. And he could not help her. He silently implored her to stay on the line. Don't give up, he thought. Say *Hello* again. Or don't. But don't hang up. Say something else. Say *I can't hear you*. Say *Can you call back*. Say anything at all. Get angry. Yell. Only: speak.

A child cried.

She hung up.

Pfefferkorn did not move for some time. The receiver was heavy in his hand. He replaced it softly. The phone ejected his card. He slid it into his pocket. He went to wait for the bus.

120.

The next morning, Fray Manuel greeted him when he came back from the market.

"You have a visitor. I asked him to wait in the vestry."

Pfefferkorn handed over the bags and went down the hall. He knocked and entered.

They stood face-to-face.

"Hello, Yankel."

"Hello, Bill."

"You don't seem that surprised to see me."

"It takes a lot to surprise me these days."

"I like the beard," Bill said. "It makes you look distinguished."

Pfefferkorn smiled. "How are you?"

"Not bad, for a dead guy." Bill glanced around. "Some place you got here."

"You want the tour?"

"Why the heck not."

They went out back to the shed.

"It suits my needs," Pfefferkorn said. "Although—a doorman. That I miss."

"You have the priest."

"That's true."

Bill's gaze settled on the hardcover on the cot. "Is that what I think it is?"

"Be my guest."

Bill opened *Vassily Nabochka* and paged to the end. He read. He closed the book and looked up.

"Well, that's shit," he said.

Pfefferkorn agreed.

"What about you? Working on anything?"

"Oh no. I'm done with that for good."

"Sorry to hear it."

"Don't be," Pfefferkorn said. "I'm not."

"Not even a little?"

"I've said everything I needed to say."

"You sound very sure of yourself."

"When you know, you know."

"And so that's that."

Pfefferkorn nodded.

"Kudos," Bill said. "It's a rare writer who knows when it's time to shut up."

Pfefferkorn smiled.

"Carlotta sends her love," Bill said.

"Same to her."

"She wanted me to tell you that she appreciated the letter."

Pfefferkorn said nothing.

"She wouldn't tell me what was in it. But clearly it meant a lot to her."

There was a silence.

"I'm sorry about that," Pfefferkorn said.

"It's all right."

"I thought you were dead. I'm sorry."

"Water under the bridge," Bill said. He tossed the book back on the bed. "You want to get out of here?"

"Sure."

They headed down to the beach. It was a cool day. The light was flat and even, sharpening the gray gulls turning circles against a scrim of gray clouds. Flaking pangas lay like casualties in the sand. The wind came whipping off the water, driving back Bill's hair and causing Pfefferkorn to snuff brine through his sinuses. They had walked perhaps half a mile when the hour began to toll, nine rich peals.

"You're back together, then," Pfefferkorn said. "You and Carlotta."

"Well, yes and no. More no than yes. I'm sort of in limbo, myself."

"What happened to you?" Pfefferkorn asked.

Bill shrugged. "I said the wrong things to the wrong people. Someone decided I was no longer reliable. Next thing I know, I'm treading water in the middle of the Pacific. Five and a half hours. I got very, very lucky someone happened by. Terrible sunburn. Hurt for weeks."

"What did you do to piss them off?"

"I wanted to write a book," Bill said. "A real one."

"Carlotta mentioned something about that to me."

"She did, did she."

"She said you were working on a literary novel."

" 'Working' is a bit of an exaggeration." Bill tapped his forehead. "Still all up here."

"What's it about?"

"Oh, you know. Trust. Friendship. Love. Art. The difficulty of meaningful and lasting connection. I don't have much in the way of plot, yet."

"It'll come to you."

"Maybe," Bill said. He smiled. "Maybe not. That's part of the adventure."

For the first time, Pfefferkorn noticed that Bill had gotten rid of his beard. He had not seen him clean-shaven since college.

"You look good, too," Pfefferkorn said.

"Thanks, Yankel."

The surf surged underfoot.

"So how come you're not in hiding, like me."

"I was, for a long time. They found me. They always do."

"And?"

"I guess they felt bad about the way things ended,

because they invited me to come back on board. They even threw me a bone and said I could write whatever I wanted. Clean slate."

"Good deal."

"There's a catch."

"I would assume so."

"They want me to prove my loyalty," Bill said.

Pfefferkorn snorted. "Figures," he said. "How."

The gulls banked sharply and dove, screaming, toward unseen prey.

"You have to leave town," Bill said.

Pfefferkorn smiled at him strangely. "What?"

"Listen carefully. You have to go. Today."

"Why would I do that?"

"And you have to stop calling her."

Pfefferkorn slowed and turned and faced him.

"That's how they found you," Bill said. He came in close, taking Pfefferkorn's sleeve in his hand, speaking quickly and quietly. "They mapped all the places you've called from and triangulated."

Pfefferkorn regarded him as one regards a madman.

"No calls," Bill said. "No books. You get on a bus and you go somewhere. Don't make friends. You stay out of sight as long as you can and then you get on another bus and repeat the whole process over again." He pulled tighter on Pfefferkorn's bunched sleeve. "Are you hearing me? Not tomorrow. Today. Do you understand? Say something so I know you understand."

"They asked you to do it," Pfefferkorn said.

"I checked the bus schedule. You can be gone by sunset. How much cash do you have?"

"They really did. They asked you."

"Answer me. Cash. How much."

Pfefferkorn shook his head admiringly. "Unbelievable."

"Stop talking and listen."

"The chutzpah . . . Unreal."

"You need to listen. You need to concentrate."

"Let me see," Pfefferkorn said. "They said something about a 'loose end.'"

"You're not listening."

"'We've got a loose end we need you to tie up.' Is that right?"

"Christ, Art, who cares? That's hardly the point."

"So? What did you tell them?"

"What do you think I told them? I told them I'd do it and then I came straight here to warn you. Now can we be practical for a minute here?"

Pfefferkorn pulled away from him. He put his hands on his hips and looked out at the ocean.

"I don't want to leave," he said. "I like it here."

"That's not an option."

"Anyway, I hate the bus."

"For God's sake. Be reasonable."

"Let's not talk about it right now," Pfefferkorn said. "Please?"

"This isn't the time to—"

"I know," Pfefferkorn said, "but I don't want to talk about it. All right?"

Bill stared at him.

"Let's talk about something else," Pfefferkorn said.

Bill said nothing.

"Let's talk about the old days." Pfefferkorn smiled. "We had some fun, huh?"

Bill said nothing.

"Play along, would you," Pfefferkorn said.

Bill continued to stare at him.

"Remember that time I was driving your car and got pulled over?" Pfefferkorn asked.

Bill's face softened, just perceptibly.

"You remember," Pfefferkorn said.

"We can't talk about this now."

"I want you to tell me if you remember."

The wind relented, allowing a stillness to rush in. The cries of the gulls were no longer audible.

"If I play along will you listen to me?" Bill asked.

"Just answer the question," Pfefferkorn said.

There was a long silence.

"I remember," Bill said.

"Good," Pfefferkorn said. "That's very good. And? Then? You remember what happened next?"

"How could I forget? My glove box smelled like a urinal for six months."

"And the thing we did, with the oars in the trees? What were we thinking?"

"I have no idea."

"I don't think we *were* thinking."

"You were always thinking," Bill said. "You probably meant something symbolic by it."

"I was stoned," Pfefferkorn said.

Bill smiled his most generous smile, the one Pfefferkorn loved and depended on, and despite the distress it concealed, it still made Pfefferkorn feel like the most important person on earth. He never wanted it to end, and to prolong its life he asked another question. "What else do you remember?"

"Art—"

"Tell me."

"I remember everything."

"Do you?"

"Of course I do."

"Then tell me," Pfefferkorn said. "Tell me everything."

They walked on for some time. The surf crashed and roared. The church bell tolled, ten peals. They went on. The sand was firm and cold. It shined like a ballroom floor. The church bell tolled eleven. They worked their way back through the years, excavating the past and rebuilding the destroyed landscape of their memories. They walked on and on and then the beach ended where a bluff pushed out into the ocean. Waves boiled through the rocks and smashed against the base of the bluff, flinging curved lines of froth like lariats. They stopped walking and leaned against the water-beaten rock.

"Berlin," Pfefferkorn said. "One night you went out around two in the morning."

"If you say so."

"Come off it," Pfefferkorn said.

"All right, I remember."

"What were you doing?"

"What do you think I was doing? I was meeting a girl."

"What girl."

"I met her on the night train from Paris."

"I don't remember any girl."

"You were asleep. I ran into her coming out of the bathroom. We got to talking and she told me she'd meet me the next night at a park near her aunt's house."

"You didn't tell me where you were going," Pfefferkorn said. "You just snuck off."

"Come on, Art. What was I supposed to say."

"You thought I would tell Carlotta."

"It did cross my mind."

"I can't believe you thought I would rat you out," Pfefferkorn said.

"I didn't say that. I said it crossed my mind."

"I may be jealous but I'm not a bastard."

"I knew how you felt about her."

"So?"

"I assumed you would want to protect her."

"Yeah, and how did you think I felt about you," Pfefferkorn said.

There was a silence.

"You loved me," Bill said.

"You're goddamned right I did," Pfefferkorn said.

There was a silence.

"I'm sorry," Bill said. "I should've said something."

"Yes, you should have."

"I'm sorry. I truly am."

"It's all right," Pfefferkorn said. "Did you ever end up telling Carlotta?"

Bill nodded.

"Was she mad?"

"A little. But, look. We never had that kind of relationship, she and I."

Pfefferkorn did not ask what kind of relationship he meant.

"Out of curiosity, what did you think I was doing in Berlin?" Bill asked.

"I don't know," Pfefferkorn said. "Something top secret."

Bill laughed. "Hate to disappoint."

They stayed there a while longer. The tide began to rise.

"There's a baby," Pfefferkorn said. "I heard it on the phone."

Bill nodded once.

"Boy or girl?" Pfefferkorn asked.

"A boy," Bill said. "Charles."

"Charles," Pfefferkorn repeated.

"They call him Charlie."

"I like it," Pfefferkorn said.

Bill hesitated, then took a wallet-sized photo from his breast pocket.

Pfefferkorn looked at his grandson. He didn't see much of himself. After all, his daughter looked like his ex-wife, not like him. The baby had black hair poking out from under a white ski cap. His eyes were blue, but that meant nothing. Pfefferkorn's daughter had had blue eyes, too, before they darkened to an inviting chocolate brown. Things changed.

"He's perfect," Pfefferkorn said.

Bill nodded.

"Does he have a middle name?"

Bill hesitated again. "Arthur."

There was a silence.

"Can I keep this?" Pfefferkorn asked.

"I brought it for you."

"Thanks."

Bill nodded.

"So you've seen her, then," Pfefferkorn said.

"I hear things," Bill said.

"And? How is she?"

"From what I can tell, she's getting along. She misses you, of course. But she's living her life."

"That's what I want. Although, I have to say, I don't feel too terrific about leaving her in his hands."

"Can you think of anyone you *would* feel happy leaving her with?"

"Not really."

"Well, there you go."

Pfefferkorn nodded. He held up the photo. "Thanks again for this," he said.

"You're welcome."

Pfefferkorn tucked the photo in his pocket. "You're a good writer," he said. "Always have been."

"You don't have to lie to me."

"I'm not lying. You have talent."

"Nice of you to say that."

"Take a compliment."

"All right."

Silence.

"This deal they offered you," Pfefferkorn said. "There's something I don't get about it. You're supposed to be dead."

Bill nodded.

"Now all of a sudden you've got a new book out?"

"They're going to put it out under my real name."

Pfefferkorn laughed. "At long last."

"If it sells more than a dozen copies I'll be surprised."

"That's not why you're writing it."

"No."

"Still, from their end, why bother?" Pfefferkorn said. "What do they get out of it?"

"I suppose it's their way of rewarding me for thirty years of service."

"Come on. Even I know they don't think like that."

"I don't have any other explanation."

Pfefferkorn mused. "Better than a gold watch, I guess."

"A lot better than being thrown off a boat."

"That depends," Pfefferkorn said. "Who's your publisher?"

Bill smiled.

"Let's say you did do it," Pfefferkorn said.

"Do what."

"Uphold your end of the bargain."

"Knock it off."

"Theoretically. Let's say you did. How would they know?"

"They'd know."

Pfefferkorn looked at him.

"They're watching," Bill said.

"Right now?"

Bill nodded.

"Where are they?"

Bill gestured all around. Everywhere.

"So they'll also know if you don't do it," Pfefferkorn said. "And they'll know if I run."

"You have to try."

"What for? They'll know. They'll just come after me again, and sooner or later, no matter how careful I am, they'll catch me. And in the meantime what happens to you?"

Bill said nothing.

"That's what I thought," Pfefferkorn said.

There was a long silence.

"Take it," Pfefferkorn said.

"What."

"The deal. Take it."

"Don't be ridiculous."

"I'd take it, if I were you."

"No, you wouldn't."

"If you don't take it, we're both finished."

"Not necessarily."

"They'll find me. You said it yourself. They always do."

"Not if you listen to me."

"No calls."

"Yes."

"And no books."

"Yes."

Pfefferkorn shook his head. "Impossible."

"It's very simple. Don't buy a phone card. Don't buy books."

"And I'm telling you, it's not simple at all. As long as she's there, it's impossible."

Bill said nothing.

"Don't be stupid," Pfefferkorn said. "If not you, it'll be someone else."

Bill said nothing.

"It'll be a stranger. I don't want that."

Bill said nothing.

"It may as well be on my terms," Pfefferkorn said. "It may as well achieve something."

"Please shut up."

"What's more important, that you be the one who does it, or just that I'm out of the picture?"

"I'm not having this conversation."

"It's an important distinction," Pfefferkorn said.

Bill said nothing.

"Well, let's hope it's the latter."

"Shut up."

"I will. Soon. Remember what you said before? In the shed?"

Bill did not answer.

"You said, 'It's a rare writer who knows when to shut up.' That's me."

"For crissake," Bill said, "it's not a metaphor for *life*."

Pfefferkorn took out the letters he carried on him at all times. The pages had taken on the warmth and curve of his thigh. "This one's for you," he said, peeling them apart. "You don't have to read it now."

"Art—"

"In fact, I'd prefer if you didn't. This one's for my daughter. Promise me she'll get it."

Bill did not move to take either letter.

"Promise me," Pfefferkorn said.

"I'm not promising you anything."

"You owe me a favor."

"I don't owe you a thing," Bill said.

"The hell you don't."

The church bell began to toll. It tolled once.

Pfefferkorn flapped the letters. "Promise me she'll get it."

The bell tolled a second and a third time.

"You can't sit here with me forever," Pfefferkorn said.

The bell tolled four and five. Pfefferkorn leaned over and tucked the letters in Bill's breast pocket. He dusted himself off and looked back at the town. The bell tolled six, seven, eight. Pfefferkorn looked at the ocean. The bell tolled nine. He stepped toward the water. He felt Bill's eyes on him. Ten. He stretched his arms. Eleven. He stretched his legs. The bell tolled twelve and he put one foot in.

"Yankel," Bill said.

Pfefferkorn advanced against the tide. The bell had stopped ringing but its vibrations could still be felt.

"Get back here."

The water came up to his knees.

"Art."

The sky was a high blank header. The horizon was a straight line of type. Pfefferkorn smiled back at his friend and called out above the waves.

"It had better be a damned good book," he said.

Pfefferkorn embraced the sea.

121.

He swam.

From far behind him came shouts and splashes. Eventually the water gave up its resistance and the splashes fell away and the shouts receded and he was alone, swimming. No one could catch him. He swam out past the bend in the shoreline. His lungs burned. His legs stiffened. He swam on past the fishing boats. He swam on until he saw nothing and nobody and then he stopped. He turned onto his back and floated, unmoored, in the limitless sea, letting the current take him.

He expected to sink. He did not sink. He drifted. Water sloshed over his chest and into his ears. Salt water ran into his eyes like he was crying in reverse, sucking up the sorrow of the world. He was thirsty. Hours passed. The sun peaked, then dropped like a slow-moving bomb. The sky became a cathedral. Night fell. He turned beneath turning constellations. The sun rose and bore down like retribution. The flesh of his face grew tender. It blistered and still he drifted on, and by the next night, his thirst had waned. His stomach closed. He felt shrunken, like a jarred specimen, at once heavy and light.

He surpassed pain. Time passed. The sun rose and fell and rose and fell. His clothes rotted away. He floated naked as a child.

Then he began to change. At first it was a change in perception. He ceased to feel his body. It was sad, like bidding an old friend goodbye. But there came a consolation. He felt new things, things bigger than himself. He felt the atmosphere like a blanket. The roll of a passing freighter. The tickle of kelp. The whizz of commuting sardines. The nuzzle of sharks. The stiff brush of cormorant wings. He heard new things, too. He eavesdropped on whales. He discerned the secrets of flatfish fathoms deep. It was as though he had become a tuning fork keyed to life itself. He gave himself over. He unfurled his limbs and beckoned life to him. First came algae. Then barnacles took up residence on his back and legs. They were joined there by limpets. He grew a moustache of mussels. He donned a crown of driftwood and trash. The tips of his fingers trailed delicate threads of seagrass. Coral cities were erected on his back and shoulders, attracting worms and crustaceans, anemones and clownfish, wrasses and triggerfish and tangs. Crabs hatched in his bellybutton. Eels curled up in his armpits. He was subsumed. He became a substrate. Mineral deposits grouted the gaps between his fingers and his toes. They spread up his shins. They locked his legs together. He calcified and collected. He was accommodating. He made room. He grew. His expanding shape created coves and inlets. The pilots of low-flying planes began to take him for a sandbar. He began to affect the tides. Organic matter composted atop his chest, creating a fertile soil. A coconut washed up onto his abdomen, cracked open, and germinated into a palm tree. An albatross dropped a mouthful of seeds. He bore wildflowers.

Later the wind shifted and he appeared off the coast, a vibrant and thriving assemblage, tilting like a giant hand in greeting. He was first noticed by fishermen. His natural beauty was taken note of. Word spread. The geological survey was divided over how to designate him. He seemed comfortable with his place, floating there in the just-beyond. An enterprising company began running tours out to see him. To prevent erosion, they limited the number of people onshore to twenty at a time. He was no longer visible except for his eyes, which peered out from the land around them, an invented land composed of many layers, some living, some dead. The people looked at his eyes and asked, *Is it him?* And the answer came: *It is.* Then they put out blankets and picnicked. They sunbathed on his shores. Children built castles and played in his waves. Pods of dolphins swam past, doing tricks. A good time was had by all.

ACKNOWLEDGMENTS

Жпасибхо бху Граф Станислав Козадаев для трансбастардизатион.

شكرا لك جاسي سي جي

Thank you: Stephen King, Lee Child, Robert Crais, Chris Pepe and everyone at Putnam, Amy Brosey, Zach Shrier, Norman Lasca, John Keefe, Alec Nevala-Lee, Amanda Dewey, Liza Dawson, Chandler Crawford, Nina Salter and everyone at Les Deux Terres, Julie Sibony, David Shelley and everyone at Little, Brown UK.

My gratitude to my wife is even greater than usual, as she made to me a gift of her idea for a casino within a casino.